Sicili and the Penniless Lad

Rachel C. Neale

Spectrum Books

Copyright © by Rachel C. Neale

Artwork: Adobe Stock – © Kathy, Martin Bergsma.

Cover designed by Spectrum Books.

Print ISBN: 978-1-915905-11-6

This book is a work of fiction. Names, characters, places and events are fictitious.

First edition, Spectrum Books, 2023

Discover more LGBTQ+ books at www.spectrum-books.com

Contents

A corset is a close-fitting piece of clothing that has been stiffened by various means in order to shape a woman's (also a man's, but rarely) torso to conform to the fashionable silhouette of the time. The term "corset" only came into use during the 19th century; before that, such a garment was usually referred to as a pair of bodies, a stiff bodice, a pair of stays or, simply, stays.

~ A Short History of the Corset

For you,
who goes against the grain because challenging the "norm"
is in every fiber of who you are.
Keep pushing for what you know to be true.

Ivy's story is for you.

And for you,
who has known a life of obedience and submission
because survival and acceptance are less scary than being
known.
I see you. Your journey matters.

Sicili's story is for you.

One

Sicili's Return

Six years. Six illustrious years of living in the heart of London and still the painting caused a conflict so deep she wanted to splash it, tear it, rip it off the wall. Every bone in her body ached to destroy it. Yet, she could not. She had not the strength to compromise such a beautiful creation. Six years since she had last seen the lovely, provoking brush strokes and the painting still ruefully fascinated her.

Sicili Windihill, wine in hand, stood engrossed by her favorite piece of art. *Grace* featured a woman commanding the attention of a courtyard of Grecian maidens. It hung at the end of the West Wing of Windsworth, her father's stately mansion. As a little girl and a lonely only child, Windsworth had been her ghostly playground. Her mother occasionally allowed her into the tea parlor with guests, while her father kept to his study. She wandered wherever she liked, as long as she left her preoccupied parents to their devices. More often than not, she wandered to the West Wing and, mesmerized, stared up at Grace for hours, studying her and wondering what made her so provokingly confident.

She sipped her wine.

Grace was a force to be reckoned with. She knew her place, her purpose. She stood tall, chest uplifted, shoulders back, attitude alert and decided. Her hazel eyes locked on Sicili, asking for *something*.

What? Certainty?

As a girl, Sicili was once drawn to Grace's confidence. As a woman, she found herself drawn to her defiance. Grace caused deep, unsettled thoughts. The imperceptible traces of arrogance behind those eyes. The texture of vibrant colors that bled into the curve of her waist. The sash meekly fallen over her left nipple. The fullness of her exposed breast.

Her glass tipped and wine splashed onto her ball gown. Frantically, she wiped it clean with her white glove. Her glove stained rogue red. She could not be seen like this. She felt frazzled enough. She did not need to look it.

She had arrived from London earlier in the day after a dreadfully bumpy coach ride from London to Wiltshire. Her father demanded she visit for his annual Windihill ball, fussing over her absence from such a grand event for the last six years. *Well*, he was the one who had sent her away to begin with. She lived with her spinster Aunt Gertrude in London. Six years of endless parties, tea sittings, literature readings, etiquette lessons, private balls in cramped apartments and "Oh, Sicili, darling, *he's* fetching. He is looking right your way. Do dance with him. *Do.*"

Dancing long past midnight, sharing smiles that meant nothing, gossiping about the latest fashion scandal, whispering little secrets never to be remembered the next day, drinking enough wine to "be fun, Sicili, dear." All in hopes of landing the *right man*, as her Aunt referred to Sicili's future not-yet-obliged husband.

At the age of sixteen, her father sent her to live with Aunt Gertrude to help with the loneliness of being an only child. "The city will do you wonders, Sicili, my angel. You shall have friends to keep you company and suitors to meet. Endless, handsome, wanting suitors. Your mother and I are rather a bore. Do you agree, my angel, my girl?"

It ought to be easier to look at Grace after six years. After surviving her Aunt Gertrude's eternal moodiness, after learning the ways of society, etiquette, and grace. After standing still and yet stiller and wondering when the stillness would cease. She waited for something extraordinary and unexpected to happen. If only Grace would come to life and dance with her.

For the time being, Wiltshire would have to do, the land of rolling hills and deadly gossip. Good heavens, why had she come back?

She swallowed more wine.

Grace's defiant eyes challenged her.

"Do forgive me, Grace," she whispered. "I fear I do not have the answers you seek. To be frank, I have no answers."

She turned from the painting just as a tall, overweight figure appeared at the end of the corridor. George Windihill, her father.

He smiled like a devil. "Sicili, my dear, you look magnificent."

"And you look evil, Father. As usual."

His eyebrows, overgrown and white as snow, were her nemesis. She used to get after him about them, but in her absence, laziness had become them. They dashed upward.

"The ball has begun. The guests are arriving. The music is struck." His voice, thick and strong, demanded the utmost attention. "Join us, my angel. The night is eager for your presence."

She forsook the painting and planted his cheek with a kiss. As she pulled back, she noticed a devious glint dancing in the right corner of his eye.

She shuddered. "What are you up to, old man?"

"Oh," he exclaimed with inappropriate delight, "a bit of fun."

"Are you allowed to have fun at your age?"

"I most certainly am. I may be white-haired, but I am far from dull."

She groomed his white brows. "As long as your fun doesn't involve me."

He winked, and the glint grew furiously passionate. She thought it might jump out of his eyes and assault her. Her father had a reputation for schemes and selfish pranks.

He kissed her hand. "May I have the first dance, my angel? I fail to see a gentleman preoccupying your arm."

"I saved it for you, old man."

He held out his arm. With a cautious smile, she looped her arm in his, and as he led her out of the corridor, she felt Grace's eyes still on her, still wanting the answers she did not have. She straightened her shoulders, held her breath and lifted her chin as they entered the grand ballroom where music, laughter, chatter, and society mingled in colorful celebration.

Two

Naughty Ivy

In the shadow of her mother, Ivy struggled to breathe. She fanned herself vigorously, scanning Windsworth ballroom for an inconspicuous escape from the Charlotte Ferthing's overbearing watch, but every exit spilled with socializing guests and platter-holding butlers. She preferred her mother's shadow over the jaws of Wiltshire's most elite.

"I can ward off the evils of society on me own tonight, Mother," she had professed on the carriage ride from Vineyard Estate. "You needn't be my chaperone."

Charlotte had pinched her elbow. "You are not leaving my sight, Ivy Ferthing."

She fanned herself harder. The corset and layers of confinement her mother insisted she wear threatened to drown her in sweat and stop her lungs from functioning. She had not missed suffocating from the grips of a party dress, and she certainly had not missed society and all its demoralizing expectations, not for one trifle of a second. The last five years of freedom had been pure bliss. Long walks, books on whatever subject she desired, endless time with her father, and relative solitude––besides Charlotte's demands that she stop slouching and smile more and "oh, Ivy, will you do your hair for once?" Now, she had to grapple with the amused glances and thrilled whispers from the other guests surrounding her.

She placed the fan over her pale, freckled cleavage. Beside her, her mother and Francine Windihill conversed in low voices. Charlotte glanced sidelong and pressed the fan down. The midnight blue frock, with lace bits escaping the sleeves and neck lining, pushed her breasts up like they were two fresh melons waiting to be plucked. She dispelled her mother's hands and shot her a glare, which was returned with Charlotte Ferthing's subtly pinched lips and glassy-eyed glower––a look Ivy knew too well. The very look she had created five years ago.

She shivered and returned to fanning herself, ignoring a group of ladies that held their chests and covered their mouths. One of them glanced at Ivy and then burst out laughing. Another one spilled her drink. Ivy turned a shoulder to them and distracted herself with the glitz of the ballroom. It sparkled from ceiling to mirrored walls to the glittering dance floor. Maroon drapes hung heavy against the windows that let in a starlit evening. She wanted to be out there, in the cool breeze.

Mrs. Windihill sipped campaign and kept her distance from Ivy. "My daughter has just arrived from London," she said.

Charlotte gasped. "How delightful."

"We do hope to have her stay on with us, only she's rather attached to London. Six years of bustling entertainment and diverting prospects tend to preoccupy a young woman's mind, or so she tells me." Francine Windihill had a laugh that sounded like a chime in a windstorm, soft and too polite.

"I have never understood the draw of London," Charlotte said.

"I feel the same. Sicili is taken with the city for the same reasons George and I found it unbearable. All that noise and no privacy. Quite ironic, if you ask me."

Charlotte pierced Ivy with a glare of regret, followed by an extravagant sigh. "Children do tend to bring about irony."

"Still, we are happy to have her returned." Mrs. Windihill called her butler over to replenish her wine.

The butler, Wilber, shot Ivy a guarded glance, as if he viewed her as a criminal and expected her to cause a scene at any given moment. She snorted. After five years of avoiding balls and dinners and lively interactions, the world still thought of her as the fourteen-year-old heathen who fell asleep under the influence. She tucked the fan inside her preposterous cleavage. Why not? They all expected it from her.

Charlotte snatched the fan before Mrs. Windihill noted the discretion and vigorously cooled her crimson cheeks. "You'll be the end of me, girl." She drank a vexed amount of wine.

Mrs. Windihill cautiously inched a step closer to her. "It is good to see you, Ivy. How awful those rumors were, but it seems they are behind you. Better days are in store for you, I am sure." She extended a hand, like royalty. "I do hope you and Sicili can meet."

Better days were *behind* her. Happy mornings in the library at Vineyard Estate. Glorious afternoons spent with her father inspecting his rows of grapes. Exhilarating evenings sneaking out of her bedroom window to visit Madam Desiree's. Mrs. Windihill kept her hand extended, poised and gracious. Ivy had no idea what to do with it. Charlotte gave her a sharp eyebrow raise. She pinched the ends of Mrs. Windihill's slender fingers and brought them to her mouth, planting a soft kiss on Francine's knuckles.

Shock replaced Mrs. Windihill's earlier kindness. A thin gasp escaped Charlotte as she clasped her neck and the fan collided with the floor.

"Why of course," Charlotte squealed. "Ivy would love to meet your daughter." She rescued Mrs. Windihill's hand and wiped it free of unwanted residue.

Mrs. Windihill recoiled, taking the step back as she reddened from ears to neck. She retracted her hand, as though it were diseased, and clawed at it with a fold of her dress. "We-we shall have to arrange a little get together. Soon, very soon. Excuse me. I must––my other guests." She backed away. "Do enjoy the rest of the night, Mrs. Ferthing and..." she trailed off as she avoided eye contact with Ivy. The diseased. She nearly tripped as she fled.

Charlotte finished her wine and gripped Ivy's arm. "The night has yet to begin and you have already offended our hostess."

Ivy shrugged. "She extended her hand like a queen does to a knight. What was I to do? I had no choice but to oblige."

"All those books you read."

"I'm convinced she'll recover. Francine Windihill is made of thicker stuff than offence. It was only a peck."

Charlotte blanched. "*Stuff*, Ivy? Where did you learn that insufficient word?"

"One of my books, I suppose. I rather like the word. It doesn't ask for much."

Charlotte's lips thinned. "A lady must use eloquent words."

"We both know I'm not a proper lady, Mother."

Charlotte and Ivy had always been opposites. She––sloppy, droopy, careless where her mother was poised, pungent, meticulous. Charlotte had never complained about these despicable contraptions called dresses. She performed, feigned laughter, and read the social cues of any room she entered with her head held high, despite the setback of having a wayward daughter. Regardless of her dashed reputation due to Ivy, Charlotte always looked impervious and untouched by age, her hair clumped in delicate ringlets and her nose powdered.

Tears threatened Charlotte's eyes. "I heard you last night, Ivy. Like I hear you every night, creaking and climbing. I have a mind to bar your window."

She fell silent. She had snuck out to the Madam Desiree's last night, just like she snuck out the night before and a week's worth of nights before and every night before that for the last year. The girls who danced at Madam Desiree's were her refuge from the storm of being trapped in dresses all day long. She had been out especially late last night, drinking away her worries about returning to society after five years of absolute freedom.

"Have you any idea how it feels, Ivy, having your only daughter sneaking out at night doing *lord knows what* while you toss and turn and fret?" Charlotte sniffled. "You have no concept of my trials. You never will because *you* are a spoiled, mischievous brat who delights in all things evil."

Ivy had a laugh. "Not *all* things evil. I have yet to run away from home. Though I have a mind to if you keep dragging me to these bores."

"You torturous girl. You ought to take me seriously."

"What is there to be serious about? I'm suffocating in a dress with my breasts displayed like melons and the entire room gawking at me like I'm the black plague."

Charlotte lowered her voice. "Everybody who is anybody is here, from the Prattles to the Evergreens."

"The Evergreens?"

"They own a share of banks. Where is your head, Ivy?"

"How should I know? You locked me away for five years."

"And you enjoyed every minute of it."

Ivy smiled. "I'll happily return to isolation."

"I regret keeping you away, Ivy." Charlotte grasped Ivy's chin and forced Ivy to look at her. "Tonight is your chance to put things right, you darling disquiet. Tonight we put those ancient rumors behind us and hold our heads high. Tonight society will see a woman, not a preposterous girl. They will see what I see."

She laughed outright. "An outrage?"

"An opportunity."

Ivy went quiet. The laughter got stuck in her throat. That glassy-eyed look had returned. "For what?"

"*You* are going to dance with every man at this ball *and* you are going to impress."

She stiffened. "I hate dancing. You know I do."

Charlotte pinched Ivy's cheeks until they stung and turned her about. "From this night forward, Wiltshire will know that you *do* like balls, you *do* know how to dance, and you *do* make your mother and father proud."

"We both know those are lies."

"There is nothing wrong with hiding the truth when necessary. Illusion is a beautiful thing."

"I'm no illusion, Mother."

"Oh, Ivy." Charlotte sighed. "I want grandchildren."

"You have three sons. I should think they would be delighted to produce bouncing bundles of shite and wails."

"They live in London. You know them, Ivy. They admire city life. They enjoy studying more than the company of women."

"Bribe them. You're good at bribing."

Charlotte directed them toward a group of tight collared gentlemen. "I am serious."

"Aren't you always?"

"You're my *only* daughter. All I want is to see you happy."

She halted and faced Charlotte. "I know what you want, Mother." She straightened from her lazy slouch. She squared her shoulders and tipped up her nose. "You want what every mother at this delusional ball wants. You want me to marry a wealthy man. You want your friends to faint with envy when you walk down the street. You want money, fame, and stature."

Charlotte let out a whimper.

"Correct me if I'm wrong."

Charlotte held her tongue.

She freed her arm from her mother's deathly grip. "I need a drink."

***

Ivy had no interest in illusions. She was who she was, and she had never been ashamed of it. The sooner her mother and all of society knew it, the better. She downed her wine in two mouthfuls and snatched another. All this talk about children. She didn't want children. She didn't want to get married. A husband would stick her with snotty, messy babies and tell her how to act. She didn't want to gossip over tea and pretend to like people she despised.

It was fact. Ivy had no desire to feign, gossip, and seduce.

Charlotte Ferthing would never admit to knowing the truth, but Ivy knew that deep, deep down, her mother understood her more than she admitted. One day she would find the courage to be out with it, to tell the world and smile at their horrified gawks. But today was not the day, not with her mother hounding after half the men in the room, whispering in their ears and receiving solemn *no's*. She did feel sorry for her mother. Her poor mother, who had tried desperately to bring up a normal, polite daughter. All to no avail.

A group of ladies tittered next to the wine table. They had given Ivy the cold shoulder after she gracelessly stuffed deviled eggs in her mouth and fisted two wine glasses. She now admired them from a distance.

They found themselves in the thick of a ridiculous dilemma.

"I shan't fill my card too fast," one of the ladies frantically wailed. "How hard it is to choose. They should give us lengthier cards. *Oh*. Mr. Evergreen has written on mine."

"No, no, not him," said another. "He has no sense of rhythm."

"What about him?"

"Awful breath."

Harriet Prattle, the matriarch of the group, tethered them with her illustrious voice. "Ladies, ladies, do hush. Dance with every man there is to dance with. You may be married next year. Once you're taken, you're doomed to dance with one man and only one. For eternity. It's a drab punishment." She had the most influence because she married a man with ten thousand pounds a year. At seventeen.

Ivy rolled her eyes and stuffed another pastry into her mouth.

"*Ooooh*, I'd rather be married than have to choose," the frantic lady wailed. "They're all so amiable."

Harriet snatched her card and surveyed the prospects. "You're much too careful."

Ivy sipped her wine. *You were never careful*, she thought. Harriet had once been young and frivolous, and she gave her heart away to more than once person. The wine tasted abnormally bitter and dry. The taste lingered at the back of her throat.

Harriet detected Ivy's wandering gaze, and she glanced away at the dance floor, at the mingling, happy couples.

"You look pretty, Ivy Ferthing," said Harriet.

She swallowed a lump of pasty before leaning against the table. "Do I? I feel like a wench in this dress. It pinches in all the wrong places and pulls at all the wrong stuff."

"Stuff? Whatever do you mean?" Harriet's eyes wandered to Ivy's preposterous display of cleavage. "I think it looks lovely on you."

Lovely? Heat crept up her neck and into her face and tickled long lost feelings in the pit of her stomach. At seventeen, Harriet married Phillip Prattle––the businessman. He filled his days with meetings and papers while Harriet spent his hard-earned money and flirted with anything that breathed. She preferred men, but when the men were preoccupied, she liked to flirt with her share of women––touching and gazing and smiling just so. A long time ago, Ivy fell prey. They were once upon a time close friends before the rumors struck the countryside.

Her elbow knocked against the side of the table, shooting pain up her arm. She grasped at it and nearly lost her glass of wine.

Harriet's amused laugh lit up the ballroom. "Are you drunk, Ivy?"

"What else is there to do at these boring affairs?"

"You could dance." Her tone chastised.

"Only if you'll do me the honor."

Harriet purred. "In your dreams, Ivy."

"Too attached to your husband?"

Harriet raised an eyebrow. "You're charming tonight. I'm not sure I like you when you're charming."

"All of Wiltshire knows you are the charming one, Harriet Prattle, with your lusty eyes and sultry webs." The girls held their mouths and giggled, but none of them came to Harriet's defense.

Harriet pursed her lips. Her eyes narrowed. "I wonder how your mother got you into a dress. I heard a rumor you dislike dresses."

The girls tittered.

"Do leave her be, Harriet," one of them said. "She's nothing but trouble."

Harriet pressed her friend away. "Your poor mother, Ivy. I do pray for her well-being."

Ivy bit her tongue. At the moment, Charlotte desperately searched the ballroom for a gentleman who would willfully cast down his pride to dance with a pumpkin stuffed into a contraption. Ivy groaned and chased the pastry with a gulp of wine. Her poor mother indeed, and the poor chap who fell prey to Charlotte's desperation.

Harriet kept her eyes on Ivy until two dashing gentlemen joined her tittering group. They had eyes for Harriet. She leaned toward them as her horrendous wedding ring sparkled and caught the light.

Ivy swept up a fourth glass of wine and turned toward the dance floor. *Humbug, Ivy. Leave the past where it belongs. Harriet's a wily trap of smiles and charm. You're a daft chump if you think otherwise.* Just as she inhaled the first sip, a nervous young fellow made his way across the ballroom and held out his hand to her. He stood as stiff as a board.

He cleared his raspy voice. "May I have this dance, Miss Ferthing?"

She choked back wine. "Me?"

"Indeed."

She scanned the ballroom for Charlotte, ready to send her an eyeful of daggers, but the witch had disappeared into the throngs.

The fellow continued to hold out his hand.

"You know," she said through mouthfuls of pastry, "I'm an awful dancer."

His stiffness looked like a soldier ready for battle. "I can do the leading."

"You jest."

He winced. "Certainly not."

"Did my mother send you?"

He blinked and stuttered and gave a whinnying cough.

"All right then." She set down her glasses and shoved him onto the dance floor with a haughty, "What's your name, fellow?"

He gulped. "Patrick Derby."

"How much did she offer you, Mr. Derby?"

"Pardon?"

"To dance with me."

"I can't quite catch your meaning, Miss Ferthing."

She pressed her heel on the toe of his shoe. Wriggled it. He grunted painfully, yet managed to keep a pleasantly stiff attitude.

"How much, Mr. Derby?"

He grimaced. "Ten bottles of your father's newest invention."

"That witch."

He recoiled. "I beg your pardon? You disgrace your mother's good name. She is no witch."

"My mother is most certainly a witch. One and the same. Haven't you heard? She cast a spell that me locked up at Vineyard Estate for five dreary years."

"I hear you prefer isolation."

"You're clever. Who told you that?"

"Everybody who is anybody. You were quite the talk these last five years."

The Windchill's head butler, Wilber, took to the stage and the music abruptly stopped. The ballroom stood still. "May I have your attention?" He pointed to the West ballroom doors. "Do turn your eyes on your host George Windihill and his daughter Sicili Windihill, who has recently arrived from London."

George Windihill, with wild hair and white eyebrows, entered the ballroom with a striking lady on his arm, and the guests cleared a path for them. A pinch of enchantment settled over Ivy. Was it the four glasses of wine finally settling into her stomach? Warmth blazed up her neck and settled at the back of her ears. Sicili Windihill owned the disposition of a royal; she had only just arrived and already she looked bored and tired. Poised, delicate, but unavailable. Her blonde curls swept across her forehead into an effortless up-do, and her hazel eyes sent a distant cool over the room. Her guarded expression, with an edge of boredom to it, ridiculed.

Ivy's mouth twitched.

The entire ballroom seemed to share her opinion. Patrick gazed at Sicili Windihill with the same expression the other men did, with a light in his eye and a grin plastered on his dopey face.

Am I wearing the same dopey grin?

George Windihill twirled Sicili. Her dusty-rose dress kicked up and swooshed like the sound of a brook, and her hair caught the candlelight as she twirled to a halt.

George steadied her. "My Sicili will be visiting Wiltshire for a fortnight," he joyously said. "She will most assuredly be here all night, gentlemen, and her card does need filling. Do continue dancing, my fine guests. Do enjoy the night."

The music resumed. Patrick pressed her to continue the waltz, and she followed his lead in a foggy daze. Her earlier malice had melted away and been replaced with aching feet and a heady buzz. Sicili had cast a lovely spell. Curiosity felt imminent, involuntary. She tipped her toes and peered over Patrick's shoulder.

George relinquished Sicili to Wilber's care for a dance with his wife. Mr. and Mrs. Windihill, cordial and devoted, sparkled across the dance floor and melded to their guests. Sicili, on the other hand, kept to Wilber's side. (She rebuffed the immediate advances of half the gentlemen in the ballroom. They nervously retreated, their tails between their legs.) Her cheek bones were cut like diamonds and her skin glowed. *Is she flustered?*

She glanced up to catch Ivy's permanent stare, and for a moment, their gazes held. The ballroom slowed and disjointed before Patrick whisked her to the other side of the dance floor.

Her throat felt dry. "She's very pretty."

"The prettiest lady in all of England," said Patrick.

She licked her lips. "Are you going to dance with her?"

"I doubt I shall get within ten feet of her. Every man in this room has the same notion. We shall all be vying for her attention."

Ivy found it hard to peel her eyes away. "Is she that important?"

He chuckled. "She's the daughter of George Windihill, only the richest man in all of Wiltshire."

She smacked his arm playfully. "Is that all you gallant gentlemen care about? Money?"

"That, and she is breathtaking. Look at the way the light dances off her skin."

Ivy tripped on her dress, and he caught her tightly in his arms. He was right, of course. Sicili's resplendence left her feeling tingly and utterly clumsy.

"Do you know..." She felt foolish asking, but she had to. "Is she single?"

He sighed hopefully. "Miraculously. Do not ask me how. She lives in London. I should think every man in London would want her hand."

"Why London?"

"Have you not heard the gossips?"

She *clucked*. "Inform me, will you? I'm a recluse, remember? Not a social butterfly like you, Patrick Derby."

He smiled with an air of pride. His stiff disposition from earlier had relaxed. "George Windihill sent her to London six years ago. She has lived there ever since."

Ivy cocked her head. "That's odd."

"No one knows why."

"I suppose she has more of a fighting chance in London. All Wiltshire does is put on balls and gossip into the late hours."

"And how would you know, Miss Ferthing? I understand you have been hiding away at Vineyard Estate."

"Happily so. I still hear the gossip every now and then. I have my mother to thank." She gave him a friendly pat on the shoulder. "I like you, Patrick. I like a man who speaks his mind. We shall be great friends."

"Friends?"

"Unless you fear me."

He straightened with a gallant smile. "Afraid of Naughty Ivy? Would you like to know what I think, Miss Ferthing?"

"Why not?"

"I think you should have stayed in society despite those ghastly rumors. Rumors are only rumors. They are not who you are."

She felt a pinch of affection for the lad. The corset scratched at the skin under her armpit. *How kind of you to say, fellow, but how wrong you are*. Utterly wrong. The rumors were exactly her. He twirled her under his arm, and as she spun, she saw Sicili in the crowd. She loved two things in the world. Her father's wine and women. Intoxicating, confident, illustrious women. If the truth came out, Wiltshire would cast a ghastly shadow over not just her, but her family. Her mother, who denied the rumors and strived to end the gossip while protecting Ivy from the evil of the world. Her father, a self-made man, who wanted naught but happiness and comfort for his wife and children.

She forced a smile. "I dare say you are one of the nice ones, Mr. Derby."

They danced the next two sets. After the third, Patrick declined a fourth. He complained of a sore knee, yet immediately got to dancing with a bright young thing. She retreated to the back of the ballroom where no one noticed her, and the wine kept her engaged. She scanned the guests and caught a glimpse of Sicili's side profile. Her diamond cheekbones dazzled. Her flushed skin glistened as she fanned her face. Ivy searched for her own fan, but she had miserably misplaced it. Looking at Sicili set fire to her world. Her knees weakened as her heart skipped a beat. *Pitter-pat–flop*. She felt uneven. All over. Her dress felt tight, yet too loose. She suffered a quick fantasy of rushing through the crowd and sweeping Sicili's hand into an earnest kiss, but then the horror of Francine Windihill's reaction when she had done so earlier came rushing back to her. She thought better of it. She was Naughty Ivy after all, the scandal of Wiltshire.

Three

Red Hair, Bright Eyes

The girl with the red hair, bright green eyes, and obnoxious lack of grace intrigued Sicili. Among the throng of dancing couples, she saw no one else.

What is it? Something inconvenient. It had to be. The growing feeling in the pit of her stomach always led to misplaced ideas and frivolous thoughts. *Is it her feet? Her feet are dragging. They ought to be cheerily skipping to the waltz.* No. It had to be the uncomfortable gap the girl had set between herself and her dance partner. Her unfortunate second. He was trying to lead, but the girl led him, and did not appear to know what she was doing.

Is it her dress? It looks uncomfortable. Not quite right. Rather, it might be the way she holds herself, with a decided scarcity of interest. I ought to look elsewhere.

She forced herself to watch her parents dancing, opened her fan and aired her face. There were too many people cramped into the ballroom. Her father had outdone himself, as per usual. Sweat slipped down the crease of her corset.

The girl danced by her again. *What is it?* She fanned herself faster.

She studied her like a painting. The girl had stunning features. An angled jaw and pointed nose, freckled cheeks with crimson soft upon them. Unruly red tendrils stacked upon her head like she hadn't spent one moment's thought on them.

The more Sicili scrutinized her, the more fascinating and out of place the girl seemed. She refused to blend into the ball.

"Who is she, Wilber?"

Wilber cleared his throat. "Ivy Ferthing."

"Ferthing? Have I heard that name?"

"Her father is William Ferthing, the celebrated wine merchant. We drink his wine tonight."

She could not take her eyes off the girl. "Truly? The very gentleman my father brags about in every letter he sends to London. He tells me of Mr. Ferthing's concoctions of brilliance and bliss with great detail. He goes on for pages."

"I imagine he does."

"I heard Mr. Ferthing grew up a tailor's son. Is it true?"

"Indeed."

"He earned his wealth from a vineyard, then?"

"Quite."

"Fascinating. He is especially famous in London. They call him an *entrepreneur*. Have you heard that term? I'm told it's a relatively new word. I have yet to meet a mouth that hasn't tasted his wine." She dabbed her neck with her handkerchief. Her fan failed to fight the overwhelming heat. "And *she* is his daughter."

Wilber cleared his throat, again.

She snapped her useless fan shut. "I would think her more refined given her position in society. She is his only daughter, is she not?"

"Indeed."

"She cannot have more than a thousand pounds a year." Miss Ferthing's dance partner held her waist firmly. His knuckles crinkled around the fabric of her dress. "She will never survive on that. Will she, Wilber?"

Wilber lowered his voice. "A word of caution, Miss Windi-hill. It would not be wise to befriend Miss Ferthing. There are rumors."

"Do you think I need friends, Wilber?"

"I beg your pardon, Miss Windihill. I assumed. You have just arrived from London."

"Yes, and I shall stay but a fortnight. No longer, and possibly not as long as that. I have a perfect number of friends in the city. I came here to relax, not to busy myself making unwanted acquaintances. Particularly not the likes of a red-haired, bright-eyed girl who cannot dance."

Wilber held his tongue.

She sighed. "You sound like my father, Wilber. That evil old man. That menace."

Timely, George Windihill slipped next to her and offered her a glass of champaign. He toasted her return to Wiltshire, and half the gentlemen around them joined in, and they drank. She glanced about at the nervously fixated eyes and felt like a showpiece in a grand circus manned by none other than her infamous old man.

He pecked her cheek. "Have any of them caught your eye, my dear?"

She looked at Ivy. The girl had managed to stumble all over her partner's toes. While he sulked, she smirked. Sicili's mouth twisted into a smile. The performance made her giddy. Ivy Ferthing was quite unlike a lady. *If* the girl could be called a lady due to her lazy, boyish air.

She sipped the champaign. "Any of who, old man?"

"Your suitors, of course." His intoxicated glint dazzled.

In truth, no one else had secured her attention. Ivy Ferthing's careless lack of skill had her entirely captivated.

George nudged at her.

"Suitors, Father?"

"I trust they are no less varied than the gentlemen in the city."

"They are... varied. I suppose."

"I knew Wiltshire would not disappoint you. Your mother had her concerns."

She pried her eyes from Ivy and did her best to survey the "suitors." They ranged from short to tall, charming and genteel to chauvinist blowhards. The country had handsome men––handsome, but not interesting. The same expression lit their faces as her attention moved from one to another, the same anxious flit of nervous admiration. Not for her, but for her father's money. She knew men.

"Tell Mother not to fret," she said. "The country is adequately diverting."

George put on a jubilant grin. "It does me good to have you back, my Sicili. Wiltshire has been in desperate need of your wit and beauty."

With that, he pecked her cheek goodbye and went off to find more wine. She growled. "Is he up to something, Wilber? His eyes are full of it."

Wilber coughed.

She stared him down, quite severely. "You know something, do you?"

"Only that he means to have a word with you in his study."

"Truly?"

Her father's study was sacred, and the idea of being summoned to it baffled her. It made her stiff and uncomfortable. In her twenty-two years, she had been granted entrance but once. Six years ago, on the day he announced she would be moving to London with her Aunt Gertrude to learn the art of being a lady.

She preferred to forget that day. Instead, she searched the ballroom for Ivy Ferthing. Watching the girl brought excitement into her world, not dread. Ivy had apparently disappeared. Her former dance partner looked relieved, to say the least. He floated the dance floor with a new lady in his arms, one much lighter on her feet.

She leaned into Wilber. "Tell me more about this Ivy Ferthing. You mentioned rumors."

He cautiously leaned in. "Far from pretty."

"I should hope so. Let's hear them."

He leaned in and whispered, as quietly as he could. When he finished, Sicili pressed her fingers against her lips. "Are you sure?"

He nodded.

"Trousers?"

"Unfortunately."

"A fisher's cap?"

"As I said."

"An oversized tailcoat?"

"Not a word of a lie."

"Naughty Ivy?"

"Following the incident, the Ferthings kept her in hiding. Mrs. Ferthing was too ashamed to let her daughter see the light of day. She hoped the rumors would subside; I imagine. This is Miss Ferthing's first appearance back in society in five years."

"How informed you are, Wilber."

Wilber smiled. He looked especially pleased.

"But why trousers?"

"No one knows."

"There must be a good reason."

"Miss Ferthing's greatest misfortune is that her ways are most unreasonable."

"I shall give her that."

His mouth hinted at a smile. "Do you mean to dance, Miss Windihill?"

"Later, perhaps."

For the present, she obsessed over the thought of Ivy in trousers. *How do they look on her?* Her lazy posture would suit a pair of trousers. Her hair, let down and wildly red, would complement a tailcoat. Better than a dress, in fact. *Does she look boyishly handsome or ridiculously barbaric in trousers?*

Wilber noticed her searching the ballroom and cleared his throat one last time. "I advise you to stay clear of Ivy Ferthing, Miss Windihill."

"I might, Wilber. I might not."

"She is scandalous. Wiltshire holds her outlandish ways as a serious disgrace."

She laughed. "How severe you all are. Your concern is noted, but I am a lady now, not the little girl who used to roam this mansion in need of a friend. Remember how you used to amuse me, Wilber?"

Her memories of him were fond. Wilber was the Windihill's oldest and loyalist employee. She had more memories with Wilber than with her own father. Wilber taught her to ride, draw, play croquet, and master the piano. The important George Windihill enjoyed the shadows in his study with a whiskey in hand and a book in his lap more than he enjoyed his only child.

Wilber thoughtfully smiled. "I do, Miss Windihill. I do." He told her the wine needed replenishing and left her side with a grateful bow.

She was neither delighted nor dismayed with the rumors of Ivy Ferthing. Curious. Drawn in. Captivated. Why would a girl of fourteen dress up as a lad? She dabbed the sweat from her top lip and caught a glimpse of Ivy's red, unruly hair from across the room. Off the dance floor, Ivy looked even more out of place.

She moved in her direction. Perhaps she could help the girl. Somehow. Perhaps she could teach her a trick or two about standing taller while still looking at ease. She attended countless lessons in London at her Aunt's bidding. She knew all about a woman's need for finesse, for the perfect stature. She had mastered the search for limitless elegance. A group of girls stepped in front of her and obscured her view of Ivy, and a lurch of unease gripped her chest. "Excuse me." She brushed between their plentiful frocks, ignoring their whispers. Ivy's red hair bobbed against the grain of the crowd and stopped to loiter next to the wine table. Her bright eyes scanned the ballroom, and Sicili breathlessly overcame the urge to wave as she stepped closer and closer toward the misplaced Naughty Ivy.

Her steps were too small and too thought out. Ivy turned and fled the ballroom for the West Wing.

Four

A Daring Match

Ivy elbowed her way through the layers and layers of guests. She snatched a glass of wine from the nearest floating tray and downed it without polite restraint. She suckled the last drop and stared at the empty glass. *Am I an alcoholic?* She shrugged. *I am the daughter of a wine merchant, after all.*

Ahead of her, two ladies whispered at the perfect pitch (to overhear).

"Did you see Ivy Ferthing dancing with poor Patrick Derby? *That* was something one does not see every day. She has no skill."

"No future."

"Did you see her lips? Blue as a blueberry. Hardly arrived and she is already drunk."

"Her father's daughter."

They laughed delightedly.

It wasn't that the conversation affected Ivy. It wasn't that it hadn't. It was her corset. The awful contraption squeezed at her ribs. Fresh air––she *needed* fresh air. A great horde of it. She fought against the guests, fought to get near the entrance of the ballroom, fought to free herself of the glares and the judgement. Her mother sailed easily through the dresses and frills, grasped her arm, and frowned at her just so.

"Look at you, Ivy." Charlotte pulled a handkerchief from her sleeve and began rubbing Ivy's lips with it. "Blue. *Blue.*"

She tried to pull free. "Stop that. You're rubbing them raw."

"Hold still."

"Mother, I need fresh air. I've been dancing all night."

"You danced with one man. One. There are plenty more."

"I don't see them flocking, and seeing as you're bribing them to dance with––"

"I certainly am not," Charlotte lied. "You're being extravagant."

"Be honest, Mother. Could you get a decent man to dance with me if you offered him half of Father's vineyard?"

Charlotte relented. She grabbed the wine glass from Ivy. "You're ruined." Distraught, she sniffled and blew into the handkerchief. "Go on, then. Get some air. Come back on your best behavior, young lady."

"I will, I will."

Balderdash. She would not. She could not. Returning to such a pretentious, crowded ball would be the end of her. Not another minute of it. Not a single ounce more. She had nothing left to give. She took the nearest corridor and scurried for an exit. A dead end. No windows––closed doors and gold-framed paintings. She slipped through the most convenient door and entered a tranquil study flanked with mahogany chairs and books to the ceiling.

She exhaled relief. A moon lit window behind an important desk beckoned to her. She hurried around the desk, moved the lofty armchair, thrashed at the latch, and peeled the window open. She gasped in the fresh, fresh air. Lovely, lovely fresh air. Only a few feet to the nicely trimmed lawn. Her puffed sleeve caught on the latch and tore. *This forsaken dress*. She unbuttoned the wretched thing and tore it off. She flung it out the window. *Dammit*. The corset stole most of the fresh air from her lungs. Still hot. So very hot. The layers of petticoats were to blame. She tore them off as well, until she wore nothing but her underpants and the nasty corset. Better, much better. She breathed a bit easier and readied herself for the jump.

"*What* are you doing?" a voice behind her said.

Ivy straightened. She turned to face the stoic Sicili Windihill, who stood in the doorway, stricken with flushed cheeks and an outraged expression.

She backed against the window. "Pardon?"

"I said, what are you doing?"

"What are *you* doing?"

"What am *I* doing?"

"Indeed." She faltered for an answer. "What are *you* doing following me?"

Sicili glided into the study. Her silk dress sighed. Her expression softened. Her eyes, not void of superiority, crinkled. The moon light illuminated her temple, her cheekbone, and her soft mouth. She need not employ makeup and jewels, like Harriet Pratte and her girls, to captivate. Her presence was more than enough. There was something different about her, something Harriet could only dream of. Something worldly.

Sicili clipped the door shut. "I'm not following you." She drew a staggered breath. "What are you doing down to your undergarments?"

She shrugged. "Escaping. What does it look like?"

"Escaping out a window?"

"Why not?"

"You're quite naked."

She smiled coolly. "Nakedness is skin and flaws and vulnerability, not this blasted corset. Count yourself lucky. I'm layers from being naked."

"Are you not cold?"

"A little. It's lovely. I was roasting."

"Your cheeks are flushed."

Ivy touched them.

Sicili floated toward the desk. "It looked like you were having a grand time dancing."

"Were you watching me?"

"It was hard not to."

They were permanently alone in the moonlit dark, and the dark seemed to move and nudge at them and poke her from the comfortable, airy window ledge and into the spot where the moon shone brightest at the side of the desk where Sicili settled, one hand hesitantly rested upon the mahogany and one hand grasping her waist––*could she breathe?*

Sicili's chin tilted. "You do know who I am?"

"Someone important, I suppose. With that air."

"What if I forbade you to leave?"

She traced a grain in the wood of the desk and rested her palm inches from Sicili's. "Would you dance with me if I stayed?"

Sicili blinked. The open window brought in a cool breeze and an eyelash melted onto her round, ruddy skin. "This is my father's study."

"Is it?" In the dark, Ivy made out the smell of whiskey, leather, and the painted portraits of ancient Windihill family members. "It's lovely." Not that she cared for anything in it but the window. And the lady.

"I never come in here," the lady said. "It looks different in the dark."

"How so?"

"It feels lonely." Her palm brushed Ivy's knuckles, and though her skin was cold to the touch, it sent a jolt up Ivy's arm. They both felt it. Sicili stepped back. She gripped her waist. "I thought I might help you."

"Help me?"

"If you're willing."

The ledge beckoned. "What makes you think I need help?"

"You are about to escape a ball through a window in nothing but your undergarments."

She crossed her arms. "It's not the first time. It won't be the last."

Sicili hid a smile. "You're quite unlike anyone I know. I have never met someone so boyish and rude and gallantly content to be so."

"Now you have," she said. "Do you wish you hadn't?"

"No. Truly. I only wish to make a few suggestions."

"Such as?"

Sicili licked a finger. "May I?"

"Be my guest."

She ran the wet finger over Ivy's eyebrows, groomed them, harnessed the strands of loose hair from Ivy's stacked mess and tucked them neatly away, uncrossed Ivy's arms, made her stand tall, fixed her corset, and stepped back to admire her work.

Ivy scoffed softly, amused. "Well? Do I look the part?"

Sicili frowned. "No. I dare say you're doomed to look clumsy and unladylike."

"Happily." Ivy backed toward the safety of the ledge. "Right. A pleasure to meet you, Miss Windihill––however, escape is calling."

"Wait––" Sicili touched Ivy's wrist. "I'm not meaning to offend you."

Ivy had to admit. Sicili Windihill was far more interesting in the moonlight, in the dark, in the shadows of a secret study.

"Miss Windihill," she said, "I've heard it all. Do you think you're the first person to offer me help? I have a secret for you." She leaned into Sicili's ear. "You're not required to fit in either." And winked.

Sicili's lips parted. She looked lovely in the pale light in that silky expression. Her golden hair was pinned to perfection. *She must look reverent with her hair down, draped over a naked shoulder.*

As if her words held some power over Ivy, Sicili cinched closer. "I've heard the rumors, Miss Ferthing."

She smiled gallantly. "Which ones?"

"The worst of them."

"I doubt that."

"You once dressed up as a lad."

"One of my finest moments."

"Is it true? You wore trousers and a tailcoat, and a dirty fisher's cap."

She tipped her invisible cap. "A pleasure to make your acquaintance, Miss Windihill. Trousers are much wiser than the confinements of a sufferable corset."

Sicili gasped. "You're proud of yourself."

"Wouldn't you be? I'm a legend around these parts. I might be more famous than your well-to-do father."

"You're gloating."

"You're pretentious."

"You're rude."

"You're quick to judge."

"You're a self-proclaimed libertine."

"You're bored. Isn't that why you followed me?"

Sicili blinked. "I didn't follow you."

They were perilously close. "I know who I am, Miss Windihill."

"So it seems. Are you decided on refusing my help? I could be of great service to you."

She leaned in. "Not in the way I should hope."

Their lips met, briefly, and the dark felt a little warmer and a little less lonely for a heartbeat of a moment. Ivy hesitated, held her breath, grew savvy, and stiffened, wary that kissing the much-sought-after daughter of George Windihill might land her behind bars––or her mother's wrath. *Ivy, you rot. You devil.* She withdrew.

Sicili lightly held Ivy's elbow. Her hold tightened softly before her hand slipped to her side.

Sicili searched her face. "Did you mean to kiss me?"

"Did you mean to hold on?"

"I..."

Her diamond cheekbones dazzled. Her eyes glossed and grew distant, dazed. Her ruddy skin looked hot, and Ivy gulped. Oh, *rot*. She should have jumped when she had the chance. Wonderful uncertainly gripped her.

"Now," she cleared her throat, "if you'll excuse me, Miss Windihill, I have a window to get back to. I'm reluctant to leave you in such a state, but truly, I cannot stay." She paused before the jump. "Should a woman with nervous habits and dewy eyes come looking for me, tell her you haven't a clue where I got to, will you?"

Sicili nodded.

She turned her back and out she slipped, landing softly on the neat lawn. She grabbed the crumpled dress and took off in long strides for a hedge of shrubbery. With a fleeting glance over her shoulder, she saw Sicili still standing by the ledge, unmoved. Miss Windihill stared longingly after her.

Something worldly, indeed.

***

Sicili hid in the study. She locked the door and melted into her father's leather armchair. Hot, so hot. *Am I flattered or am I enraged?* Not only had she walked in on Ivy stripped to her corset petticoat and tried to help her and failed, but she had also suffered a kiss––a *kiss* from a woman. Her cheeks burned. They felt on fire. She feared they would burn off into little heaps of ash and sizzle at her feet. Her chest felt raw and reborn, and her heart frantically endeavored to break free.How dare a trouser wearing, bold, hotheaded Ivy Ferthing steal a kiss from her? *Humiliated. I'm humiliated.*

She managed composure, after her breathing slowed to an acceptable pace, and exited the study, all while fighting off the hot memory of Ivy leaping out the window, red hair lashing at her back. When the cool air of the hall hit her damp skin, she leaned against the wall for support. *Am I so deprived of human touch?* Plenty of gentlemen in the city touched her, pressed their hands against her back and squeezed her arm, planted a delicate kiss on her hand. None received the reaction Ivy had stolen. Not one caused such a tumult of hot emotions.

Where is my fan? I'm a sticky mess.

"Are you well, Miss Windihill?" asked a gentleman who stood at the end of the hall.

She touched her wrist to her forehead. *Feverish. I'm feverish.* Her Aunt Gertrude's discerning voice pricked at her conscious."In the face of adversary, stand tall in a confident posture and precise attitude." She tried her best, but she felt off. Discombobulated.

"You look quite ill." The man drew near. He would do. His put-together look and steady eyes would distract her from the thought of Ivy's lips.

"I only needed a moment of fresh air," she said.

"I shall not ask you to dance, then." Concern etched his otherwise even voice. "Your state is most alarming."

"You shall. I would be delighted."

She accepted his friendly arm. He led her back to sanity, gaiety, music. As they danced, he held her tight. He brought her a little too close for a waltz. Dizzy and dazed, she looked up into his steady brown eyes and stale, structured face. *Is he the sort of man a woman wants for a husband? Would his handsome charm last?*

They moved across the dance floor, and heads turned, and she caught her old man's eye. George smiled broadly as he watched her dance, a drink in hand and pure delight on his evil face.

She mustered a smile. "Who do I call you?"

"Princeton Evergreen."

"Do I know your father?"

"You would." His smile glistened. "Paris Evergreen. He owns a franchise of banks, mainly in London."

"I do know him." Her sanity gradually returned. Her heart slowed. Her cheeks cooled.

His arm tightly gripped her waist. "How pleased I am to finally meet you, Miss Windihill."

"My friends call me Sicili."

A sparkle lit his eye. "Are we to be friends?"

"Possibly." His forward attitude made her wary. Not to mention that sparkle. She had seen it one too many times in many a man's eyes, and had known the displeasure caused by dashing it all too forcefully. "I make no promises."

"Then I will not hold you to any." He tightened his arm around her waist. "Your father speaks highly of you."

"Does he often speak of me to you?"

"He does."

"I assure you I am not as important as he makes me out to be."

"You are. Look around. You own every opinion in this ballroom." He whispered in her ear. "You are the belle of the ball."

They danced two more sets. He knew every step and every turn. He was a genteel dance partner, though a bit too persistent with his eyes. She was flattered, but not impressed, and far from enamored. When another gentleman cut in, Princeton kissed her knuckles and held his lips to her skin. "I look forward to our next meeting, Sicili Windihill."

"Mr. Evergreen," she said with a practiced smile.

She wiped her knuckles.

As she danced into midnight on the arms of trite suitors, she fell into a warm, buttery stupor. With Ivy. No matter how many eager gentlemen her father encouraged and sent her way and no matter how late she waltzed, the thought of Ivy Ferthing down to her corset and petticoat persisted and conquered. The breathless conversation they shared in the moon lit study stuck to her skin. By the end of the night, her cheeks were hot again, not from dancing the ball away, but from the memory of Ivy's lips.

Five

The Rumors

Five years earlier: 1835

Ivy Ferthing was fourteen when society turned its back on her.

From a young age, she preferred garments tailored for the male sex. Back then, she had no idea know why. Childhood did not expect answers from her. She simply relished the freedom of a large pair of trousers––the comfort to move around and be herself. It could have been the difference in fabrics: men's clothing was made of durable suedes and cottons, whereas women's garments were constructed of flimsier, scratchier materials combined with restrictive undergarments. She felt solid and protected under an oversized tailcoat. In a dress, Ivy had to stand tall and exude elegance. She had to be the woman society told her to be. She had to pretend that slouching and letting her gut lose did not come naturally to her. For Ivy, *pretending* (a word she refused to believe in) could be equated to living with her tongue and her arms lopped off. Pretending simply did own a place in her world, which was why she embraced her preference for the unusual––an attitude that was most certainly frowned upon.

When she was a child, Ivy's whims, like those of most children, could easily be thwarted. When she dressed up to impersonate one of her three brothers and marched around Vineyard Estate, her mother would give her a harsh scolding and send her upstairs to change. As Ivy grew older, however, her will to emulate the male sex proved harder to control. She became clever with it. She stole a pair of this and a set of that from here and there. She made herself a nice collection and hid the secret garments under her bed in a trunk marked *Do not meddle, Mother*. At night, when Vineyard Estate hung in darkness and slumber, she would pull on her stolen clothes and assume the role of a gentleman. She would dance with a make-believe lady, and every now and then, lean in to kiss her.

Soon, though, Ivy grew bored with dressing up in secret. She wanted to be free to wear whatever she liked, wherever she chose. One night, during her fourteenth year, she disguised herself as a penniless lad. She hid her unruly red hair under a ratty old fisher's cap and, to fatten up her tiny figure, wore a hideous, bulky tailcoat with worn trousers. She snuck into the night and roamed the countryside of Buckingham until dawn.

It became a devilish habit. And Ivy grew to love the freedom. While all of Wiltshire slept, she would gallivant from road to field, from street to alley, at her leisure, brimming with delight. That is, until one Sunday morning.

***

Ivy woke up feeling adequately rested, but thoroughly confused. She lay in a lush field of dew and grass, the rising sun her blanket. A man with a gruff scowl stood over her. A flock of *baaaing* sheep accompanied him. One leaned in and licked her face.

The man poked her with his cane.

"Wake up, lad," he scowled. "Up. That's it. Up with you."

She sat and looked about. The field stretched on for miles. It was none other than Mr. Barney's sheep field. The man poking at her was Mr. Barney himself.

"Can't you read, lad?" Mr. Barney said.

"I can," she declared.

"Didn't you read the signs? They say, 'Private property.' See?"

"I'm sorry, Mr. Barney. I don't quite––"

The night before came back to her with terrible clarity. She had barely survived a fight with her mother. Charlotte Ferthing had grown more and more suspicious of her daughter's desire to be alone. "Not to mention, Ivy, your lack of interest in young, *worthy* men."

"None of them are worthy of me," she had lashed back.

"Such balderdash, girl. Look at you––"

"Stop fiddling with my hair, Mother."

"––how young and capable you are. Will you try? You must show men––"

"Stop pinching my cheeks, Mother."

"––that you care."

"I could care less."

"Why, Ivy? Tell me why?"

"I haven't a clue." She had thrown her arms up in exhaustion and accidentally back-handed Charlotte in the face. Her mother had wailed and retreated to her tea parlor, assuring the entire household that she would not be speaking to Ivy for the rest of the day.

Being the answerless adolescent that she was, Ivy had sought refuge in the comforts of her secret wardrobe and stolen a bottle of her father's oldest wine; Mr. William Ferthing was a celebrated wine merchant and would not miss it.

She had drunk her sorrows back and stumbled out to roam Wiltshire.

And now she was being poked and prodded by Mr. Grumpy Barney. Not only had she trespassed on his sacred pasture and fallen asleep under the influence, but she had also done so wearing her guise of being penniless and of the opposite gender.

"I'll have you explain yourself, lad," Mr. Barney demanded. "Out with it."

There was no good explanation, Ivy knew. She blinked up at the man. She searched for a likely answer, scratched her head for it.

Mr. Barney bent down and pulled the half-empty bottle from the grass.

"What's this?" he asked.

She stuttered.

"A lad of your age drinking," Mr. Barney scowled. "And on my property. I'll have you be thrown behind bars for this, you scoundrel."

"You have me confused, Mr. Barney."

"Where'd a scoundrel like you get this drink, anyhow? Did you steal it? You little––"

"I'm no lad," she said, getting up and feeling brisker than she had in a good while. She smoothed down her tailcoat, brushed off some stray wisps of grass. She adjusted her cap. "I'm a lady," she said, all too carelessly.

Mr. Barney howled a good long spluttering laugh. "A lady? A lady never dresses up like penniless lads."

"Who says?"

"Good society says so."

Ivy pulled off her cap. Her red hair fell out in long naughty tendrils. Mr. Barney stepped back. His sheep wobbled about, *baaaing*. She beamed with pleasure at how her transformation affected Mr. Barney's face. He went whiter than Charlotte Ferthing's table linens drying in the afternoon sun: the ones her mother used for special occasions like Christmas and if ever the Queen of England came for a tete-a-tete.

"Is that you, Miss Ferthing?" he said, gasping.

"It's me, all right."

His eyes filled with shame and dread. "Does your mother know you've been prancing about disguised as a lad?"

"She doesn't need to."

Mr. Barney scratched his head, clearly at a loss for what to do, clearly bewildered by Ivy's bold choice of clothing.

"Really, Mr. Barney," she said, feeling more like herself than she had in weeks. "She truly doesn't need to know. Mothers should be kept in the dark about these sorts of shenanigans. Let's make this our little secret. What do you say? Shake on it?"

Mr. Barney did not shake on it.

The cart ride to Vineyard Estate was a dreary one. Mr. Barney refused to say a word. He chewed away at a bit of straw. Given his silence, Ivy knew she would be in grand trouble with her mother and the rest of Wiltshire. She abided the ride in squirming apprehension.

Charlotte Ferthing must have seen the cart from the end of the drive, for she was out front waving her hands frantically when Mr. Barney pulled to a halt.

"Oh, Ivy, you outrage," Charlotte said, near tears. "Where have you been, girl?"

"Out and about," Ivy said and dismounted with a boyish stride.

"Mr. Ferthing and I have been worried sick. I sent him scouring the countryside for you." Charlotte looked her up and down, suddenly becoming aware of the situation. "Well, now. That's a lovely dress. Where did you get it, Ivy?"

"It's not mine."

Dread overtook Charlotte. "If it's not yours, whose is it?"

Mr. Barney cleared his throat. "The dress belongs to my daughter, Anna. She lent it to your Ivy due to——well, Mrs. Ferthing..." He cleared his throat again. "...unfortunate circumstances."

Charlotte's face paled, then flushed with anger, then came to a medium hue alongside a sickened expression. "What circumstances, Mr. Barney?"

"I'm vexed to tell you, Mrs. Ferthing."

"Go on," Charlotte said, her voice shaky.

He couldn't stop clearing his throat. "Miss Ferthing——ahem——was found fast asleep on my property with a half-drunk bottle of wine at her side."

"A bottle of wine, Ivy?" Charlotte's color drained. "Do explain yourself."

Ivy took a great breath. "I stole it from the cellar, Mother."

"Oh, Ivy..."

Mr. Barney stepped closer. "That's not the worst of it, Mrs. Ferthing——"

"I'll tell her," Ivy up and said. She of sudden felt a surge of pride. "I was wearing these." She held out the folded penniless lad's costume, which Mrs. Barney had conspicuously wrapped in an old newspaper and hemp against Ivy's wishes. "Open it, Mother."

Charlotte clawed the bow to shreds. One by one, she lifted the garments into the light and eyed them with immense terror.

"These... Ivy," Charlotte said, her voice low with despair. She pressed a hand to her now-pale cheek. "A lad's clothes. And so worn and of such a stench. Trousers, Ivy. A tailcoat, Ivy. This hideous fisher's cap!"

"All of it," Mr. Barney said. "She was dressed as a penniless lad, I tell you. That's how I found her this morning––to my shame––just as the sun was peeking over the hills. Now, I'm not quite sure what to think of all this, Mrs. Ferthing. I reckon––"

"Dear Mr. Barney. How kind of you to return her to me. I assume this little incident will stay between the three of us." Charlotte grasped his hand, working her charms on him.

Mr. Barney shook his head. "I'm afraid my wife and girls have already seen Miss Ferthing at her worst, and I can't be sure my wife will keep quiet on the subject."

"Surely you could ask her to keep it between our two families?" A desperation lit Charlotte's eye. She gripped Mr. Barney's hand now, digging her thumb in. "Let me fetch a few bottles from the cellar. The best of them. Surely your good wife could use a splash of wine in her stew. Mr. Ferthing's drink is quite a delight to curl up to at the end of a hard, long day. You must work such long, hard days."

Her charm had failed. Mr. Barney reclaimed his hand most righteously. Charlotte had held it so tight that there were red fingers marks on his skin. "I'm not one to be bribed, I'll have you know. And we're not much for drinking, us Barneys. I've got sheep to herd and fields to plow. My dear wife is busy all day with the girls and school. We don't have much time to sit down to a glass of wine, however fine it is."

Charlotte was desperate. "Surely there's something I can do to keep this little incident between us. Ivy... well... Ivy's only a girl. Only fourteen."

"What's that got to do with it, Mother?" said Ivy.

"Everything, girl. You weren't thinking right. Children never think right."

"My girls think just fine," Mr. Barney said. "They'd never be caught wearing men's apparel. They're good girls."

"Are you calling me evil?" Ivy said. She crossed her arms.

"Not evil, Miss Ferthing," he said, choosing his words. "Deranged, maybe."

"That's the word," Charlotte gasped. "Deranged. Not herself. Not right."

"You're describing a mad person, Mother. I'm perfectly sane."

"Are you?" Charlotte hurled at her.

Mr. Barney began backing toward his horse and cart.

"Mr. Barney," Charlotte cried out, "you will keep this a secret, won't you?"

He gave Charlotte a tip of his hat. "I can't make any promises, Mrs. Ferthing," he said, solemn as a judge. "Not in these parts. If this were London, perhaps... I'm sure this sort of thing happens all the time in the city, but it can't be allowed to happen in the countryside."

"I understand you completely, Sir. But, please, do think of my daughter's reputation. If this gets out, it will be the ruin of her."

Mr. Barney climbed into his cart with a forced, "Good day to you." He couldn't be persuaded, Ivy knew. The man had made up his mind. He lashed his horse, and the cart creaked down Vineyard Estate's drive and over the hill.

She was right, of course. By midday, the rumor of her indecent disguise had been unleashed. Like wildfire, whispers of her strange behavior spread across the countryside.

On his way home, Mr. Barney crossed paths with Beatrice Doily, a long-time servant of the Prattle family who happened to be rushing to work. Mr. Barney couldn't be expected to keep his tongue on such a scandalous matter. Beatrice, whose second occupation was the butter-mouthed tattletale of Wilthshire, saw it as her duty to inform Mrs. Prattle first thing. The Prattles were, of course, outrageously delighted.

It had been a few years since the last scandal, which had centered around a servant involved with a high-class fellow. The Prattle family heaped their scorn on Ivy over breakfast. They said a prayer for poor Mrs. Ferthing. All the while, the servants eavesdropped. At afternoon tea, the Prattle servants visited the Dainty servants, where they tittered long and hard. The Dainty servants, that same afternoon, whispered about Ivy in the kitchen, and as they did, Vivian Dainty strolled by. Vivian, being the most curious of the Danitys, demanded they speak up and tell-*all*. By the end of the week, Ivy was named "Naughty Ivy" and giggled at by children a third her age and half her height.

From there, rumor launched itself into various ingenious forms. One idea was that Ivy was a spoiled youngest child who couldn't be kept out of her father's wine cellar. Another adaption was that Ivy figured herself a boy, a fourth brother—thus the trousers and tailcoat and fisher's cap!

At the core, the rumors were true. Ivy liked to drink to escape society. Ivy liked to dress up as a lad so she could one day kiss a lady. Ivy was ridiculous. She was awkward with boys. She was tall and lanky and bereft of ladylike inclinations.

Ivy embraced the rumors, realizing the rumors were more her than her mother's inept version of a lovely daughter who wanted to read and sew and learn the piano and simper over boring boys with boogers up their bottoms from listening to their nannies and mothers all their lives. She was not like the other children her age. This was a comfort. This was her true disguise, the one that kept her safe from being someone she would never feel whole as.

Charlotte Ferthing, of course, suffered a broken heart. "Surely a daughter with such a tarnished reputation can't be expected to properly enter society. You're never leaving this house, Ivy."

And so, out of shame and self-preservation, Charlotte kept her daughter at home, hidden behind books and protected from the malicious tongues that blemished Ivy's once good name.

And that was how the rumors began. And that was how Ivy Ferthing became known as Naughty Ivy. Ivy relished the rumors. She delighted in her newfound solitude. She had never been overly fond of society. It had so easily disowned her, so she, in turn disowned it. She kept herself fully occupied at Vineyard Estate, helping her father perfect his wondrous wines. Of course, she didn't stop with her disguises. Nor did she stop sneaking out at night.

Six

An Outrageous Proposition

Sicili halted in the East Wing in front of a regal portrait of a younger, happier George and Francine Windihill. Though his eyebrows had been peppered with brown back then, they still carried a disarrayed alarm about them. Had her father always been evil? A terrible headache plagued her, and she braced the wall. Wilber, on his way to the sunny breakfast parlor, exited the kitchen with a tray of steaming sausages, crumpets, and tea.

"Are you well, Miss Windihill?"

She touched her lips. "I feel grossly sore, Wilber, and my head." She touched her temples. "I danced more than twenty sets last night. Father had me up to my elbows in clawing, predictable suitors. I do wish he would let me breathe."

"His intentions are amiable."

"Are they?"

He cleared his throat.

"I had the strangest dream, Wilber." Her lips tingled.

"Do you wish to share it?"

"Not all of it, no. Quite horrendous. Would you believe I dreamed about Ivy Ferthing?"

Wilber frowned. "I would. You were rather taken with her at the ball."

"Taken? Wilber, you exaggerate. She happened to be the most interesting person present." She laughed. "Mainly for her lack of skill. Nothing more."

He nodded. "If you are certain."

"I am, Wilber."

He went on his way and left her simmering in the shadow of the kitchen. She pursed her lips. They tingled and tickled and reminded her of a red-haired, bright eyed outcast of a girl. *Stop that*. Last night, in the heat of the crowds and the cool of the study, her emotions ran away on her. Today was a new day with new promises and a new sunrise and the glorious company of her family. She would cherish them. She would bask in the presence of her mother. She would think well of her father, despite her weighted distrust of him.

The portrait on the wall loomed. George Windihill's heavy-lidded eyes fixated on her.

She followed Wilber to the breakfast parlor and sat with her mother by the Persian draped window that faced the West Wing. Sunshine embraced them. She shaded her eyes and gazed across the lawn at her father's half open study window. Pigments of colored light reflected off the glass.

Wilber poured tea.

Francine cleared her throat. "You seem preoccupied, Sicili."

"Do I?"

Wilber held a saucer and cup to her. She grasped it. "Forgive me, Wilber. Last night has me in a state."

Francine studied her. "Did you have a favorite, darling?"

"A favorite?"

"Suitor, of course. From the ball."

"Oh." Her temples throbbed. "It is difficult, Mother, when they come flying from all directions. Where is Father?"

Francine thoughtfully sipped her tea, and Sicili saw her share a secret look with Wilber before he straightened and left the parlor. "Your father will join us for lunch, darling. He's accustomed to waking early and walking in the morning. It's good for his heart."

The old man taking care of his heart. How strange. Six years ago, while she yet lived under his roof, he owned the habit of sleeping until noon and spending his day indoors with a game of chess and a whiskey in hand. He had clung to the dark of his study. She had so rarely seen him.

"He has changed, Sicili," Francine said. "Your absence has made him... more thoughtful."

"Impossible." She snorted. "George Windihill? Thoughtful?"

Francine reached across the couch and squeezed Sicili's hand. "He wants you to return permanently to Wiltshire."

"Permanently?"

"We both do."

"Out of the question, Mother. My home is in London now. All my things and friends are there."

"We miss you dearly."

"A price you must pay for sending me away."

Francine returned to her tea. "Are you so impartial, Sicili?"

She rubbed her temple. "Forgive me, Mother. I suffer a terrible pounding, and sometimes I forget how delusion-ally you love that old menace."

Francine sheepishly smiled and plastered a crumpet with jam. Her mother owned the habit of staying calm when George imposed himself on the innocent. Whatever he had been brewing up with that devilish glint was out of her mother's control.

Francine took a delicate bite of the crumpet. "Sicili, do refrain from despising him."

Her skin tingled and her lips itched. "Will I have a reason to?"

Francine shrugged and turned to the window. "Your father wants to see you in his study. Finish your breakfast and go to him. He thinks it urgent."

"Does he? What is he up to, Mother?"

Francine raised the porcelain teacup to her lips. "You know I never know."

***

George Windihill could be described as a persistent man. When he had an idea––the strangest, smallest, wickedest of such––he preferred to chase that scant notion to the moon and bring it swinging back into orbit. A man who owned a capital reputation, wealth, and a civil attitude toward those less fortunate was not easily thwarted.

Sicili described her father as obnoxiously selfish.

She knocked thrice on his study door.

"Come in, my angel," George sang from within.

She caught her breath, jiggled the knob, and reluctantly stepped into her father's sanctuary of tethered leather, whiskey, and mystery. He sat in his great armchair behind the mahogany desk with a copy of *How to Create the Perfect Marriage by Uniting the Perfect Union* by Mr. Cody Ale and Mrs. Ann Misery pinched between his fingers.

"Here you are, Sicili." He licked his thumb, folded his page, and snapped the book shut.

She gave a start. The door moaned shut, and when it clicked, fear settled over her in a thick haze. *Oh, forbid. There it is. That devious glint.*

His face twisted with delight.

"Here I am, Father. I do hope that book is a light read."

"This old thing?" He grinned from ear to ear. "Have a seat."

"I prefer to stand."

"I insist, my angel. We have much to discuss."

"Have we?" She crossed her arms.

He laughed, and the glint grew and conquered. "You have been away these six years."

"I'm beginning to fear my return was a mistake."

"Nonsense. You have nothing to fear. I have your best interest at heart."

I doubt that, old man. She relented her position at the door and settled into the chair across from him. He leaned in. Though the sun peeked through the window and warmed the edges of his moustache and his crazy white hair, she felt particularly cold in his shadow. She shuddered.

It felt like a business meeting. Him across the desk from her, one hand resting on the book. Her hands twisted in her dress at her side. It felt like their meeting six years ago when he told her she would be sent away from the only home she had ever known. She felt small again, and she loathed the feeling.

His eyebrows dashed upward. "How about a sip of whiskey to take the edge off?"

"Mother said you gave whiskey up."

"I did. While you were away. Now that you have returned, we have much to celebrate. A skimp of whiskey is well due." He popped the crystal bottle on his desk and poured himself a drip and offered her half a glass.

She gulped it back. "Shall we get on with it, Father? I see that glint in your eye."

"A glint?" He poured her another half glass. "Is it a frightful glint? I dare not scare you off with it."

"Devious. I call it devious. And I am frightened."

"Of me?"

"Need I remind you? The last time you summoned me to your study was six years ago. You announced my departure to live with my aunt. You gave me no say. You had Wilber pack my things and deliver me to London the next day. I recall it distinctly, Father, like a cold winter wind biting the bone. You waved from the window––your face in the shadows. Mother stood in the front entry, gripping the door, full of uncertainty and sadness."

George leaned back. His brow crinkled. "You make your fortunate life sound so decidedly dreadful. You had education and comfort and safety."

"What is comfort and safety without family?"

He heaved a great gust of a sigh. "You do make a valid point. I admit, my angel, I was wrong to be so bold. I refused to consider your happiness."

She blinked. *Wait for it.*

He leaned forward, rapped his fingers on the book and poured himself another drip of whiskey––the wood groaned, and his moustache lifted while his eyes crinkled. "While you have lived in London these six years, I have pondered a great deal and come to the conclusion that you have been away for far too long."

"Have I?"

"I never expected you to keep away for six *excruciating* years."

"You are to blame. You sent me. *To meet friends and endless, handsome suitors.* Do you remember those words?"

"I do. You have met friends. You have met suitors."

"I was sixteen."

"You were lonely."

"I was equally lonely in the city. Aunt Gertrude burdened me with her strange moods and high expectations. I was a child. Do you remember my tears?"

"I do."

"I learned the ways of the world with a heavy heart."

"I do regret causing you pain, my Sicili. However, to this day, I am pleased I did not let your tears persuade me otherwise. The world has done wonders for you. Look at you. Look at your bright face and wild eyes. You are a star, a light in the dark. Men of the greatest reputation and class are after your affection."

"My fortune," she corrected.

The glint twinkled. "Fortune can be used to trap the wisest of men. You must look at your disposition as my daughter as an advantage, not a burden."

"You old wry."

"You will marry someday."

She scoffed. "Not if I can help it."

He stood, moved around his desk in a jiffy of jubilance and caught up her hand, squeezing it quite firmly. "My Sicili. You are my one and only child––my only heir. I sent you to London to learn to ways of the world and be educated by your aunt, yes––but I must confess, I had ulterior motives." He kissed her palm. "I had hoped you would catch the eye of a great lord, and fall in love, and..." he pinched her knuckles. "Quite the romantic I was."

"Quite." She wriggled from his deadly hold. "A great lord?"

"An earl, perhaps. The prince, I dare."

"Are you not rich enough, old man?"

He laughed, deep and full. "You see, my angel, you were born with the position and beauty to enchant whomever you please, whomever strikes your fancy."

A breeze, brisk and kind, rushed in and stirred the smell of leather, whiskey, and disappointment. She looked past him at the open window. The all too recent memory of Ivy dashing out of it braced her. Her cheeks flooded with unprecedented warmth and her gut gave a squeeze. She gripped the armrest.

The outlandish sight of Ivy stripped to her corset had set something in motion. Something deep. Something diabolical and lovely. Something she could not quite comprehend. *What is she doing to my mind?* The present situation was much too disconcerting for silly memories. She glared back at her father. "Are you admitting to sending me to London to get married? Is that the only nonsense that motivates you?"

"Indeed, at my age. Your mother is motivated as well. You are twenty and two, Sicili. Well passed your single years. A woman should be married by your age."

Her knuckles whitened around the arm of the chair. "Says who?"

"Society, my girl. Centuries of it. I wish to see you happy, with children and joy and a fine husband at your side."

"How do you know a husband and children will bring me joy and happiness?"

He cupped her cheek with a laugh. "They bring every girl your age fulfillment and purpose."

Do I have no purpose without a man and children in my life? Truly? Is that all I am good for? She rose and recoiled from his jubilance, into the shadowy corner by a bookshelf of unread books. *Am I truly unlike the girls my age? Am I so different?* Such tumultuous thoughts struck her, and cut deep, and hurt. Her dress pinched. Her corset, without due warning, suddenly felt too tight and constricting, and she strove to catch her breath. She was glad to know the truth. For years she had wondered why he had treated her so trivially, like a nuisance, why he had ignored her for whiskey and books and his dark, twisted ideas. She had been too afraid to ask--too afraid to face the truth. Deep down, she had always known how selfish he was.

She had recoiled too far into the shadows, and George Windihill could no longer see her. He danced about the study, eyes dazzling, arms flailing, frothy at the mouth with a scheme. "You have standards, Sicili, which I am aware of. As is your mother. We have taken your ways into much consideration and have put together a list of gentlemen with the finest occupations and most diverting families. Quite a list it is. Quite!"

"I am different," she whispered to herself as she glowered at him from the shadows. A hiccup sprung to her lips. Her cheeks burned, fierce and hot, and a twisting. Her heart fluttered in a deviant way. Aunt Gertrude had told her something once. Something strange: "Love feels like a twist in your organs, a shift, really. Raw and poisonous and habitual. Once you have tasted it you shall not go back, Sicili."

The old man was caught up with himself. He had failed to hear her, and her profound words had no effect on him. He skipped about the study with exaggerated gestures. "You shall be up to your neck in their sweltering company, my Sicili. I made the appropriate arrangements. It has all been taken care of. Each of them will meet you at a different event. You may decide for yourself which one you prefer. You see, I do have your best interest at heart. Mr. Evergreen was the first of many. Did you like him? You danced most of the night with him. He was quite captivated by you, I must say."

Her corset rubbed. Her ribs felt raw. "Princeton Evergreen means to marry me?"

"Every man means to marry you. Have you not been listening, my girl? *You* are what every man wants."

"Men are far from what *I* want." It came out abruptly. *Raw. Poisonous.* Hearing it out loud startled her. Had she been holding her breath her entire life? Little hiccups of air elapsed. Her lungs were brand new, and she had yet to learn how to use them. She felt tingly and alert and clearheaded. Her world came alive all at once. *Have I been in the shadows all this time?* The window called to her. The sun rolling over the hills beckoned her outside of her little, quiet world of confusion.

"Are you hearing me, Sicili? Are you listening?"

She reached from the shadowy corner for escape, and moved toward the light, forgetting to note the desk. Her hip slammed against a sharp corner, and the bottle of whiskey shattered as it hit the floor.

"*Oh.*" Dazed, she crouched and brushed the broken crystal into a pile and sorted the pieces of glass in means of size. Biggest to smallest. Most dangerous and sharpest to least frightful.

George jumped. "Good riddance, my angel. Leave that to Wilber."

"I must clean this up."

"You might hurt yourself. I insist you stop." He dashed into the hall yelling, "Wilber, Wilber, do come at once."

Too much. It was all too much. The light reflecting off the window onto the shattered crystal, the new fluttering of her heart, the twist in her organs. Her throbbing headache. Last night's memories. Her sore legs from dancing too many sets with too many men she cared so little for. Her father, this list of his, Ivy intruding on every thought. A distraction––that's what she needed. Something fun and lighthearted. In London, she visited her good friend Catherine when in need of an uplifted spirit. Catherine was a lively, charismatic girl who harnessed just the right energy to take one's mind off pressing matters and replace them with joyous, fascinating ideas. Why had she not brought Catherine along?

In her hurry to sort the mess on the floor, her hand grazed a shard of crystal. She flinched. Blood trickled down her finger, over her knuckle, and splattered on the white rug.

Her father gasped and came to her aide, spluttering nonsense about blood and a ball and his list.

She bundled her finger in a fold of dress. Blood spread over the floral print and diluted a pink flower.

"It's deep," she said.

"Try not to look at it, my angel. Looking at it will make you ill."

"I'm surprised, not ill."

Wilber rushed into the study. "Are you well, Miss Windihill?"

"Fine, Wilber." She forced a smile. "I collided with father's desk and managed to cut myself. Silly me."

Wilber disappeared for half a second and returned with a basin, cloth, and some gauze.

Her father slugged into his chair. "Quite the morning," he groaned, as though he suffered from his own cut.

Wilber exposed her wound. It bled anew. Deep, red, gushing.

"We have to stop the bleeding," he said.

George held his chest. "Do hurry, Wilber. Her blood is precious. She has only so much of it. Her legacy is in great demand."

She glared at her father while Wilber mended her finger, the same way he had mended her loneliness as a little girl, and wound the gauze tight and even.

He offered her a sympathetic smile. "That should do, Miss Windihill. If the bleeding persists, I recommend you see a doctor for stitching."

"Quite the butler you are," she gratefully whispered. Wilber nodded, cleared his throat, and took his leave.

"Is that better, my angel?"

"It stings."

He stood. "Shall we continue our meeting?"

"Goodness. Is it not over?"

"Of course not. You have yet to hear my proposition."

"You called me to your study to proposition me? I think you mean *bully*."

He huffed. "I resent your resentment, Sicili. That word *bully* will not do. No. I am a doting, concerned father who has one daughter. You are my only offspring."

"We have been over that."

"Not to the full." Brimming with pent-up schemes, he ran a hand through his wild hair and adjusted his cravat. "My Sicili, I propose you stay in Wiltshire." He paused. "Indefinitely."

She drew out a sigh. "Mother said as much. For what cause, Father?"

"For the befitting cause of a husband."

"Did you not hear me? A husband does not strike my fancy. I have everything I desire and love in London. Everything."

"Indeed." He leaned onto the desk. The wood creaked under his weight. His eyes blazed intently. "You have made your sentiment for London clear——*but* you would have nothing you desire and love without *my* fortune."

His earnest, resolved eyes met hers.

Her wound painfully pulsed. The gauze pressed into her skin and cut off the blood supply to the tip of her finger.

The headache had become a persistent band of pressure jabbing at her skull. She needed the dark, and covers, every cover known to Windsworth. "Did I hear you correctly, Father?"

"I said you need my fortune and generosity in order to survive."

Blinking sunlight sent shadows over the side of his face, then it dipped behind a formation of clouds and left the study cool and ominous. "You have my utmost attention."

He smiled. "Good. You may go on living how you desire and spending my money on whatever indeed strikes your fancy under one condition. You must marry."

Wind struck the window and gusted into the study and blew the book he had been so engrossed in open. *How to Create the Perfect Marriage by Uniting the Perfect Union* was not a light read after all.

She cleared her dry throat. "You demand I marry."

He slammed the book shut. "Indeed. If you provide me with grandchildren, all the better."

"You are unbelievable."

"And thoroughly serious."

The wind persisted. It howled against the side of the mansion. Dark clouds gathered outside, and the sun hid behind the East Wing. George closed the window and exaggerated a shiver. "It looks like rain, my angel."

It feels like cruelty. "Let me clarify, Father. You plan to disinherit me if I do not do as you command."

"That is a harsh clarification."

"But it is the truth."

He swished his hand like a famous composer, or painter, like she might better understand his cruelty with a flare of tumultuous motions. "Plenty of daughters love to please their fathers. They love to settle down and start a family of their own. When did you decide to be so different? I think it perfectly normal to get married. Perfectly."

She rose. "Truly, Father. I cannot stomach this." She headed for the door. "I need a day's worth of rest. I suggest you speak with mother about a more appropriate way to welcome me home."

He cleared his throat. "Your mother is aware of my proposition, and she agrees. Your choice in the matter is nonexistent, I'm afraid."

His words were meant to cut, but they hardly phased her. She had learned young to fortify her heart against George Windihill's passionate words. She paused in front of the door.

She was tired, so very tired of his schemes and delusional ways of showing her love. This latest ruse of his had taken everything out of her. She turned to him. "You? Afraid?"

His laugh held no constraint. "You do have the choice of your husband. I shall not force you into wedlock with someone you despise."

"You do realize you are forcing me into wedlock to begin with."

"I think coaxing is a better word. *Force* sounds so... force-ful."

She scowled. "Oh, Father. I am on the edge of hating you."

He slapped the desk. His books and quill jumped. "You have until your twenty-third birthday."

A new wave of fatigue gripped her. She stuttered. "My-my twenty-third birthday is three months near."

His head wagged with elated apprehension. "Plenty of time for you to choose a fitting husband. Plenty. If you dislike my list of suitors, you are free to chase down your own, as long as you consult me first."

"In other words, I might as well stick to your list."

"It would be easier. I have done a grand job with it."

"A grand job of making yourself a villain."

"Go ahead, darling. Be angry with me. It will pass. You shall thank me in the end. I dare say you shall love me more."

"When I am unhappily trapped and hating you? I think not, old man."

George Windihill, the villain, returned to his great, comfortable leather chair, crossed his legs, picked up his book, licked his thumb and unfolded the page where he had left off. He vanished, quite rudely, right in front of her––right into that heinous book and left her steaming and glaring and plotting to strangle him. She turned from the corrupt sight, composed her hate, smoothed down her blood-stained dress, and trudged out of the study before her imagination prevailed.

***

Sheets of grey rain licked the front garden and plastered the winding, shrubbery flanked drive up to Windsworth. Sicili sat on the stone steps out front, staring into the fated rain. Fistfuls of wet dress eased the ache in her shoulders and the fluttering pain of her new lungs.

"Sicili?"

She closed her eyes. Her mother's voice.

"Sicili, darling, how very cold it is out here."

Francine draped a shawl over her shoulders. It slipped off. She made no attempt to retrieve it. The cool helped. It made her corset feel looser and her heart colder.

Francine pressed wet bits of hair behind Sicili's ear. "Your father is worried for your health if you stay out here."

Her throat tightened. "Father's worries are my demise."

Francine sat next to her. She clasped her hand. "I take it your little meeting went poorly."

She growled. "He forces me to get married. He threatens to disinherit me if I fail to choose a husband in three months. *Three months*, Mother."

"Oh dear. He has gone rogue."

"Is he serious?"

"We cannot be sure." Francine twirled a strand of her limp, damp hair. "He is a man of his word. When he puts his mind to something, however ridiculous, he rarely strays from his course of action."

"You seem less than concerned."

"Frankly, darling, I cannot say I'm horrified." She squeezed her hand. "I have been worried about you, alone in London with your aunt, with her strange moods."

"I adore London."

"But... your lack of interest in men––"

"Mother."

"If you need to talk––"

She ripped her hand free. "I will not talk to the woman holding me captive." She stood, kicked the shawl down the steps, and marched inside.

Seven

The Distraction

Sicili locked the door to her room, pulled the drapes, and refused to see anyone for the rest of the afternoon. Her mother was rebuffed. Her father was severely ignored. Wilber, who offered to change her bandage and bring her a refreshment, was told to "come back in the morning when I have bled out and starved to death".

She had to get out of Windsworth. A worthy distraction would do――something fun, something lighthearted and risky, something so unlike her and so bold her father would frown about it for days.

Outside, thunder crackled.

An idea struck her. Madam Desiree's happened to be the most risqué location in all of Wiltshire. Burlesque girls were in high demand at Madam Desiree's. They danced and taunted and kissed. Indecent men emptied their pockets to watch them late into the night and to sneak a private meeting behind a drawn curtain with their sweet lips. Indeed, Madam Desiree's would do the trick. A lady of her reputation would never, *never* be seen in that part of town.

She sorted through her wardrobe and found a dangerously low-cut frock with puffed rouge sleeves and a black lacy corset. *Who might accompany me?* She held the dress up to her reflection in the mirror. Princeton Evergreen. If he still wanted a chance at her hand, surely, he would accompany her wherever she desired. She threw on the dress, pinched her cheeks, let down her hair, and picked her best riding jacket.

She ordered Wilber to saddle one of her father's many neglected horses and marched downstairs in a decided manner.

"Where are you going, darling?" Francine called to her from the dining room. "You need to eat."

She paused in the foyer. "The taste of betrayal is more than filling. I shall be satisfied for days to come."

As she slipped outside, she heard her mother saying to the old man, "Quite the mess you made, George. Our only child refuses to dine with us."

"Let her be. She'll return in good time. The taste of betrayal always wanes, my dear, and sooner than later."

"You have such hope in your little games."

"A little game? Not this time. I entirely plan to——"

She slammed the door shut. Grey rain had eased to a light drizzle, and the air tasted fresh and smelled of wet hay and crisp grass, and she breathed in the newness. Ten yards from the East Wing, a stately stable glowed in lantern light. Wilber stood by a saddled horse in the tall grass, reins in hand and mouth pressed.

"Be careful, Miss Windihill."

She snatched the reins. "I exude constraint and composure in all areas of life, Wilber. Why stop now?"

She rode toward the horizon, her cheeks hot with fury. The sun stretched thin over the rolling hills of Wiltshire and settled in the distance beyond reach and beyond grey clouds. Dusk conquered when she reached the Evergreen estate. The residence had a pleasant, quiet look about it——humble and nothing in comparison to Windsworth. The garden leading up to the entry was well kept and the lawn freshly trimmed.

She knocked boldly. Princeton delightfully answered her demanding raps. He wore a cozy robe and wool slippers and reeked of firewood.

She stifled a laugh. "Have I called at the wrong hour, Mr. Evergreen? You're quite bundled in for the night."

"Miss Windihill." He swept up her gloved hand and kissed it twice.

"Sicili," she insisted, "just Sicili. Have you forgotten about our friendship?"

He smoothed back his curly dark hair. "Of course, of course. I had no reason to expect you. To what do I owe the pleasure?"

"Spontaneity and a dash of revenge. Do forgive my inadequate warning."

"Indeed. I am adequately charmed."

She forced a fake smile. "Would you care to join me for an impromptu adventure?"

His face glowed. His eyes lit up. Charisma oozed from his pores. A pinch of guilt for using him ebbed at her heart, but nothing she couldn't dash with the thought of her father forcing her mother to endure listening to the extravagant cruelty of his latest scheme over dinner.

She had no idea how Francine Windhill loved that man.

"I would." He kissed her hand anew. "Where to, my lady?"

"Madam Desiree's."

His face fell.

"Do you know the place, Mr. Evergreen? I hear the fun is endless. Incredibly entertaining... if you like that sort of diversion."

"Madam Desiree's?" He shuffled uncomfortably. "I hear they have... lady companions there. Do they?"

"Have you never been?"

"Madam Desiree's is a single man's pastime, I should think, not a lady's."

"I am single. Too single, according to father. Besides, I visited Madam Desiree's on several occasions in London, and with ladies and gentlemen alike." She exaggerated, of course. She once accompanied Catherine to a famous brothel in East London and failed to survive the smoky atmosphere and exotic costumes. "You can play cards if the entertainment is too provoking for you. Plenty will occupy your fancy."

He hugged himself against the cold. "I do enjoy cards."

"Live a little, Mr. Evergreen. Adventure awaits us."

"Right. Indeed. Right. Adventure with an astounding lady. How unpredictable you are. You fascinate me, Miss Windihill."

He led her into the lobby and offered her a seat while he rushed upstairs to dress. She tapped her foot and glanced about. His was a simple home. Simply decorated and painted. It lacked the touch of a lady's influence.

"Do you live alone, Princeton?" she called to him.

"I do. My parents live in London. They used to reside here, but they found the journey back and forth too demanding."

"And you have no siblings?"

"I did. A brother. He passed away several years ago."

"*Oh*. My condolences."

"My condolences for dampening the mood."

"Do take all the blame."

He skipped down the stairs, dressed in a grey riding coat and beige trousers.

And winked. "How do I look?"

"Dashing."

"Dull compared to you."

"I am wearing a dress."

"You could be wearing anything. You astound me regardless."

His charm filled the room and teased the corners of her mouth. She gave him that. He knew how to make a woman feel important. She tapped her foot and studied him from every angle. *What bad habits do you have, Mr. Evergreen? How will your nose look in a certain light? Is that the trace of a unibrow? Will you stay this agreeable, or will you age horribly?*

They rode swift and hard toward the moon and into the tiny town of Westbury. Madam Desiree's dwelt on the far end of the only street of little shops. Save for the cranky music drifting out of Madam Desiree's, the town slept. The gutters dripped and the wind from earlier crept between the old buildings and tapped Sicili on the shoulder.

They dismounted and tied their horses to a rail in front of Madam Desiree's. Princeton led her safely clear of puddles and insisted she hold tight to his arm. *Am I so frail?* She could see the street just fine with her own set of eyes. Besides, a little muck and a water might do her riding jacket good. She owned twenty more just like it.

He paused at the swinging doors to Madam Desiree's. The sign out front creaked. Smoke and music wafted from the open shutters on the second floor.

A shrill laugh from upstairs startled him. "Are you sure you want to go in?" He coughed. "We could go someplace quiet. Somewhere more... ideal and private."

"That sounds ideally boring." She wanted noise and ruckus and the taste of whiskey at the back of her throat. "Come on, Princeton. Let's be daring."

She shoved him inside. Balmy, fragrant smoke filled the dimly lit Madam Desiree's. A lethargic mood enchanted the wide-open room. Men lounged in booths with woman at their sides, giggling and touching. Princeton stumbled in, caught his fall, and went uncomfortably stiff when a lady with heavily jeweled cleavage sauntered up to them.

"Good evening," the lady said, her voice as soft as silk. "My name is Eveline. Sit wherever you like."

"Wherever we like?" Princeton repeated with a stutter.

"That's right, handsome. Ten shillings a lady."

His neck and cheeks flushed bright red. "Ten shillings a lady?"

Eveline pawed his arm. "You can do whatever you like with her. We offer private rooms upstairs. Twenty shillings for a lady and a room."

"Twenty for both?"

"That's right." She winked at Sicili. "The gents come next Thursday."

"Me?" Sicili looped her arm in Princeton's. "I have a perfectly decent gent right here." He loosened a little.

Eveline didn't seem to care. "The Sultry Sisters are on in half an hour. They're a delightful duo. Once they finish their set, you can have your pick. Very flexible the two of them. Twenty shillings an hour, or thirty-five for both. Come find me if you fancy a drink." She smiled and strutted off.

Princeton's jaw had dropped to his collar.

She brought his ear to her lips. "Mr. Evergreen, you might want to close your mouth."

"Right, right."

They took a booth next to an old fellow who stared at Sicili for a good five minutes before he blinked and turned his back on them. Princeton, a hot mess, stiffly hugged his side of the booth and dabbed his forehead with a handkerchief. Clearly, she chose the wrong companion for such a spontaneous deviation.

"How old are you, Princeton?"

He looked ready to faint. "Twenty next month."

"My, quite the fledgling you are."

He flashed a weak smile. "I happen to be very mature. Mature and handsome."

"And arrogant."

"Arrogance is a virtue."

"Is it?" She laughed. "Do you want to know my age?"

He clasped her hand. His skin felt cold and clammy. "Sicili, age makes no difference to me." Beads of sweat dribbled down his temples.

"Are you well, Mr. Evergreen?"

He swallowed hard. "Possibly not. This is my first time, you see. And..." He stuttered and failed to finish.

She liked seeing him sweat––it was selfish and cruel, but she reveled in his discomfort. He tugged at his cravat. The fledgling could hardly breathe, and what a glorious sight. After all, if he wanted to marry her, he would be getting all of her––an independent, uncertain, dissatisfied wife.

She shuffled out of the booth. "Shall I get us a refreshment?"

"Nothing for me. I'm not one for drinking."

"And why not?"

"I race horses as a hobby. I must keep a certain figure."

How posh and stodgy. A rich man with consuming hobbies. "Stay put, Mr. Evergreen."

"Whe-where are you off to?"

"I shan't wander too far."

Smoke settled heaviest at the back of the room, where girls in exposed corsets and lacy undergarments lounged on bar stools, dripping off them like frothy milk. One girl smiled sweetly, spun a ringlet and waved. "Are you looking to fetch one of us for your friend?"

Sicili tensed. The girl's legs were fully exposed, and Sicili hadn't seen a woman so naked since Ivy in her father's study in the pearly moonlight.

The girl ran a hand up her thigh. "Or are you looking for yourself?" She got up and sauntered toward Sicili, her hips rolling like waves as she approached.

Sicili stared, mortified at her own weakness. Her mouth had gone dry. She needed whiskey badly, which was all she managed to say. "W-whiskey."

The girl pouted. "Go see Eveline, beautiful." She pointed to the far end of the bar. "Don't mind Ivan. He's a regular." She winked. "If you change your mind, I'm here all night."

A scrawny, squeaky-voiced lad in a top hat and overbearing tailcoat leaned over the bar and chatted Eveline up while she washed and dried a row of crystal. "Not tonight, Ivan," she said to him. "Have any of the other girls."

He huffed. "What other girls? I'm struck by you and only you. Let me take you upstairs."

"Upstairs? You can't afford me."

"I'll give up every penny for you, Evie. I'll give up my life, my entire life."

She teasingly hit him with her rag. "What life? You're here every night drinking your heart out."

"I could be the wealthiest gent alive, for all you know. I could own a mansion on the East side and sip on a brandy in the morning and play croquet in the afternoon."

"That's unlikely." She set down her rag and straightened his top hat.

"The way you dress and all. Trust me, I'm too much for you."

"How much?"

"*Too* much."

Sicili settled next to the lad. His freckled cheeks glowed crimson red. He scratched his pointed, pretty nose. His thick mustache twitched.

"What can I do you for, Miss?" Eveline said. She dismissed the lad.

"Two whiskeys, thank you."

"A whiskey for the lady and her gent. Coming right up."

Her corset squeezed. "The last person Mr. Evergreen is is mine. Anyone but. Both whiskeys are for me, thank you."

Eveline poured a heaping glass. "Two whiskeys for the lady. I assumed he was your gent––my apologies, love."

She peered over her shoulder at Princeton sweating in the booth. "He might be a candidate, I suppose."

"He's a handsome devil, if you ask me."

In a certain light, he could be considered handsome. He charmed, and flirted, and raced horses as a hobby. A plethora of women desired to be his wife, no doubt. Yet, her organs failed to twist at the sight of him. "I suppose."

"You sound ill convinced," the lad piped in.

"I am." She sipped her whiskey. "A man wants two things in the world. Money and a wife. If he can achieve both in one woman, what else is he in want of?"

"Love," the lad said. "If he cares for that sort of thing."

Eveline giggled. "What do you know about love, Ivan?"

"Very little. I do know it exists." His voice had softened from its earlier contrived masculinity.

Sicili turned to him and tapped her fingers on the sticky countertop. "Love?"

"That's right," he said.

His petite figure looked a little too small for the over-bearing tailcoat. His jaw, hairless and elegant, reminded her of a bright eyed, red-haired someone. He stepped back, into the smokey shadows. *Is his mustache red?* She stepped in for a better look. "Do I know you?"

He cleared his throat. "Wouldn't you like to."

Something not quite right about his voice tugged at her. It sounded an octave too high for a lad's, and a bit too expressive to go undetected. She closed the step between them. A tendril of red hair slipped from under his top hat. "Ivy?"

His arms flew to his hips. "Ivan's the name, Miss."

She laughed. "Ivan. As in Ivy?"

"As in no indeed."

"Indeed or no?"

He blinked. "Is that a trick question?"

"Could you not have thought up something less like your actual name?"

"Ivan is positively my name."

"Are you positively absolute?"

His elegant jaw clenched. "I'll not have this conversation, Miss."

"Would you happen to go by another name? Say, during the day when you drink brandy in your mansion on the East side?"

"Certainly not."

She flipped his hat off and red, naughty hair flowed over Ivy's petite shoulders and down her back. Ivy Ferthing, *indeed*, the fraud. Sicili hiccupped a laugh. The sight of Ivy dressed in a thick mustache, trousers, and a heavy tailcoat proved more alarming and much more unnerving than seeing the girl in a corset and underpants.

Mortified, Eveline's hands flew to her mouth and the whiskey bottle shattered at her feet. She squealed. The girls at the other end bolted upright, and half of Madam Desiree's patrons reared and gawked, including Princeton. Eveline fled around the bar and out the swinging front doors.

Ivy pursed her lips. "How kind you are, Miss Windihill, to expose me with such unfeeling."

"I own a great many feelings on the––"

Ivy grabbed her by the hand, ran past the gawking, pulled her into a dark hall, and spun her against the wall. She pinned her tight. A narrow staircase led upstairs, and a potent amount of smoke gathered at their ankles.

Ivy placed a hand on the wall. "Evie's my favorite, I'll have you know, and you *had* to march in here with that air and unhinge my disguise and scare her off."

"With what air?"

"That staunch air."

"Pardon me? You and your arduous tailcoat and your makeshift mustache scared her off, not I."

Ivy grinned. "You think me makeshift in this mustache?"

"Frightful is the word I prefer."

Ivy ripped the fraudulent thing off. "How about now?"

"Better. Might I make a valuable suggestion?"

"Might you refrain?"

"Miss Ferthing––"

"Ivy."

"––oh, not Ivan?"

"Bullocks. Here we go."

"Playing the part of a gentleman at Madam Desiree's is far worse a transgression than dressing up as a penniless lad at the age of fourteen. You do realize?"

"Actually, I never thought of it, seeing as I kept my identity concealed––hence the top hat."

"You are *too* bold."

Ivy's lips eclipsed hers. "And you look lovely with your hair down. Has anyone told you?"

Ivy smelled of musk and grass and a heady wine, and her lips tasted buttery and tangy––*like a pastry*? She forgot where they were and how they had arrived, where the wall ended and where it began. Ivy caught her up and folded her into her lips, and kept her warm and breathless and caused a fiery ache in her bones. It felt wrong, utterly wrong. And divine, and powerful, and perfectly right.

Ivy broke the incomprehensible lip-lock.

She hiccupped. "*Oh.*" She braced the wall. It felt paper thin and off to the left. Or was she off?

"Well?" Ivy whispered. "Has anyone told you?"

She blinked. "Told me what?"

"How lovely you look with your hair down."

"Not recently."

"That's a shame." Ivy cupped her face, and they blinked and smiled weakly and breathed in unison. "Do you remember when I was down to my corset in your father's study and you barged in on me?"

"How could I forget?"

"I should have kissed you harder." Her green eyes crinkled. "Your lips are quite agreeable."

"Only quite?"

"I have yet to acquaint myself with them. Perhaps once I do, I shall find them *very* agreeable."

She pressed a finger to Ivy's confident mouth. "I like you better without a top hat. You could be yourself, you know, instead of stuffed inside a musky old getup."

"And I suppose you still want to help me."

"Certainly not. Not now that I know you."

Ivy gasped. "What happened to your finger?"

"My finger? Oh, nothing––nothing of any consequence." She withdrew the wounded hand, but Ivy clasped her wrist and lifted the knuckle to her lips. Warmth tickled the nape of her neck. "That's three," she said.

"Three?"

"Kisses. You have stolen one too many. I'm counting."

"Good. I can steal another."

She gripped the musky tailcoat and pulled Ivy in for a fourth inescapable kiss, but Ivy froze inches from her lips when

Princeton appeared at the end of the hall. Quite the surprise. He had mustered the courage to leave the safety of his booth.

"Sicili, is that you? Are you well? Is he−−" He gaped at Ivy's red hair, fists clenched at his sides. "Is he bothering you?"

She freed Ivy's collar. "No, Mr. Evergreen. I'm well−−more than well." Her skin tingled and her organs twisted and her heart pumped firm and wild. Regretfully, Ivy stepped back, crossed her arms, and attempted a lower pitch.

"She's invigorated, my good man."

Princeton's eyes narrowed. "Are you−−?"

"Ivan." Ivy strode up to him and shook his hand. "Pleasure to meet you. Miss Windihill is all yours. Best of luck, chap. She certainly is a keeper if you go asking me."

He took his hand back. "I'm well aware."

"Good." Without adequate farewell−−not even a look back at her or a wink−−Ivy shoved passed him, ran for her top hat, and dashed out the front swinging doors.

Princeton relaxed his fists. "Blimey. Was he a woman?"

Why do I feel so off? Her cheeks burned with the same fiery passion they had that night in her father's study. A deep, unsettled part of her wanted to dash after Ivy and head into the night−−anywhere and everywhere, wherever the moonlight beckoned them. "Come on, Mr. Evergreen." She steadied herself on his arm. "What an awful idea this was."

"Did you get your refreshment?"

"I did, and much more."

Arm in arm, they cleared the hall and escaped the smoky Madam Desiree's for the crisp night air. Grey clouds had vanished, and stars and moon twinkled overhead. In the distance, Ivy bolted up the only street in Westbury−−red hair flicking at her back and the moon her guide. *What a strange and lovely sight.* Down the street, Eveline came swiftly with a man in uniform at her heel and halted in front of Madam Desiree's.

"There, Officer. After that man. He's an impostor. A fraud, a fraud!"

The officer unleashed his pistol and took off after Ivy.

Sicili's heart thumped wildly. "I hardly think a pistol necessary. The lad is harmless."

Eveline gasped for air. "Did he harm you, love?"

"Far from it."

"At least he has a good set of legs on him," Princeton said.

She felt ill.

Eveline composed herself and pried up her cleavage. "I do hope you two had a lovely time. Come again soon." She swung through the doors.

Princeton belched a hearty laugh, right from his gut. The night's air had cooled his earlier nerves. He tipped his riding hat to her and laughed until she laughed with him.

"Tell me, Princeton. What are we laughing at?"

"You, Sicili Windihill. You do impress."

He swept off his hat altogether and kissed her beneath the moonlight on the only street in Westbury. The crinkly music from Madam Desiree's enveloped them and the lingering taste of smoke tickled the back of her throat. Frankly, and somewhat to her dismay, she felt *nothing*––complete and irrevocable nothing. Compared to Ivy's buttery lips, his thin, firm mouth failed to satisfy. She clung to his neck, tipped her toes, and pushed into him. *Nothing*. On several occasions in London, the opportunity to share intimate and fragile moments like this with a suitor had often arisen, but she had never gone through with them, making excuses about being tired or too under the influence. She once wondered why a pair of genteel lips so rarely tempted her. *Now I know*.

She pressed him back with a gentle shove.

He was breathless. "I just realized." His face shone with adoration. "We missed the Sultry Sisters performance."

"Shall we go back in?"

He smiled ear to ear. "Not on my life, Sicili Windihill."

***

Princeton insisted on seeing her safely home. He galloped far ahead of her to show off his talent, as if she claimed to be an avid fan. She rode hard against her thumping heart. She saw passed him. She saw moonlight. When they arrived at Windsworth, the stable doors hung wide open and Wilber fed the horses. Princeton helped her dismount, despite her being capable on her own.

She forced a smile. "Goodnight, Princeton. Thank you for the adventure."

He pulled her close and kissed her with all his might and passion. His lips felt less romantic and more demanding, more rough and daring. His tongue brushed her lips.

"You are greedy, Mr. Evergreen."

The look in his eyes devoured her. "Goodnight, Sicili."

"Goodnight. Until we meet again."

He mounted and took off with perfect form. She scowled. Madam Desiree's had temporarily done the trick. Windsworth loomed over the stable, and she coward in the shadow of windows and stone and perfect hedges. The old man's evil plot gripped her anew and squeezed at her ribcage. She led her horse into the stable. Wilber untied the saddle and groomed the horse.

She tarried. "Did you witness Mr. Evergreen's daring advance on me?"

"I did, Miss Windihill. It was lovely. Very romantic."

"Was it?" She pulled at her riding gloves. "He believes he's won me over. I saw it in his eyes."

"Has he not?"

"Do I look won over, Wilber?"

His knowing smile answered. He knew her better than her mother and father combined.

She bid him goodnight. As she strolled up the path to Windsworth, tense and tired, the thought of Ivy running up the street in trousers struck her. She chuckled and relaxed and felt a tad guilty. Perhaps she ought to call on the Ferthings in the morning. Just to make sure Ivy had fared well. *No, Sicili. Wilber is right. Ivy Ferthing is a reckless girl with unreasonable ways. You best steer clear of her.* Besides, they were far from being friends. Only friends and lovers called on each other.

What were they?

Not until she entered the well-lit foyer did she notice her finger. Fresh blood spotted the bandage on her knuckle. *I must have held the reins too tight.* She kissed her finger and smiled. Ivy's preposterous courage and undone disguise made her giddy.

The girl truly was a laughing matter.

***

George and Francine sat in the drawing room. With the fire lit and the rest of the room dark, shadows danced off her father's face and spilled onto the book in his lap. Her mother painted a teacup.

Sicili reluctantly settled at the door.

George, very much consumed by his book, looked up. "Where were you, my Sicili?" His white eyebrows demanded an explanation. They looked quite evil in the firelight.

She tore off her riding gloves. "You might be happy to learn, Father, I went riding with Princeton Evergreen."

He smiled delightfully. "Did you? How was it?"

"He kissed me. Twice."

"And? Is he a good kisser? He must be a good kisser to last."

Her mother simpered but kept to her painting.

George flipped his page. "Be meticulous, Sicili. Now is the time. I would rather you be exacting than forever bored."

"I *am* bored. Wiltshire has no sense of fun. You all go to bed at eight o'clock and frown at the idea of adventure."

"There, there," Francine scolded. "You speak ill too fast, Sicili. There happens to be a croquet tournament at the Dainty's next month. You're expected to attend."

"Next month?" She yawned. "What a long way off. I shall have to fill my time with something. Father?"

He looked up.

"I accept your proposition."

"Do you?" The surprise in his voice was contrived. "How glad I am, my angel."

"I'm quite ready for your next suitor. Toss him my way."

"There my girl is." He winked. "You shan't be disappointed."

She crossed her arms. "I hope not, Father, for your sake not mine. I am exhausted. Goodnight, you two."

"Goodnight, dearest," they said in unison.

The old man lifted his book. Just as she feared. It was the book he read earlier in his study. Something ridiculous, something about marriage and unity. She held her tongue. She blew her mother a kiss and shot her father a glare, which sadly went un-noticed.

She hovered for a moment outside the drawing room in the dark, lonely corridor.

"See? I told you she would come around," George proudly gloated. "It was only a matter of time."

Her mother sighed. "She looked unhappy."

"How can you tell, darling?"

"A mother knows these things, George."

In her room, Sicili undressed methodically, laying her riding clothes out on the bed for inspection. Not one strain. Not one rumple. Not one thread out of life. Rather like her life, she realized. She stood in front of her mirror for a long while, and the candle on her night table flickered in the cold. Her naked figure frightened her. *Have I always been afraid of myself?* Red corset marks caged her ribs and under-breasts. Blue veins squiggled under her pale skin and webbed up her neck, looking drained of oxygen. Her breasts ached from being trapped all day. The left was bigger than the right, and they both looked too small for her chest.

The old man might be right. Was she too old to be single? Would a husband want her in ten years when she could no longer bear him children? Would she be ready in ten years? She slipped on her nightgown and turned from her reflection.

Would Ivy want her in ten years?

She blew out the candle and fell asleep to a reluctant thought: Ivy Ferthing knew how to kiss. Her lips were kinder and more genuine than Princeton Evergreen's by miles. Whether Ivy kissed better than all men, she had yet to find out.

Eight

Charlotte Meddles

Charlotte woke to the sound of Ivy scraping her bedroom window open and climbing down the side of Vineyard Mansion. Years. It had been years since she enjoyed a proper night's rest.

The time had come to confront her unruly daughter.

Stiff with the sore muscles of a mother who constantly worries, she lit a candle and ambled to the kitchen to make a pot of tea. She poured a cup with a long, tired sigh and sat blinking herself awake in front of the old kitchen hearth.

The Windihill's ball had changed nothing for Ivy. No one but Patrick Derby had danced with her, and the Derby's were a poor lot. The stares and whispers had been insufferable——even the servants had given Ivy dirty looks. Charlotte squeezed the bridge of her nose in memory. And the rumors! Her great undoing. They had followed Ivy out of hiding and bedeviled the festivities. Five years of solitude and penance should have put those monstrous rumors to rest. Apparently, not. Apparently, Wiltshire was as unforgiving as it was conceited. Ivy's damnable transgression of dressing up as a penniless lad haunted her, just as Charlotte feared.

She drank the last drop of tea and glanced at the clock above the mantelpiece. Quarter after midnight. *Oh, Ivy, you will be the death of me. My utter ruin.* She lit another candle, creaked upstairs to Ivy's corner overlooking the vineyard, and waited. She left the window open. The night air soothed her nerves.

She sat on the edge of Ivy's bed, held a hand over her heart, and sobbed into a pillow. Despair washed over her. She wanted happiness for Ivy. A normal, seamless life with smiles from society. A husband to care for her, pamper her, and put her in her place, and grandchildren to redeem the hard years of raising an ungrateful daughter. But——she heaved a great sob——Naughty Ivy persisted. Ivy would be Ivy, and the chances of normality and happiness were slim. Ivy would rather ruin herself than seek traditional contentment. Always smiling at girls, always making a fool of herself at balls, always stuck in books intended for men, always running off at night *doing*——

Charlotte sniffled. She refused to think of what Ivy did out there at this godforsaken hour.

Charlotte wiped her nose on the pillowcase. Did she expect too much from Ivy? Could the girl change after nineteen years of the same shenanigans? Was she set in her obscene ways——set to make a fool out of her family and continue the disastrous path she had chosen?

As all suspicious mothers of a wayward child are eventually pressed to do, she rose and smoothed back her hair and searched Ivy's room. Every corner and every nook. Her daughter had secrets, deep, unsettling secrets. She felt them in the cracks and the shadows. She clawed through Ivy's wardrobe and dresses. Everything appeared normal, smooth, and pristine. The handiwork of the housekeepers. Ivy was anything but pristine. She opened every drawer to Ivy's vanity. A brush, a notepad (which she flipped through and gasped from shame: there were drawings of naked girls), a quill and ink. In the bottom drawer, severed tendrils of Ivy's red hair were placed in neatly arranged piles.

Mystified, she moved chairs and furniture and tore off covers and found a green trunk under Ivy's bed. One of William's missing luggage pieces from way back when. A boldly written discolored sign said *Do not meddle, Mother* in Ivy's finest print.

She took a deep breath, flipped the latch, and meddled. The trunk harbored a collection of outrageous clothes––all designed for the male sex. They were positively the worst possible fashions. Several top hats and berets and a dirty fisher's cap. Heat rose to her cheeks. Shoes of various sizes, and bundles of draping that Charlotte refused to figure out. Tailcoats with large, square pads tucked into the shoulders. Plaid trousers, striped trousers, and fancy trousers. All hideous. All monstrous. All things a proper lady would never wear. She envisioned Ivy in them and fretfully dabbed her forehead with a large shirt. Lastly, and most concerning: Neat packages of Ivy's hair hid at the bottom of the trunk. She opened one and held it in her shaky palm. Ivy had transformed her locks into fake mustaches.

She slammed the trunk shut, fastened the latch, and shoved it under Ivy's bed. She had a mind to burn it. After five years of preserving her daughter's dignity and trying and failing to guide the wretched girl toward the light, her hard work had yielded a trunk of mismatched outfits and a hideous truth:

Ivy was incapable of propriety and love.

She spent the remainder of the night pacing and wringing her hands, and when the sun came up and stretched over the vineyard below Ivy's window, she dried her eyes and resolved to keep trying, to not give up like most mothers would have done.

Staggered footsteps crunched outside the window. A fuss of mumbled words and the sound of clumsy movement up the side of the mansion followed, and soon Ivy pulled herself up through the window and flopped onto the floor like a fish. The girl, disheveled from head to toe, smelled like whiskey and evil, unmentionable deeds.

Tears scratched at Charlotte's throat. Ivy wore one of the many outfits the trunk had to offer––mustache and all.

"Mother?" Ivy fumbled up and tripped on her own feet.

"Are you drunk, girl?"

"I cannot tell. Do I look it?"

"*Oh*, you slop of a girl."

"Likely. An officer of the law chased me down. I hid in a field. I had to, Mother. You know, until it was safe."

"Spare me the details, Ivy. You're a horrid mess. At the moment, nothing else matters."

Ivy stumbled to the bed and collapsed. "I know all that. Haven't I always been? The daughter you never wanted."

"Hold your tongue, girl."

Charlotte clung to her resolve. She composed her tears, helped her drunken Ivy under the covers, closed the drapes and banished the morning sun. She wandered downstairs to the kitchen and put the kettle back over the fire and waited for it to boil. She prepared a tray of tea with crumpets and sausage and delivered it to snoring Ivy. Dewy-eyed and full of love, she watched the girl sleep, dabbing her sweet face with a hot cloth and trying not to weep.

When Ivy moaned and opened her eyes, they shared a devastating look.

Charlotte leaned back. "The tea is cold, and the crumpets are dry."

"I'm not hungry." Ivy turned over.

It had to be said. "What are you doing dressing up as a gentleman?"

"Do you really want to know?"

"No."

"I'm not like the rest of the girls, Mother."

"You certainly are not."

"There's no stopping me."

"Indeed. A fact I am all too aware of and have suffered from for the last nineteen years." She broke down. She wept long and hard. Ivy turned back to her, face somber, and squeezed her arm.

"I'm sorry--"

"How dare you? Take it back."

"I'm sorry I'm not the daughter you want."

"You, girl, are far from sorry." She blew her nose. "You're unstoppable." Charlotte cleared her tears and composed herself. "So. I shall let you keep your incorrigible clothes. Who am I to stop you? Do whatever you like in them whenever you like. On one condition."

Ivy retracted her hand. "What condition?"

"You will attend every social event there is to be had. Do you hear? Until I can find you a gentleman who will take you for what you are."

Ivy slumped against the pillow. "Quite unlikely."

"Promise me you will try."

"All right, Mother." She sighed. "I'll do it for you."

"You will do it for yourself, never mind me. You will do it for your reputation and your future. All of Wiltshire deems you unruly and out of control."

"I am. I would rather them know it than think it."

"You ghastly child." She used the wet cloth to wipe her nose. "*Oh*, you shall be the end of me."

***

Not a week later, to Charlotte's delighted surprise, the Ferthing's received an invitation to dine with the Windihill's the Friday next. She read the invitation over breakfast and pressed her daughter with a firm look.

Ivy ventured a smile. "An evening with the Windihill's is far from advisable, Mother, especially if Sicili Windihill is present."

"You tragic girl." She caressed the card. "It will be a quiet evening, I assume, with little for you to destroy. You did say you would attend social functions for me, remember?"

Ivy's smile broadened. "Fine. I suppose there won't be any single men to harass me."

"There *will* be the opportunity to make friends with Sicili Windihill. She must know half the men in London, even the poorer half."

Ivy stuffed toast in her mouth and spoke through mouthfuls of rolling food. "You really want me to travel as far as London for a match? And you want me to be poor?"

Charlotte held back a scolding for Ivy's horrible table etiquette. She was too tired to get after the girl this early. "Status is beside the point. Connection is of true value, and especially when it comes to Miss Windihill's influence over *all* men."

Ivy laughed. "All men, really?"

"Indeed. *All* men. Besides, I would rather you marry a poor gent than..." She cleared her throat. She had surprised herself. She sipped her tea and re-arranged her serviette, avoiding the girl's eyes. When finally, Charlotte looked up, she met Ivy's curious expression.

Ivy had raised her eyebrows. A hopeful look wavered in her eyes. "You can't say it, can you?"

"Can *you*?"

The wretched girl dove into her eggs. "I'll go. But I warned you. Remember it, Mother."

She dismissed the warning, quite happily. Ivy had no right to be right. The girl desperately needed connections and a second chance, and as a mother, Charlotte felt pressed to take advantage of the right opportunities. Sicili Windihill––fair skinned, hazel eyed, intoxicating to *all* men––might be the token Ivy needed to get back into the good graces of society.

Nine

The First of Many

Sicili lounged on a pillow covered chaise in the corner of the drawing room, one leg draped over the edge. Sunlight tickled the nape of her neck and danced off the gold mantlepiece, warming her soul. She traced the sparse freckles on her right arm, up her wrist and stopped at her nearly healed finger. She smiled. Little, harmless thoughts of Ivy were becoming a persistent dilemma. They refused to leave her be. She kissed her finger. Ridiculous memories in dark halls and moon lit studies were far more amusing than all the suitors on her father's list combined.

The list went on and on.

Last week, she accompanied Henry Fuller to London for a gallery exhibit of paintings inspired by political events. She had strolled from one painting to another and wondered how bored a person could be when the memory of Ivy leaning in to kiss her wounded finger had struck her. Even now, she remembered the feeling on her cheeks, the stir in her stomach, the hunger for more as it drove her wild.

"Are you well?" Mr. Fuller asked more than once. "You look flushed, Miss Windihill."

"I'm engrossed," she managed to conjure.

"As am I. History depicted by the stroke of a brush is most engaging."

Henry Fuller, a dull gentleman, had thirty thousand pounds a year. He loved to talk about art and politics. She feigned interest. Unfortunately, he had called twice since the exhibit and assured her he planned to call again before the end of the week. What a dull husband he would make, and what a somber wife she would be. The mix of his tedious talking and her inevitable boredom would surely make a lifeless marriage.

Her father's list irked her. The fact that it existed infuriated her.

She sat up and sipped at her morning tea. *I shall find something better to do than devote my attention to the incorrigible Ivy Ferthing.* Riding would do the trick. The morning promised blue skies and a sunny afternoon.

A ruckus in the foyer, followed by passionate footsteps, startled her upright and produced Princeton Evergreen. He barged into the drawing room without introduction.

"Mr. Evergreen?"

He said nothing. He removed his top hat, flung it on the chair next to her and adjusted the collar of his tailcoat––something had gone disastrously wrong with it on the ride over. Two weeks had passed since their impromptu adventure to Madam Desiree's. She had no reason to expect him, not after turning down his several calls to Windsworth. Had she not made herself clear?

He wrung his hands and paced in front of the hearth, greatly agitated. The love in his eyes ached. "I just heard the most devastating news."

She tried to avoid them. "Can I offer you tea, Mr. Evergreen?"

"I'm refreshed just seeing you."

"Oh." She managed a polite distance to her voice.

"I understand you have been too busy to take my calls."

"Do sit, Mr. Evergreen. You make me dizzy with your pacing."

"I'm not here for tea. I'm not here to sit." Hearth to chaise, chaise to hearth. "Tell me, Sicili, is it true?"

"Is what true?"

"Are you courting Henry Fuller?"

She set her teacup on its saucer. The clank made him wince. "Your knowledge of my private affairs is rather disconcerting. Who told you such?"

"All of Wiltshire is talking about you and that artsy baboon."

She pinched her lips. "What if I am courting him?"

"I would be most devastated." He ran hands through disheveled hair. "I am in love with you, Sicili."

She stiffened. How? And when? She felt pity for him, but nothing remotely close to love. "We only just met."

"Indeed, and it only took seconds for me to fall for you."

"Nonsense, Mr. Evergreen."

"Have you kissed him?" He stopped directly in front of the chaise. His eyes beseeched her. "Have you? The way you kissed me?"

To be frank, she struggled to recall his lips on hers. She remembered very little from that night other than Ivy and her mustache and her long, naughty hair. And a kiss they had shared in a smoky hall. Nothing about Princeton's lips. "If I have, it is certainly none of your business."

"Make it my business." He fell on one knee.

"Princeton, do get up."

"Marry me, Sicili. Make me the happiest man in the world." Just as he opened his palm to reveal a ring, Wilber came in with a tray of tea.

"Wilber," she said. "Will you give us a moment?"

"Certainly." Wilber backed out of the drawing room, his eyes wide with curiosity.

Oh, grand. She returned to Princeton, still on his knee, still holding out the diamond ring to her. His lip quivered and his eyes were ruined with love. "Marry me, Sicili."

She closed his fingers over his palm. "Do put that away and do get up."

His face fell. "Is that your answer?"

"My answer is *no*. I hardly know you, and I certainly do not love you."

"But... Madam Desiree's."

"What about that dreadful night?"

"You were testing me." He seemed sure of it.

"Testing you?"

"My chastity. You had to know if I was a lustful man, if I would be true to you. I passed your test with flying colors. I give myself to you willingly. I shall have you as soon as I can." He rose abruptly and swept her up in his arms.

"Hold your tongue." She wriggled free. "You misunderstood me."

"Did I?"

"I had no intention of testing you, or making you believe I was. That night had nothing to do with you. I was angry with my father. I wanted to enrage him. I wanted to do something bold. It was a selfish plan, and I was afraid to go alone, so I thought of you."

He let her go. She slipped closer to the door, prepared to flee if he advanced again, but her cruelty had settled over him. He stood by the fireplace, steadied himself with the mantelpiece. He stared at the embers from the early morning fire Wilber had lit and fell silent for an excruciating minute. It was a lovely ring. She wondered if she should tell him to keep it for a lady who would take him without a moment's hesitation, but he jabbed the ring into his pocket.

The truth had ravaged his eyes. "It *was* bold."

"We had a grand time, Princeton, and *my* what a fine gentleman you are and *oh* what a fine..."

His eyes welled. "Do you love him?"

"No. I dare say I love no one."

"I see. Are you playing us both a fool?"

"*No*. How harsh. Need you think of me that way?"

"I dislike games, Miss Windihill. I dislike feeling a fool. I should think Henry Fuller will feel the same when you break it to him." He gathered himself. He snatched his hat from the chair and headed for the door.

"Princeton, please. You are a wonderful man. You will find yourself a wonderful girl." She followed him to the foyer. "You will forget about me. You will––"

"Good day to you, Miss Windihill." He slicked his hair and placed his top hat. "If we cross paths, I shall warn Henry Fuller to flee if he wants to keep his heart whole."

"You are a wonderful man," she repeated.

Wilber held the door open, and Princeton slammed it on the way out. The damage of taking him to Madam Desiree's to spite her father had backfired. *Oh, what a backward human I make*.

"He is a wonderful man, Wilber."

Wilber resumed his dusting. "Indeed. Which is why you turned him down, I assume."

Her mother hovered on the foyer stairs, her bosom held and her expression elated. "Goodness, Sicili. What was that about?"

She glared up at her. "I just received my first proposal."

"*Oh*." Francine squealed. "My darling, darling girl."

"I refused, Mother."

"Did you? He was handsome."

"And eager. Too eager."

"Sicili. You will have to marry one of them."

"One. Not all. He claimed he loved me after two weeks' acquaintance. Father is to blame for this. I will have that man's neck."

"Some men are more passionate than others. Take your time, Sicili. Choose wisely. Try not to share your bed with a fool."

"Such sound and caring advice, Mother."

She desperately needed a ride. She finished her tea and picked out her finest riding gear. Wilber offered to ride with her, and she distractedly declined.

"I need to be alone."

"Understandably, Miss Windihill."

"Tell Mother I might be late for supper."

"Should I tell her what direction you ride?"

"I have no idea which, Wilber. No idea. Does anyone know? Do you?"

She rode for hours. Against the brisk English air as the morning sun stretched over rolling hills and golden orchards. Against farm lands, and the smell of old things and manure, and against rippled pastures of sheep and cows and horses. The uncomfortable aftermath of Princeton's visit sat sour in her stomach and left a tickle in her throat, a tickle urging her to laugh or belch, or do both. She had been cruel and wicked to him, and marvelously she hardly regretted it. What made her weak and ill were his aching eyes, not her own cruelty. Impeccable love had overwhelmed his young face.

Was she his first heartbreak?

The sun, mid-sky, sweltered. She tore off her riding jacket and flung it at a hoard of sheep. They yelled and gathered. "Have it, for all I care!"

She flicked the reins in hope of escaping the heat and rode and rode and lost herself in angry thoughts having to do with an evil old man. Damn George Windihill, damn his proposition and his cruel ultimatum of wealth and marriage versus happiness and rags, damn his schemes and inability to be a proper, loving father. Her cruelty toward gentlemen such as Princeton prevailed because of her father's unfeeling toward his only daughter. If not for George, she would be back in London, dodging Aunt Gertrude's strange moods, laughing about mediocre opera performances with Catherine, and writing the occasional letter to Mother.

She halted in a grassy meadow, a mile off from a vineyard. *Where am I? Have I lost my way?* A stately residence––blue shutters against white––governed a hilltop. Colonial pillars welcomed weary travelers in need of a heady glass of wine. Rows and rows of lustrous vines cascaded down the hillside. She shaded her eyes, and her organs twisted. Her breath caught. At the bottom of the vineyard, a girl with red, unruly hair carefully inspected clusters of grapes. Ivy. She wore a pretty summer dress with boots up to her knees. Her hair flew about with the wind.

The horse whinnied. In the distance, Ivy straightened and shaded her brow. Despite the mile between them, they reflected off each other and illuminated and somehow they infused, and it felt as if the mile had disintegrated. Ivy waved a brazen hand in the air. *At me?* Her corset attacked her lungs, and her heart leaped wildly in her chest, and the feeling of staring at an outlandish girl in a foreign meadow made her kick the side of the saddle. The horse reared and took off against the grassy meadow.

The sun blinked behind a cloud.

At home, Wilber met her in the stable.

"Do you rest, Wilber?" She dismounted her horse.

"Not when company is expected."

"Company?"

In her room, she tore off her riding dress and sticky under-garments. She brushed them into a pile under her bed. They reminded her of Princeton Evergreen, an unhappy memory. When all this fuss about being betrothed subsided and she returned to London, she planned to shop for a new outfit. In fact, many new outfits. The city had the most magnificent boutiques. She missed them. She missed Catherine and noisy, endless streets and the routine of life with her aunt.

She slipped into a silk corset with blue detail and a cream petticoat when a knock came at the door.

"Come in."

Her mother entered, flushed and preoccupied. "Where have you been, darling?"

"Nowhere special." She sat in front of her vanity and forced a pink hue into her pale cheeks. Messy, sweaty hair clung to her forehead and neck. "I needed to think."

"You had all morning to think."

"Will you brush my hair?"

"The Ferthings are expected for dinner and cards tonight and you look a fright."

"The Ferthings?" The disaster of more memories of Ivy was the last thing she needed. "You forgot to tell me, Mother."

Francine yanked at her hair. "You were gone all afternoon, darling, and that business with Princeton Evergreen had me forgetting what day it was."

"I would have bought a new dress or… something fresh." She pinched her cheeks until they were rosy red.

"Something fresh? What do you mean by fresh?"

"Oh, something bright, I suppose." *Something Ivy might like and be drawn to.* "All my dresses are dark and foreboding."

Francine braided her hair and pinned it tightly at the nape of her neck. She sighed like mothers do when they are taken with the reflections of their daughters. "How beautiful you are, Sicili. No man will be able to resist falling in love with you."

"Resistance is preferred."

"How blasé you are. You should feel flattered by Mr. Evergreen's proposal."

"Or trapped."

"Your father has been difficult of late, I know, and I mean to talk to him about his selfish games——"

"Do you truly think he plans to go through with it?"

"——but be on your best behavior tonight. The Ferthings are good friends."

She snorted. "Since when does Father have good friends?"

"Do think better of him."

"Why should I? He forces me to hand my life away."

"Not your life, Sicili. Only your happiness."

Sicili's brow crinkled. "Are they not one and the same?"

"You can do without the latter. Trust me." On her way out, Francine turned and said in the mirror, "Our guests will be here in an hour. Try not to fuss over what dress you wear. The Ferthings are simple."

She cleared her throat. "Will Ivy Ferthing be joining them?"

"I believe so. I confess she's akin to a serf at social situations, but I told Charlotte you two might get along. Be good to her, Sicili."

She brushed her hair. She had to keep her hands busy. "I have heard the rumors, Mother."

"Have you? She could have been wed by now if not for those rumors."

Francine shut the door. A smile tempted her. *If she liked men.*

She fussed and fretted and tried on several different dresses. She pinched her cheeks until they stung, powdered her nose, let down her hair, only to braid it and wear it over her shoulder. She held up a dress with a plunging neckline. Would Ivy look? Would tempting a heathen condemn her? She slipped into a maroon dress detailed in gold sequence.

There.

She looked foreboding.

Ten

The Start of a Lovely Tryst

The Ferthing's had arrived and settled in the drawing room when Sicili made her way downstairs. Her mother engaged Mrs. Ferthing with chatter about the latest shop in town––Mr. Stellaway's Fashions––"Do stop in, Charlotte. Tell him I sent you." Her father and Mr. Ferthing debated the complexities of wine. They winked and laughed.

Ivy sat by herself with a cup of tea. Firelight danced off her cheekbones. Their eyes met, and Ivy smiled, and that feeling from earlier, that implicit feeling of infusion and illumination––

"There you are, Sicili," Francine said. "Charlotte, this is my daughter. Tardy but always stunning."

Sicili gave a vague curtsy.

Mrs. Ferthing was elegance, ringlets, and glowing skin. Naturally, Sicili had imagined a sour-faced, hunch-backed woman as Ivy's mother, not a picture of flawless extravagance and refined manners. She sat tall and proud.

"We missed you at the ball, Miss Windihill," Mrs. Ferthing said. "Unfortunately, Ivy was indisposed. A pleasure to finally make your acquaintance."

Sicili smiled. "The pleasure is mine."

"This is my Ivy," Mrs. Ferthing said. "We have three boys as well, but they live in London."

Ivy took a polite, knowing sip of her tea. "Pleasure." The edges of her mouth lifted in a playful, roguish design.

The girl *actually* looked pretty. Too pretty, Sicili regretted, because now she would have to spend the remainder of the night trying not to stare at Ivy's bright cheeks and exposed shoulders. The floral dress she wore highlighted her freckles and, in the firelight, made her look inexperienced, not worldly and wild. A pleasant improvement over her last memory of Ivy sprinting down the street wearing trousers too big for her stride.

She had no choice but to engage Ivy and settled next to her with a heaviness at the back of her throat. Her voice felt far off and small. She debated several conversations. *"How lovely you look, Ivy."* No, too forward. *"Have you been back to Madam Desiree's?"* No, too disastrous. *"I see you drink tea. Tell me your favorite kind?"* No, too desperate.

She managed a shallow, "How are you?"

Ivy sat tall and elegant. Her usual stooped, untamed self was in hiding. "Healthy. Are you well?"

"Indeed. More than well."

Silence. The lull in conversation tortured her and forced her to notice lovely little details about Ivy. Her collarbone, dancing with golden light from the fire. Her freckled shoulders. Her chest as it rose and fell in perfect succession and pushed against the ruffled neckline of her dress. *Careful, Sicili.* A dress suited Ivy just fine. Much better than an overbearing tailcoat.

Wilber delivered her a glass of wine. She smiled most gratefully. He knew her all too well. Wine helped. A little. It made her heart light, but her forehead damp with perspiration. She should have taken a cold bath.

After several minutes of torture, Ivy leaned in. "I saw you riding in the field today. Did you see me wave?"

She took a long sip of wine. "Did you wave?"

"I waved, and you took off against the hills. You're a good rider, you know."

She glanced at Ivy's lips. "How did you know it was me?"

"Your hair. The sun hits it flawlessly, and makes you look quite like an angel. You should wear it down more often."

"Should I?"

"I think so."

The space between narrowed, and a heaviness tugged. "Do refrain from calling me an angel, Miss Ferthing."

Ivy smiled. "I meant it as a compliment."

"I took it as an insult. My father calls me angel, and I detest it."

"Very well. For as long as we are acquainted, I shall never again use that detestable word to describe you. You have my word."

Ivy's ease with conversation helped to relax her nerves, and the wine felt lovely against her throat. "Is ours to be a long acquaintance?"

"If we last the night, possibly." Ivy sipped her tea. "How is that fellow who accompanied you to Madam Desiree's?"

"He stopped calling."

"How dare he stop calling on Sicili Windihill."

"Are you mocking me?"

"Yes. I think you need to be mocked from time to time."

"You do a great deal of thinking for me."

Francine rung for more tea and Wilber appeared in seconds. The conversation of the room lulled, and Francine took a moment to lean toward them. "What are you two whispering about? You seem to be getting along quite well."

"Only about short acquaintances with grotesque men," Ivy belted, a little too loud for their intimate gathering.

Sicili giggled without thinking better of it. Half her mouthful of wine spluttered out. Wilber ran for a cloth and water. Mrs. Ferthing stared with a ghostly expression at Ivy. The rest of the room held their chests and inquired if Sicili had drunk too much in so short a sitting.

It was a gallant start to the evening.

Sicili tried to brush off the sensation of finding Ivy quite diverting in the face of a long evening of stiff conversation and cards. "I'm pleased I chose my maroon dress," she teased. "Imagine if I had chosen the baby blue."

No one laughed.

Ivy looked at her mother and fell silent.

Heady, and a little embarrassed at her failed humor, Sicili savored her wine in the hope of appearing de-tached and cool. Indifference had treated her well in the city––rescued her from uncomfortable situations and te-dious talks with vivacious men. Next to Ivy, with her heart light and her skin itching to get closer, indifference felt im-possible. She endeavored to stop glancing at those bright eyes and that pointed nose and the way Ivy's locks fell free of her up do and grazed those freckled shoulders––but the simple task of neglect proved too difficult to achieve in the presence of Naughty Ivy.

She leaned in. "Your behavior is faultless tonight, Miss Ferthing."

"Sadly. I endeavor to impress my mother."

"I assumed you impressed *only* your unreasonable self."

Ivy's eyes crinkled. "Touché."

Wilber cleared his throat and announced supper, and Ivy set aside her tea at the same moment Sicili slid her wine onto the side table. Their hands brushed.

Ivy's chest rose. "Your finger healed nicely."

"It was only a scratch. Nothing of consequence."

"It was something. I remember. In the hall at Madam Desiree's after I——"

Her hand graced Ivy's knee. The movement felt natural, inevitable. "Please, Miss Ferthing. Let us keep that disastrous night to ourselves."

Ivy moved to the edge of her seat. "As you wish, Miss Windihill." She followed her parents into the dining room and left Sicili in a flustered mess of unreasonable emotions. She needed more wine. More wine and a large fan.

At the drawing room door, her mother looped an arm in hers. "You two seem friendly, Sicili."

Her corset pinched. "Not overly. We met at Father's ball. In his study."

"In a study? That's an odd place to meet."

"By mistake." *In fact, I followed her there because she makes my heart wild, and tonight I'm quite full of lies.* "She needed fresh air and I..." *I'm not sure what I need.*

"I find her very obscure. I try not to let it show in front of Charlotte. Wiltshire thinks her graceless disposition stems from Charlotte's lack of discipline, but I cannot conform to that frame of thought. I know Charlotte. She has endlessly strived to set that girl straight. It must be something altogether different. Would you agree?"

"Mother, I prefer not to talk about our guests while they sit in the next room."

Francine cupped her cheek. "How sweet you are to your new friend. It pleases me you two are getting along."

Mothers and daughters sat side by side at the candle lit dining table, and the gentlemen sat at either end. She and Ivy faced each other, most unfortunately, and shared a subtle look. She wistfully smiled, doomed to notice lovely details about Ivy for the entirety of dinner. Ivy returned her smile, briefly, and ignored her thereafter, as if they had not shared secret words in the drawing room and sat close and spoke low. She drank her wine and picked at her food and bowed out of conversation––something about a busy road set to be built from London to Wiltshire.

She saw no one but Ivy at the table. The flicker of candle light intensified the red of Ivy's hair and the floral against her skin and––

Wilber stood over her shoulder. "Shall I top up your wine, Miss Windihill?"

"Right to the top, Wilber."

"Is the duck to your liking?"

She hadn't touched her meal. "The view is lovely, Wilber. Thank you."

He tarried long enough to witness Ivy's glance––a restrained glance, but a glance nonetheless. And her blush––rosy, honest, and unmistakable. He cleared his throat and moved on to replenish Francine's wine.

The girl, quite unlike her true self, engaged in conversation with just the right amount of poise and knowledge. Subtle interjections of "oh, indeed" and "I do agree" and "may I mention?" escaped her buttery lips. She nearly lapsed when the subject turned to society and the notion set upon women to be kind and polite and obedient to their superior gender. Her cheeks took on a warm hue, and her natural vigor surfaced for a gasp of air––"Mr. Windihill, I will have you know, not all women in their right mind desire the oppression––" only to be silenced by a stiff look from Mrs. Ferthing.

Ivy's jaw locked, and she soberly returned to her last bite of duck.

Francine rested a hand on Sicili's shoulder. "Speaking of marriage––"

"Please, Mother."

"––Sicili received an offer today."

George raised his wine glass. "A toast," he bellowed. "To my angel's influence and beauty."

The table toasted and cheered; Ivy included.

"And when do we expect the wedding?" Mr. Ferthing asked.

Francine laughed. "She refused him, of course––"

"Mother, you speak as if he proposed to you."

"––Mr. Evergreen is not quite her type."

Mr. Ferthing lowered his glass. "Oh?"

Francine nudged her. "Am I right, darling?"

"Indeed." She compulsively glanced at Ivy. "Not quite."

"Poor lad," Ivy said. "At least he attempted the impossible. Cheers to courageous men who are rebuffed by Sicili Windihill." Ivy held up her glass. No one joined her. The rest of the table gawked. Unfazed, the heathen took a sip.

Sicili set down her fork. "I, too, have a toast." She raised an eyebrow at her father. "To those who think they know what is best for me."

He lifted his glass. "Indeed, my angel."

After dinner, they moved to the parlor in the West wing where they played two rounds of whist. George won both. Francine teased that he had the cards rigged, and Sicili seconded the notion, to which George replied, "*Shhh*, my dears, you mustn't alarm our guests." Charlotte and William joined him for a merry laugh. Wine flowed freely. Wilber devoutly encouraged intoxication.

Ivy sat beside her, less than an arms-length away, and made no attempt to engage in conversation. They touched several times in the reshuffle of cards, an electricity sparked between them, and they both felt it––she was sure Ivy felt it, but the girl refused acknowledgement by avoiding her gaze.

By the third round, she knew she had to focus on something other than Ivy's wrists.

"I am curious to know, Mr. Ferthing," she said on the fourth round, "how did you become the successful winemaker you are today?"

Mr. Ferthing's eyes danced with happy memories. "Are you certain you care to know?"

"Very certain."

"I would have become a tailor by trade if not for my generous father, God rest his soul. He was a frugal man. Not rich, but frugal. Over the years, he saved enough to send me to university in London. He wanted his son to be anything but a tailor. To his dismay, I studied agriculture. I graduated at the head of my class, having fallen in love with the art of plants."

George piped in as if the story belonged to him, "That was only the beginning."

"Then I thought to myself," William went on, "what plant, if cared for and nurtured, would produce the most rewarding fruit? What fruit would yield the greatest profit for me? Strawberries, blueberries, huckleberries? Too sour, too sweet. A fruit with a balance of citrus and sugar? A few months after I met my gracious Charlotte, it came to me. Grapes."

"Grapes," George echoed.

"I started myself a small vineyard, and cared for it day in and day out."

"Even in the wee hours," Charlotte said.

The party all laughed.

"Within a year, Wiltshire had gone mad over my grapes. We needed more space, a bigger vineyard, a barn to make and store the wine. So my dear father sold his tailor shop and came to live with Charlotte and I. He passed a few years later, the proudest he could be. He––humble, frugal, generous––was the origin of my success."

The party clapped. Mr. Ferthing wiped a tear from his cheek.

Sicili offered him her handkerchief. "I imagine tending a vineyard is no easy business. Does it tire you?"

William patted his obtrusive gut. "I shall never tire of a marvelous cluster of grapes pressed into a tall glass of wine." He laughed.

"Hear, hear," George roared.

"Besides," Mr. Ferthing added, "I have my Ivy to help with the workload. What would I do without her?" With a light in his eyes, he patted Ivy's hand and they shared an endearing smile.

The party fell silent over the thought of Naughty Ivy being helpful.

Sicili took a sidelong glance at her evil old man. The only light he let off was the glint of his plan to hold her captive until she unhappily married. He gave her a drunken wink. *You scumbag.* He resembled a lump of lard in comparison to Ivy's frugal, selfless grandfather. She envied their way of life––the hard work, the dedication, the sacrifice.

Halfway through the fifth round, Ivy set down her cards. "Mind if I sit this round out? I need to powder my nose." As she rose, her knuckles brushed Sicili's arm. "I dare you to win, Sicili."

Her arm tingled where Ivy had touched. "Dare me what?"

"A penny."

"Only a penny?"

"You might get lost," interrupted Francine. "Whoever built this mansion had no sense of the necessary."

George thundered a laugh. "Francine––our guests."

"It is true, George. You know it to be true. It takes ten minutes to find your way."

"Wilber, my wife will have another glass of wine."

By the sixth round, euphoria trumped, and laughter reigned supreme. George's masterful hand refused to let up, and every card placed on the table, except his, suffered. Wilber served tea and cake, possibly to detour further inebriation and the longevity of gaiety.

Mrs. Ferthing inhaled her piece of cake. "Where did Ivy get off to?"

"She went to powder her nose," Francine said.

"That was hours ago? Was it not?"

Francine giggled. "Was it? How hard it is to remember."

Mrs. Ferthing dabbed her mouth. "She ought to be back by now. She must be lost. William, will you find her? She's up to no good. I can feel it in my bones."

Mr. Ferthing obediently nodded.

"Sit down, William," Francine said. "Windsworth is a nightmare to navigate, especially at night. Sicili will bring her back to us. Sicili?"

Lovely details about Ivy had finally let her be, and now her mother wanted them to be alone. "Are you trying to foil me, Mother? I plan to win this round."

"Dubious," George chuckled.

Her mother tapped her leg. "Mrs. Ferthing is in suspense. Go at once, Sicili."

Sicili folded her cards. She could win later. As Sicili left the room, Charlotte Ferthing finished her cake.

***

The library doors hung wide open. How like Ivy to seek solitude in the loneliest corner of Windsworth. On the dreary days when clouds hung over the garden and wind raked the fields, Sicili used to seek refuge in her father's grand maze of decrepit books. That was before he sent her to London. The library––dark, disorganized, cold––symbolized his betrayal.

Shelves of dusty books rose to the high ceiling, tethered by age and neglect. Narrow aisles led to a hidden bay window overlooking the back garden.

"Miss Ferthing? Are you in here?"

A muffled voice down a distant aisle, "Over here."

"I thought you might have escaped out a study window."

A cackle. "Not tonight. Mother would crucify me. She wants us to be friends."

"Us?"

"She thinks your influence over men is bountiful."

"It is large."

A softer cackle. "Not as large as your suppressed desire for..." Ivy trailed off.

"Pardon?"

"Do you read?"

She followed her voice. "Not often. My father devours books. Naturally, I despise anything he adores, except my mother. Do you read?"

"Adamantly," Ivy answered. "Mother thought books would tame me. They only fed my fury. I did little but read while she imprisoned me at Vineyard Estate. Theodore Pyniing says woman should refrain from literature. They should learn the skills necessary to win a man and provide him with children, then be content to live a quiet life."

"Who is Theodore Pyniing?"

"A moralist who calls himself an author. What a loaf."

"Where are you?"

"Over here. By the window."

"You found the window?"

The aisle opened into a cozy area of furniture. A starless night peered through the tall bay windows. Ivy leaned against an armchair, consumed by an ancient book. They had sat side by side and played whist in the parlor, and maybe fifteen minutes had passed since she last saw her, maybe. Somehow, Ivy's hair looked wilder in the dim light of the library.

Ivy looked up. "Did you prevail at whist?"

"Of course not. My father is a cheat. You owe me a penny."

"What if I'm penniless?"

"Then you owe me something else."

"Another kiss?"

Sicili clucked. "You can dream." Heat and feelings and memories rushed to her cheeks. "Mother sent me after you. She's so very intoxicated. I never see her this way."

"I find her charming."

"Unlike me?"

"Now that you mention it, you do take after your father."

Her eyes narrowed. "Did I say something to offend you? In the drawing room before dinner?"

Ivy shrugged. "Not that I recall."

"You ignored me all evening."

"Did I?"

"At dinner and at whist. Quit playing daft."

A smile. "Am I?"

"I know you."

Ivy snapped the book shut. "Oh, really? Do you?"

"You can be brilliant and sly when not bored, and you happen to be the perfect little actress. I watched you at dinner. You have my family convinced you are good and proper and cured of your devious past."

The girl smiled ear to ear. "You were watching me at dinner," she stated. "Do you find me irresistible, Miss Windihill?"

Yes. A hundred times yes. "I find you formidable. And vulgar."

"Vulgar enough to forsake whist and wine for my company?"

"Presumption is ill advisable, Miss Ferthing."

"Ivy. Just Ivy."

"Not Ivan?"

Ivy set the book down and blew a runaway tendril out of her frightfully beautiful eyes. "Have you thought about that night?"

"No," she lied. "Have you?"

"Yes." Ivy returned the book to its shelf and strode toward Sicili, closing the distance between them like someone who knows what they are about, who never once doubted themselves.

Sicili felt a pinch of envy. She retreated and hit a dusty shelf. Dust billowed down. With a subtle smile that made Sicili squirm, Ivy rested a hand over Sicili's shoulder and contemplated her lips.

They were inches apart and still not close enough. Ivy tucked a loose lock of hair behind Sicili's ear. "I'll have you know, Miss Windihill, your exhibit of courage that night managed to get me banned from Madam Desiree's. Eveline refuses to serve me."

Sicili played with the lace of Ivy's extended sleeve. She played with the idea of bringing her closer. "I did you a favor. Madam Desiree's is no place for a woman."

"I could tell you the same, but I won't, because I know how it feels."

"How what feels?"

"The need to escape life as it is." Her thumb brushed Sicili's jaw. "Did you have a grand time with Mister Whatshisname?"

"Mr. Evergreen."

A light went off in Ivy's eyes. "*Oh*, that's right. Mr. Evergreen. The gent who proposed. Poor fellow."

She snatched a book from the shelf and leafed through the pages to distract from Ivy's proximity and tormenting eyes. The book added a nice gap between them. "He would have been worse off had I accepted him."

"Why is that?"

"I shall not make a humble wife."

Ivy laughed. "Perhaps he wanted an impartial wife."

"Perhaps. The last thing *I* want is an overbearing husband." She lost herself in a paragraph, despite her innate desire to lose herself in Ivy's eyes.

Ivy seemed to get the hint and backed off. She strolled down an aisle. "What *do* you want, Sicili Windihill?"

The bold question gave her great pause. Had she never been asked it before? It felt new and frightening. It made her antsy. She wanted for very little in life. Whatever she desired, she received without effort. It was never a matter of *what* she wanted, but more a question of: Was she missing something? Why could she not look at Grace without guilt and displeasure?

"Never-mind me," she said after too much deliberation on the matter.

"I rather like the subject of Sicili Windihill." Ivy's voice faded as she turned and disappeared.

"In comparison to you, I'm as drab as a stick."

"I highly disagree."

"How unfortunate."

"For you or for me?"

"Where are you?"

"Over here. By the plant."

Sicili found her after deliberately taking her time. She wanted to appear cool and detached, not as curious as she felt. Ivy had returned to the window, and she stared out it with a listless manner. The view overlooked the needless sprawl of Windsworth Estate, an expansive lawn engulfed by an overbearing box of a mansion, pressing its shadow onto everything green in sight. Sicili had always felt the mansion much too large for a family of three. She preferred the neat corners of Aunt Gertrude's apartment in the city with nowhere to go except one's room and the sitting parlor. It forced her to engage with her aunt and the servants. At Windsworth, one could purposefully get lost and not be found for days.

Ivy leaned against the wall in a boyish fashion, her arms crossed, and one leg crossed over the other.

Sicili ventured closer. "Shall we talk about the infamous Naughty Ivy?"

Ivy's eyes shone as she gave a bow. "What would you like to know?"

"I know a great deal about you already."

Ivy's grin was dubious in nature. "Do you? Enlighten me."

Sicili touched the plant. "You dress up as a boy."

"A man," Ivy said with dignity. "Ivan Miller. The man. You'll have to do better. Everyone knows I dress up. I said it when I first met you and I shall say it again: I'm a legend in this part."

"Very well. I know you like to woo women into dark halls while dressed up as Mr. Miller. See? I know more than most people know about you."

Ivy's face got bold. Her grin went soft. "Have I wooed you?"

She moved to the other side of the window. There needed to be space between them. Without it, she feared a remake of that night at Madam Desiree's. "Not a chance."

The girl looked from defeated. "I'll have to try harder."

"Or not at all. I think you give yourself too much credit, Miss Ferthing."

Ivy smiled. "Just Ivy."

Just Ivy. Not naughty, not Ivan, not Penniless, not obtrusive—just Ivy. She lowered her eyes to the book. *The male's vocal cords are crass in nature when he lets forth his call. The female calls back in a shrill high-pitched song. Her agenda is clear, stating that she is drawn to his calls and ready to mate.*

Male and female will mate for days, long after conception has been achieved--

"Only two?" Ivy said.

She looked up from the fascinatingly dull read. "Pardon?"

Ivy tarried by the plant, arms still crossed, and face still preoccupied with a curious glow. "You know two things about me. I dress up as a man, and I occasionally woo women." She shook her head with feigned disappointment. "There is more to me than my getups and my love for the intoxicating female figure."

She placed a finger on the spot where she had stopped reading. "I do want to know one more thing."

"Yes?"

"Do you desperately want to be a man?"

Ivy shrugged the question off. "Desperately? No. I might like such a role, I might not. The male sex gets away with everything--I envy them that--while woman fuss over tea and pretend to like it."

"Most women do."

"Not me."

"You *are* extraordinary."

"Am I?"

"I meant it as an insult, not a compliment."

"Are we insulting each other now?"

"We better, before we get carried away."

Ivy's laugh was softer than her usual cackles. "We are alone."

Laughter sailed through the open library doors from down the hall where their parents played whist and waited for the return of their daughters. As if awaking from a dream, Sicili realized she had been gone for far too long. The others would begin to worry soon, even in their drunken stupor, and she had wrongfully kept Ivy Ferthing in suspense given the circumstances of her father's plans and why she stayed

on at Windsworth until her twenty-third birthday. Though
she wanted to stay in this neglected library, alone, with the
wayward scandal of Wiltshire, knowing she would very much
enjoy every moment of it, their little tryst had to come to an
end. For Ivy's sake, if not for her own. For in waking, she saw
that Ivy had begun to look at her in a certain way that affected
her bright eyes. In fact, a way that made them even brighter.
And it was blinding and confusing.

Sicili snapped the book shut. "Henry Fuller and I are courting."

The brightness in Ivy's eyes faltered. "You are?"

She made up a lie. She was good at lies. She was wonderful
at shrouding her heart behind falsities and formalities. "And it
has gotten quite serious over the last week. He means to call
on me tomorrow, and we plan to spend the day in London."

Ivy straightened from her comfortable stoop. It looked
un-natural to see the girl serious and stiff. "You moved on
from Mr. Evergreen rather quickly."

Sicili shrugged, holding Ivy's eyes and pretending it didn't
feel awful to lie to the girl. "You know what it's like when a
woman means to settle."

Ivy gave her a stupefied look. "I thought you were impartial."

"I am, but so is Henry Fuller. I will have the city and my
darling Charlotte, and he will have his galleries. I think we
shall fit each other quite seamlessly."

Ivy bit her lip. She turned and looked out the window. "You
sound like quite the match." She huffed. "Do you want to know
what I think?"

"Hardly."

"I think if you were any other person besides Sicili Windihill, you would be named a charlatan for how quickly you
disposed of Mr. Evergreen and swept up Mr. Fuller."

Sicili gasped. "A charlatan? You make it sound as if I set traps for them."

Ivy spared her a glance, her eyebrows raised.

"You cannot mean that," she argued.

"I can. I know what it feels like to be outed for you who are."

"Truly, Ivy. This coming from you, someone who prefers the company of brothels and dancers."

"I own who I am."

"I wonder, sometimes, at how you became *so* bold."

Ivy proudly raised her chin. "My father is an infamous winemaker. He may have had a drink too many before letting me loose into the world."

She closed the intentional space between them, getting dangerously close to the girl. "Your boldness is going to get you in trouble one day."

"It already has."

"Take it back."

"Or what?"

"Or I plan to tell you what I think about *you*."

"Go on," Ivy chided.

What had Charlotte told her about women who loved women in the city? What had she called them? Sicili dug into her memory for the worst possible word she could call a lady. And she found it. She stepped toward the girl. "I think you are a hot-headed, preposterous––" a deep breath, "tomboy."

Ivy stood her ground. In fact, she looked pleased. In London, tomboys cut their hair short and dressed in rags and lived on the streets. They were disowned by their families, and they ate scraps and huddled together and endured foul words from high-class citizens. They did unthinkable acts in the shadows of allies just to make a shilling for bread and the warmth of ale.

Ivy left the window and stood close. "You pretentious, vulnerable spinster."

"Spinster?"

Their lips were inches apart. An unsettling urge to relive that night at Madam Desiree's erupted into unforgivable passion. She shoved Ivy hard against the nearest shelf. Books fell at their feet. Dust assailed them.

"You selfish twig," she yelled.

Ivy shoved back. "Did you tell Mr. Evergreen *why* you refused his hand?"

"You, Miss Ferthing, are the one who sneaks into Madam Desiree's while your mother frets and worries."

Ivy grabbed her braid and yanked. "You hate dancing with men, but you do it despite yourself because your father expects it of you."

She screamed. "How dare you?" She pinched Ivy's nose so hard it turned red between her fingers. "You attend private whist parties to appease your mother and soothe her nerves when you would rather be flirting with half-dressed girls in dark lit parlors. You and I are not so different."

Ivy ripped the gold detail from her neckline. "Have you been trapped for half your youth at Vineyard Estate because your mother is afraid you might be a monster?"

She gaped at the ripped fabric. Her favorite foreboding dress. How dare the *little*––she grabbed a handful of Ivy's hair and pulled. Pins and naughty locks spiraled out of place. "I shall never put my mother through the disgrace of thinking I might be a boy."

She tripped Ivy and they both went down. She fell on top, and Ivy grinned from ear to ear.

"If you dare get the wrong idea––"

Ivy gripped her waist and rolled on top. Wide-eyed, they stared and blinked and searched for words. Ivy's knees pinched her sides. Red hair draped over Ivy's shoulder onto hers and had the audacity to tickle her collarbone. *Should I move? Should I kiss her? Should I scream?* Part of her wanted to stay shielded behind Ivy's hair for the rest of eternity. It felt wholesome and right to be pinned beneath Naughty Ivy, and so very foreign it frightened her into laughter. She sighed and allowed herself to giggle as the sensation of Ivy's hair flooded her. "Your insults are devastating."

Ivy huffed. "So are yours, Sicili Windihill."

Eleven

The Ruin of a Gay Evening

Just down the corridor, Charlotte reveled over a splendid hand of cards. William, full and laughing, sat to her right. Francine told stories, and George winked and puffed at his pipe. What a marvelous time they enjoyed. The fire crackled, Wilber played the pianoforte in the parlor over, and Ivy had conducted herself perfectly all evening. What more could a mother want? *I have not one complaint. Not one.* With the magic of wine in her gut and a seamless night winding down, she found herself drunk on confidence and ease.

To top it all off, she was about to win the eighth round of whist.

"Where have the girls gone?" said Francine. "You would think the facilities had swallowed them whole."

George puffed. "Francine––what a foul idea. Do contain your imagination."

"It is hard, George, when three bottles lie empty, and you insist on conquering every round."

Charlotte raised her winning card––a scream came from the corridor, followed by tumultuous yells. A hot sweat broke across her forehead. She knew Ivy's voice. She slapped her cards down and guzzled the last of her wine, knowing she had foolishly given Ivy the benefit of the doubt. Let the girl wail. Let the bells ring. Let all hell break loose.

The yelling increased.

Francine rose a hand to her bosom. "Are those our girls?"

George snuffed out his pipe.

William's laugh stalled.

All three rushed out of the parlor. Charlotte reluctantly rose and followed, weary of the sight to come. Dread. So much dread.

Francine gallantly led the way to the corridor, William and George at her heel. The yells originated in the library. "Sicili?" She dashed through the library doors and down a narrow aisle yelling, "Sicili, is that you? Are you ill? Are you hurt?" and halted in front of tall bay windows overlooking the Windsworth gardens.

Sicili and Ivy (*oh*, Ivy) struggled off each other. Dresses torn. Arms scratched. Heads tussled and hair in disarray. Ivy cradled her red, swollen cheek. Sicili fidgeted with the ruined gold sequence on her bodice. They both looked up at the same time.

And Charlotte knew.

She knew.

Ivy refused to look her in the eye.

Her ears buzzed; her legs weakened. She felt feverish and light, and her mind raced with all the right words to defend her daughter, but nothing came out. Ivy had foiled a perfectly seamless evening. Yet again.

Her legs buckled. Someone caught her. The carriage ride home passed in a blur of stern silence and airy dread. It jostled them about, pushing at her to wake up and see the ruin that her daughter was, to stop trying to change the foul girl. She groaned and came to in her own cold drawing room. The ash-stained mantlepiece glowered, and the fire cackled at her for allowing herself to dream that Ivy had one speck of a chance.

William fed the flames. Ivy kneeled at the head of the chaise. How surreal to see concern on the girl's face. "We're home now, Mother."

She fretfully sighed. "What happened?"

Ivy pressed a cool cloth to her forehead. "Wilber caught you right as you fainted."

She sat up. The room swirled. Her ears still buzzed. "What *happened*, Ivy? Between you and Sicili."

Ivy lowered her eyes. "We fought, Mother. She's pretentious and impartial and cruel to men, and she knows it."

"What does her cruelty to men have to do with you?"

"She ought to be true to herself is all..."

"True to herself or true to you?"

Ivy's lips thinned. She soaked the cloth in a basin, wrung it damp, and pressed it to her forehead.

Charlotte shuddered. "You were meant to be friends, Ivy, not..."

"Say it."

"*No*. Never."

Ivy's cheeks glowed––peachy and blithe and full of life. The way they had when she and Harriet Prattle used to sneak out to the vineyard. Charlotte wanted to slap those precious cheeks until the color drained. She wanted to see Ivy suffer and wail and pace––atonement for all the years of fretting and trying and failing to set the girl straight.

William leaned against the mantel and stared stoically into the flames, hardly ruffled.

"What do you have to say, Mr. Ferthing?"

He looked straight at her. "What would you have me say, Charlotte?"

"Something. *Anything*. Tell the girl to get a hold of her wild fantasies before she puts us both out of business and home."

He stoked the fire. "Are we certain fantasies are what they are?"

"Indeed. Wild and dangerous fantasies."

He ruffed. "Give her some credit, Charlotte. She's not a little girl anymore. She knows what she wants."

"Credit? I shall reward credit where credit is due. Our boys––our decent, hardworking boys deserve credit. They live normal, everyday, successful lives. They abide the law and refrain from wild tendencies and irrational––"

"And they want nothing to do with us." He shook his head. "We see them once a year at Christmas. Humbug. Ivy is kind and helpful and intelligent. She will be the one to take on the vineyard. Not them. They turned their backs on the years I slaved to send them to London and university. Not Ivy. We both know Ivy will stay at Vineyard Estate and take care of us in our old age."

She snatched the cloth from Ivy and draped it over her chest. Ivy withdrew to the fireside. *Her* Ivy, tending the vineyard and running a man's business? She felt another fainting spell coming on. "She's a lady, William. *A lady*. She needs to marry a fine fellow and migrate to her own household. What sort of rumours will taint her if you have her managing a vineyard? What sort of fellow will put up with her?"

William usually let up. They usually argued about Ivy's future late into the night, in the privacy of their bedroom, with shadows and fears crouched under their bed. Not tonight. Tonight, he stood firm. "Ivy will make a competent businesswoman, and I will personally see to it. I've taught her everything there is to Vineyard Estate. Charlotte, she shows promise and devotion. If you would stop dragging her to balls and bores, you might notice how bright and confident our Ivy is. She is far from the treachery society and rumors make her out to be." With that, he stomped his foot and took his leave.

Ivy trailed behind him, but Charlotte cleared her throat in a motherly way and Ivy paused at the drawing room door.

"Yes, Mother?"

"You, young lady, are going to tell me exactly what is happening between you and Sicili."

Ivy crossed her arms. "Stop your fretting, Mother. Miss Windihill is courting Henry Fuller."

"Henry Fuller? Are you lying to me, Ivy?"

"Does it look it?"

Apart from the blithe glow of her cheeks, Ivy's eyes danced with a lovely, rare light−−a light she once possessed as a girl. Charlotte feared the return of what that light meant. Without avail, she had tried and tried to shield the girl from its power. Five years of books and solitude failed to beat it out of her. She had to dash the light before it got away with Ivy, before she could begin to hope.

She blew her nose into the damp cloth. "There is something you should know, Ivy."

Ivy kept to the door, halfway out of Charlotte's reach.

"What is it, Mother?"

"Something Francine Windihill revealed to me tonight." She paused for dramatic effect. "Sicili Windihill means to be married by her twenty-third birthday, which is barely two months away."

Ivy stiffened. The light noticeably dimmed, and though Charlotte had done all she could to protect the girl, she felt ill for it. She fell back against the chaise. The wine had turned bittersweet in her gut. "People like Sicili Windihill do not stay single for long, Ivy, and when they did, it is because there is something infallible about them. There had to be a reason she returned to the countryside, and I can only imagine this is why."

Ivy hung in a dreadful silence. "So she means to marry Henry Fuller?"

"I have no idea. I imagine she will court as many men as she desires. It would be unwise to..." Charlotte couldn't bring herself to say it. "The Windihills are too far our superiors, Ivy. They would never..." That was all she could manage. She dabbed the sweat from her forehead. "If only you had been another boy. I could have managed four sons. I know boys. I know how passive and nostalgic they are. But you. I had to want you, and so badly. So terribly that I prayed day and night for a tiny, beautiful me." She rubbed her temples. "And this is how I am repaid. With you––a terrible, witless, ungrateful daughter who would rather have fun than make her family proud."

Ivy stared at her for a long while, tears sailing her precious, bright eyes. There, Charlotte had done it. Diffused the last of the girl's hope, smothered it with cruelty. But it had to be done. She had to be protected from herself.

After several minutes of irrevocable silence, Ivy clapped. "Well done, Mother. Your finest speech yet. A wonder you haven't driven me out with contempt by now."

"A wonder I haven't kept you under lock and key."

"Questionable."

"Where are you going?"

"For a walk."

"At this hour?"

A somber expression drained the glow from Ivy's cheeks. The light in her eyes slowly faded. "I can stay clear of Miss Windihill if you want me to. Do you want me to, Mother?"

"I want you to stop with your games."

"It was never a game. Not with her."

Ivy turned on her heel and strode into the hall, and the click of the front door weighed heavy on Charlotte's heart.

Depression gripped her. She mourned being the one to dash Ivy's light. What a lovely, caring light it was——but it had to be done. The Windihills were considered royalty in Wiltshire, not to mention London and most of England. They were well thought of, respectable people who were fully capable of ostracizing Ivy if she got away with herself, which she would.

Oh, how hard she had worked to restore Ivy into society.

As for Sicili, she reminded Charlotte too much of Harriet Prattle. Harriet and Ivy were inseparable as young girls. They had tea parties and made forts in the drawing room and played dress-up——Ivy wore her brother's clothes and Harriet played the pretty housewife. When they grew, they giggled in Ivy's room and snuck out of her window, climbed down the side of the house and shared whispers in the vineyard and held hands when no one watched.

And then Harriet matured and the boys her age noticed and grinned at her, and she must have decided she liked their attention more than Ivy's. She pinched her cheeks and batted her eyes and obsessed over suitors twice her age. Ivy listened and smiled, but never obsessed back. The light in Ivy's eyes grew strong and wild and passionate.

Oh, the way Ivy looked at Harriet when she thought no one else could see.

Drunk on fear, Charlotte stumbled up from the chaise and fumbled her way to the drawing room window. At the bottom of the vineyard, William inspected a row of vines. Grapes were his refuge from all things chaotic and emotional. She smiled. She married him for his goodness and his kindness, and for the light she saw in his eyes. Ivy trudged down the vineyard, shoulders stooped, hands pocketed, and stopped to give William a kiss on the cheek. He waved her goodbye as she stooped off into the golden sunset beyond Vineyard Estate.

She pressed her hand against the window. Ivy kept walking and slipped out of her palm.

Twelve

To Hardly Know

The old man had gone to bed with a jolly "All this fun has exhausted me, my dears." Sicili and her mother sat in utmost silence in the parlor––whist cards scattered on the table and rug, wine bottles half empty, a fresh fire licking up the cool night. The library incident hung over them. Sicili's shoulders and arms stung from being tossed about, her throat felt raw from yelling ridiculous insults and her scalp ached from Ivy's awful yanking. How had she let herself get so carried away?

It was as if the girl had cast a ridiculous spell on her.

Wilber brought them tea and left with a polite cough.

After some time, Francine grasped the teapot and poured a cup and set the saucer delicately on Sicili's lap. "I thought you two were friends, Sicili."

"Far from it, Mother." *What are we? Fated to quarrel? Hopelessly drawn to each other. Two prisms of light reflecting off the other?* Their disastrous relationship asked for no description. It just was. It began in the moon lit study with Ivy down to her corset and petticoat.

Francine watched her closely. "I am confused. Why did you two tear at each other so?"

"We were intoxicated, I think."

"You *think?*"

"I still am, possibly, and she *always* is. And you––you were severely inebriated at whist."

"The sight of you and Ivy wrestling on the library floor sobered me. What were you two quarreling about?"

"She bothers me. She makes me confused and tormented and passionate all at once."

Francine's expression jumped as she sipped her tea. "Passionate?"

"I'm tired, Mother. I'm not sure what I'm saying." She sighed. "When this ordeal with Father passes, I shall return to London and forget about Miss Ferthing and never think on her again."

A distressed look pulled her mother's brow. "Oh, Sicili, you do realize your father is serious about..."

Dread settled over her like a cloak.

"Perhaps I never told you, darling. When I was but sixteen, I fell in love with Gregory Simmons. He was a political man. Nothing like your father. He joined the military during our first year of courtship and got himself killed six months later. I thought I would die of a broken heart. My parents refused to let me, so they arranged for me to marry George Windihill. I fought it at first. I disliked like your father. I thought he was arrogant and had too many runaway ideas. I still dislike him, some days." A wicked smile. "I was so young and confused, and I feared my world would never be the same without my Gregory. Your father was good to me. He loved me. Cared for me. Gave me Windsworth and wealth and reputation--"

"Is that all you two care about?"

"--and without him, I would cease to have you. Sicili, darling, he does not force you to marry a man you dislike. He gives you the freedom to marry whatever gentleman you choose. You might find his oppression a blessing over time."

She plated her tea in a clutter of emotions. "How do you mean, *over time?*"

"Over many years of memories and balls and breezy social affairs. Do you not want a comfortable, stable life free of hazardous rumors and scandal?"

"Scandal, Mother?"

"Trust me, darling." Francine severely pinched the bridge of her nose. "If you continue to engage with Ivy Ferthing, a life of confusion, torment and suffering will be yours. That outrageous girl is cursed."

"You told me to be good to her."

"I changed my mind. I realize she is trouble. She has always been a troubling character. I do pity Charlotte, but I cannot entertain the fateful idea of you and——"

"Mother, please."

"Is that what you want, Sicili? Torture and confusion?"

"No..."

"Do you want comfort and stability and your father's blessing?"

"I do... possibly." *But how can I be sure?*

"You do, Sicili. Every young woman wants stability." Her mother clasped her hand and squeezed. "We want to see you settled and happy. Every mother and father want such." She released her hand. "You're cold, darling. You should have Wilber light the fire in your room."

She nodded.

Francine retrieved the saucer and cup from her lap. Neither of them had finished their tea. "What a disaster. That girl was the ruin of a lovely evening. Remind me to never again invite Ivy Ferthing into my home." Her mother took a deep breath.

She had stopped breathing all together.

"Promise me you will stay away from her, darling?"

She looked up, shocked at how long she had been staring at the ripped neckline of her favorite dress. She had the gold detail wrapped tight around her finger——the one she had wounded the day she visited her father in his formidable study. The finger Ivy had kissed in the smoky hall at Madam Desiree's. Francine stood by the parlor door. A tense expression hardened the soft edges of her face.

"I promise, Mother."

Francine nodded, and her smile was far from relieved.

When her mother slipped away, Sicili brushed a silly tear from her cheek. She laughed. The parlor lulled and the fire embers glowed and faded, and she whispered, "Can you not see how unhappy I am?" She tarried in the cold, silent and breathless, for far too long. Her skin and her veins and her heart abstained warmth and her organs cooled.

Wilber gathered wine bottles. She blinked. When had he come in? They shared a hopeless look. His expression filled with concern, and she hated seeing lines torture his brow and sadness pull at his mouth. He placed a throw from the sofa over her shoulders.

"Are you well, Miss Windihill?"

She forced a breath past the heavy threat of tears. "I hardly know, Wilber."

Thirteen

The Tournament

Once a year, the benevolent Dainty's hosted a private croquet tournament to which only the wealthiest and most popular in Wiltshire were invited. Louis Dainty, an avid player, owned a lovely estate of flat, green lawn that stretched to the horizon and back. Wagers were struck and pooled toward a small charity in aid of the poor. Wiltshire loved to empty their thick wallets the lesser folk of the countryside. In fact, if an invitee did the unthinkable and refused to attend, they were considered greedy and shunned until the next year.

Charlotte pinned Ivy's hair in a grand display of neat curls and shoved her into a restrictive dress. The fabric pinched and accentuated and felt all kinds of wrong, especially since Charlotte had been allowing Ivy to strut about Vineyard Estate in trousers and a linen tunic. The corset delighted in torturing her on the carriage ride across Wiltshire.

Ivy swished her fan while her mother and father sat across from her in the carriage. Mr. Ferthing whispered something private and crass in Charlotte's ear. She gasped in horror and swatted him before breaking down in hot giggles. He snatched up her hand and planted a wet kiss on her knuckles. Charlotte's face went as bright as her apple-colored dress. Ivy smothered a grin and gave them privacy while she looked out the window. She liked seeing them flirt. They seldom did with her mother fretting about Ivy's reputation from dusk till

dawn, but the last few weeks of Ivy behaving had afford-
ed her mother some respite, and laughter looked good on
Charlotte Ferthing.

The Dainty's tournament was a laughable farce––a reason to socialize rather than benefit the less fortunate. If the
wealthiest of Wiltshire wanted to forsake their coin, they
could go and do it in person any day of the year, not by taking
part in a tournament only the affluent were invited to attend.

Ivy's party arrived on time, just as the patio tables were
being decorated with colorful pastries and iced tea. They
were rushed through the Dainty's breezy summer residence
and brisked onto the back terrace where Harriet and her Mr.
Prattle sat under an umbrella and watched Louis Dainty test
the croquet field.

"It is hot today, Mr. Dainty," Harriet said. "I feel quite
slippery."

Phillip Prattle ran a finger down her arm. "Slippery, darling?"

"You know, uneasy."

Louis leaned into his gold embellished mallet and adjusted his spectacles. "Not to worry, Mrs. Prattle. There is plenty
of iced tea. You may take to the parlor at any time. I had Mrs.
Dainty open the windows."

Harriet shaded her eyes. "How kind of her." Dissatisfac-
tion edged her slippery voice.

"I have several rounds set up," said Louis, and quite
proudly. "The entire competition should take a complete six
hours, if I calculated correctly. That includes intermissions."
He lined up his ball and struck it through a hoop a mile down
the lawn.

Harriet fanned herself. "Despite this heat?"

"Indeed, Mrs. Prattle."

"It shall pick us off like flies."

"The winner of the previous round plays the winner of the next round, and so forth. Until we have a champion."

"We might get bored after so long in the sun."

"Impossible." He chuckled. "You shall be more than entertained. The players I have lined up come in all shapes, sizes, and reputation. Here the Ferthings come this very moment." Chipper, he pointed his mallet at Ivy. "Welcome, my fine friends. Welcome to my humble charity for the impoverished. Do sit in the shade close to Mr. and Mrs. Prattle."

Ivy obliged, reluctantly. She selected a lawn chair next to Harriet. The umbrella was rather small, and she had to get close. Her elbow jived with Harriet's, and Harriet spared her a quick smile. Charlotte settled to Ivy's right in a huff of anticipation and bade Mr. Ferthing fetch them a round of iced tea. He hurried off to the colorful tables.

Harriet fanned. "You look uncomfortable, Ivy." She motioned for Mr. Prattle to fan her as well.

"Thank you," Ivy said.

Charlotte pinched her. "Stop that slouching."

She straightened. "Are you playing, Harriet?"

"Of course." Harriet pursed her lips. "Do I look like a ninny?"

Mr. Ferthing returned with croissants, an array of cheese, a pitcher of iced tea, and two more parties. The Beckers and the Peacocks. Mr. Peacock immediately engaged Mr. Prattle in business talk, in low voices only businessmen understood.

Harriet fanned faster. "Will you step in for me when I get too hot, Mr. Prattle?"

He pecked her cheek. "Darling, that would be pointless. My skills at croquet are minimal."

He turned his back and continued in low murmurs with Mr. Peacock. The Becker's picked a viewpoint on the other end of the terrace, after several un-necessary glares in Ivy's direction. She picked at her gloves. She wore the proper formalities and sat poised and politely sipped iced tea despite impending dehydration. The perfect display of constraint for a sweltering day of croquet.

What a dreadful cage. Her ribcage groaned. Damned if she complied. Damned if she rebelled. She glanced toward the terrace doors. Attendees fluttered in, jittery and dabbing their sweaty brows, mallets swung over their shoulders.

Harriet followed her gaze. "Who are you waiting for, Ivy?"

She wiped her cleft. "No one."

"No?" She leaned in. "I heard a little rumor."

"Everyone knows I wear trousers, Harriet, it's old news."

Harriet's eyes dazzled with mischief. "I heard a rumor you and Sicili Windihill had an unfortunate mishap."

Charlotte glared at Harriet. "When is the tournament to start, Mr. Dainty?"

"Soon," Mr. Dainty exclaimed.

Harriet pinched Ivy's elbow. "Is it true?"

Ivy cleared her voice. "Are you going to pester me all day, Mrs. Prattle, or should I sit somewhere else?"

Harriet pouted. She sighed and slumped in her chair. As a married woman, she could slouch and pout all day without agitating the formalities of what single ladies are expected to adhere to.

"Do stay," she whined. "My husband is a bore. I need someone to keep me company."

The Windihills arrived last, and in the grandest display of croquet finery. Lace gloves and white umbrellas and silk sun hats. A tall gentleman, who looked more like an awkward tree than a human, accompanied their party. Sicili floated on his arm. Her diamond cheekbones glinted with sweat. Compared to their tussle in Windsworth library, Miss Windihill's complexion had paled, and she looked more forbidden than ever.

Charlotte tensed.

Ivy swallowed hard and wiped her palms on her dress. Mr. Ferthing brought her iced tea, and she swallowed it without discouragement from her mother.

Despite their tardiness, the Windihills were welcomed with immense celebration. Louis skipped up the terrace and aggressively shook George Windihill's hand. "At last," he exclaimed. "A competitor worthy of my time."

George patted his shoulder. "You mistake my presence, Mr. Dainty, though I am pleased to be a part of this charitable day. Moral support is the meaning of my attendance. You shall be playing my daughter, and I dare say you will find her quite my equal."

Sicili offered a cool, hospitable smile. "Not quite."

"She plays all the time in the city," George went on. "Tell them how extravagantly you play, Sicili."

"*Used* to play, Father. I have been detained in Wiltshire for the last month. Under your command."

"Detained?" Louis lost a bit of chipper.

George laughed. "Never mind all that. Shall we start the wagers?"

Sicili stole a glance in Ivy's direction. The sun eclipsed Sicili's bonnet and illuminated the curve of her shoulder while the bonnet cast a delicate shadow over her mouth. A slight line of perspiration hugged her top lip.

Ivy avoided her eyes and vigorously swallowed iced tea.

"Is it quite hot, Mother?"

Charlotte handed her a fan. "This will help."

The tall gentleman whispered something in Sicili's ear, and she smiled. Her half-shadowed face offered no expression. He led her to a selection of playing mallets, where they laughed about the appropriate sticks for their height.

Sweat slipped down Ivy's nose. "He must be Henry Fuller."

Charlotte held a glass to her cheek. "He looks put together."

"Rather ugly," Ivy blurted.

Her mother pinched her elbow.

"Ouch!"

"Mr. Fuller and his lady are none of your business."

"You know, he proposed last week," Harriet interjected.

Ivy bit her tongue. She almost said, "I wonder how many hearts she plans to break?" But it would have been cruel, and though she wanted to be cruel, she abstained for her mother's sake. It was none of her business. Sicili had made it quite clear at Windsworth that she had every means of saying yes to him, and she appeared happy enough. Who was she to get in the way of someone's happiness? Still, the corset squeezed at her, and she find herself eyeing Mr. Fuller up, wondering what he had that she did not. His trousers were tight and obnoxious around the waist, showcasing his full assets. She envied his ability to wear them without the disdain of society. Otherwise, he looked a common sight. Common hair brushed commonly back from his face. A commonly clean-shaven face with common sideburns, a streak of grey to them. A common tailcoat with flaps at the back and a common set to his jaw. There seemed nothing interesting about the man. With an inward grin, she recalled the way Sicili had looked at her in Windsworth library, in the light of the window, with curiosity and fear, as if Ivy could tear her a part and make her someone different.

There was no fear on Sicili's face as she engaged with Mr. Fuller. Ease, yes, and perhaps boredom? Ivy relented. Did she want to see boredom, or did she actually see boredom?

Harriet's eyes were on Ivy. "She has yet to accept, you know."

The heat pressed down on her like oppression, like society. "They look dashing," she managed.

"A woman has to be sure," Harriet said.

"Like you were sure about your Mr. Prattle?"

Harriet's eyes narrowed. "How mean you are in the heat, Ivy Ferthing."

The Windihills kept their distance. Francine waved her handkerchief at Charlotte but skirted the edge of the terrace, far from where Ivy and her mother lounged and suffered the heat. Without doubt, the library incident had compromised their relations.

Ivy picked at her glove. "I am contrite, Mother."

"You, Ivy? Contrite?"

"I am."

"Do enlighten me."

"I never meant to compromise our friendliness with the Windihill's."

Charlotte sighed. She brushed damp curls from Ivy's forehead. "Perhaps it is for the best. Being at a distance, I see quite clearly. All this time I hoped to be their equal, somehow, and now that I see them glistening in the sun, as if they own it, I am quite reserved."

"Reserved?"

"No one should own the sun, Ivy. No one."

Across the terrace, Sicili engaged Henry Fuller under a private umbrella. She leaned into him, a perfect proximity between them, and through that polite space a stitch of sunshine leaked and blinded. Ivy shaded her eyes, willing Sicili to look at her.

But Sicili's face was turned toward Mr. Fuller.

***

The tournament began. The first round carried on for an hour. Harriet Prattle effortlessly conquered and beamed like a goddess after her triumph. She gave a little curtsy to the many gentlemen who cheered and winked at her, none of whom was her husband.

At intermission, they gathered on the terrace in the shade, dabbing their chests and necks and foreheads with handker-chiefs and sucking back iced tea. Blocks of ice wrapped in cloth were passed around and gratefully accepted.

Louis leaned against his mallet, at ease despite the heat. "Now that we have had a look at the players, wagers ought to be struck. The rule is you cannot wager on yourself. Let me start. I wager Sicili Windihill shall be victorious."

George held up his tea. "Well said. I concur. Ten shillings toward my angel's victory."

"Only ten shillings, Father?" Sicili teased. "How stingy you are."

"I shall wager on you, Mr. Dainty," Charlotte said. "This is your sport, after all."

Louis modestly tipped his hat. "How kind, Mrs. Ferthing."

The wagers were struck, and coinage scooped up into hats.

"Hold up," said Louis. "One player has yet to be wagered on: Ivy Ferthing. Will anyone put a price on Ivy Ferthing?"

The spectators and players fell silent. No one looked Ivy in the eye. Her own mother fidgeted and fell as quiet as a mouse. A haze of heat settled over the lawn, and she concluded that a day in the shade would be better on her health and heart than a day next to Sicili in the insufferable heat.

Sicili stepped out of the shade. "I will wager on Miss Fer-thing. Ten pounds."

She glanced over at Ivy, squinting in the heat. It was the first time Sicili had addressed Ivy in the hour since arriving. The sun sat at mid-day, and the heat had turned insufferable.

Ivy's chest had begun to burn, and she feared Charlotte might see her heart hammering against her skin. She avoided Sicili's direct gaze, but she felt her eyes nonetheless, willing her to look up and be grateful.

"Ten pounds," Louis repeated.

"Ten pounds?" George echoed. "Sicili, how generous of you. Are you certain?"

Sicili dabbed her forehead. "Is it not for the poor?"

"Surely, but——"

Sicili dropped ten heavy coins into Louis' top hat.

Ivy held a block of ice to her nape. Charlotte had gone silent. Harriet watched Ivy with a meticulous curiosity, as if she thought Ivy had put Sicili Windihill under a contrite spell. Uncomfortable at being the target of Sicili's soft smile, Ivy got up and in swift strides went to the mallets. She picked out a tall mallet——one taller than Mr. Fuller's. She had to get away from the shadow of that a soft smile and the confusion that came with it. The crowd on the terrace seemed to watch her, waiting for her to thank Sicili for such undo generosity.

"Quite the vote of confidence, Miss Windihill," Charlotte finally said.

Sicili squinted. "No one has seen Miss Ferthing play. She could be twice the player that I am."

A carefulness edged Charlotte's voice. "My Ivy does know a thing or two about croquet."

Sicili's polite smile bloated with confidence. "The rule is I cannot wager on myself, Mrs. Ferthing."

The parties diffused over the terrace and the lawn. Sicili remained on the terrace in her own quiet world. Ivy stayed by the mallets. They hung in the silence, their dresses swaying, lips pressed, moved by each other but resigned. The second round began. Mallets struck balls and spectators cheered, and Louis' chipper voice rang out the scores. They existed away from it all, alone in the chaos of their ill-advised awareness of each other, refusing to look directly at each other in the silence.

Louis saved them from each other. "Miss Ferthing," he called out from the croquet field. "Miss Ferthing––will you prove Miss Windihill right?"

Sicili's chest rose and fell at a troubled rate. "I best return to my party," she said softly, and withdrew into the shade.

The last time they had spoken to each other had been at Windsworth library, on the floor, tangled up in each oth-er––an unfortunate misadventure that has set Wiltshire in a whole new rash of rumors about Naughty Ivy.

Ivy would always pay the price, and she refused to pay it today.

Determined, she strode down the terrace and took up her position. Henry Fuller, her opponent, leaned against his mal-let in a nervous fashion. In the shade, whispers crackled. "Miss Ferthing takes the lawn by storm. A familiar sight," one of the Becker girls laughed. "And in a dress, not trousers."

Though none of them would be caught saying "Naughty Ivy" in public—a disgraceful name in society––she knew they all wanted to. She knew they said it in private, over tea and over dinner gossip.

Ivy shaded her eyes and glared at the terrace. Her mother, fretting with her fan, sat alone next to Harriet Prattle, who tittered into her handkerchief. She saw only her mother. She placed her ball and turned her back on reckless opportunity. The Beckers and Prattles and Daintys and Windihills assumed they knew her. They had concluded that her only guise was that of a boy in trousers and a fisher's cap, that she owned nothing else to her name but a silly set of rumors, that she could be governed by them and held back and trapped by societies desire to disown her, that she could do nothing normal and acceptable. There, she could prove her audience wrong and make her mother proud.

"We *are* waiting," Mr. Dainty said. He tapped his pocket watch. He had a schedule.

She brought up her mallet. She grinned. It wasn't that she *could* adhere to society. Quite the opposite. The truth was prediction and normality were boring sisters that puckered and flaunted and lived at ease while the less fortunate suffered.

She tapped the ball, sinking two hoops, and quickly a third and a fourth. The voices of her discouraging audience waned, and the terrace lulled as she flew through the course, doubling the score of Henry Fuller and two of Harriet's admirers. A wind came up and patted her on the back.

She turned and gave a boyish bow to the terrace. Only her parents cheered her on. "Hurrah, Ivy, hurrah!" Mr. Ferthing hollered. "Hurrah!" Charlotte patted his back, squealing with unbecoming glee quite unknown to her.

The sight filled Ivy's heart. She defeated Henry Fuller on her next round. He wiped his forehead, easily resigned, and sulked back to the Windihill clan, seeking comfort from Sicili.

Sicili's eyes were set on someone else.

Finally, Ivy thought. *The only eyes I want on me*, and then she thought better of the thought and dashed it from her mind.

Louis announced the second intermission and kindly rescued the terrace from Ivy's further reign. She had quickly matched Sicili's score.

After intermission, Sicili played against Mr. Peacock, Miss Becker, and Harriet––who forfeited due to heat exhaustion. Mr. Fuller nobly stepped up to fill the gap. The crowd went wild for his gangly legs and long, oak-ish trunk.

"Good show, Mr. Fuller," George hollered from the terrace. "A little to the left, now. Good form, good form."

Henry swung like a broken branch in the wind. His ball missed the wicket and skimmed off the field into Mrs. Dainty's duck pond. A pity clap from the spectators spurred him on. He waved and shaded his eyes to see if Sicili noticed his noble humiliation. Sicili returned his wave. He smiled awkwardly and bowed. The clapping picked up pace and grew to a thunderous chant: "Henry Fuller, Henry Fuller, Henry Fuller!"

One would think he had won the entire tournament.

Sicili floated across the lawn. Her form was immaculate, her white dress, bonnet, and gloves stark against blue sky and green lawn. She tapped her ball ever so lightly; it whisked down the field and sailed through the first iron ring.

Mrs. Windihill squealed.

The crowd roared praise. Sicili waved and smiled over at Ivy. Henry noticed, as did Mrs. Windihill--they simultaneously looked over at Ivy with expressions that demanded an explanation.

She rose.

"Ivy?" her mother said.

"I believe I just realized something, Mother."

"You must wait until intermission to go off on a tangent. People are looking."

"Something formidable, Mother."

"Miss Windihill is in the middle of her turn."

"She has enough eyes on her."

"*Oh*, I thought you would want to see her play. She is the highlight of this tournament, as much as I resent admitting to such."

"I need to think, Mother."

Charlotte blinked up. "You do look hot, Ivy."

"My chest is burning."

"Go powder your nose, girl. Quickly."

***

The breezy powder room helped her think. Though her mother thought of Ivy as an incorrigible girl without a decent thought in her head, Ivy was, in fact, a heavy thinker. Every window hung open, every shimmering curtain fluttered and sighed––her own fluttering oasis from intolerable longing. Silver framed mirrors lined the walls and hung level with the chaise in the middle of the room.

Ivy stared at her sweaty, troubled reflection. Her chest, nose, and cheeks glowed bright red. Freckles multiplied by the second into mass colonies up her arms and neck and under her eyes. Her mother's lovely, tight up-do now hung in damp folds of perspiration and dread. She looked a fright. No wonder the wealthiest, snottiest, most pretentious of Wiltshire whispered and snickered about her. She looked nothing like them. *They* with their pristine gloves and silk bonnets and scarves and lace umbrellas that let in just the right amount of sun.

The truth stared back at her. Naughty Ivy. She would always be Naughty Ivy to them.

Being the disgrace of Wiltshire suited her, and she had accepted it without a fight, had let it sink and allowed it for so long. And she liked it. She liked being sneered at and left to her own devices. She liked being judged and ridiculed. She would always be the scandalous daughter of a self-made wine-merchant, and that would never change, whether she surrendered to it or not. In the eyes of society, she would always be Naughty Ivy.

Sicili Windihill was her exact opposite. They had been born to oppose each other. Miss Windihill would always be above her, would always be her superior, would always be beyond reproach. Sicili was the sought after, the ideal reflection, the always seen. The eyes of society would always be upon her, and they would always esteem her, expect the best from her. The utmost. I didn't matter if Ivy won a silly croquet tournament. It didn't matter if she behaved and kept her tongue. The Windihills would always protect Sicili from the darkness of rumor and ridicule. They had always used scapegoats like Ivy to keep Sicili's reputation silky white and clean, without damage, without reserve. Sicili had never known the feeling of society turning its back on her. She never would.

I do not envy you, Miss Windihill, Ivy thought as the breeze cooled her cheeks. *But I do pity you. What a great responsibility.*

She splashed her face with water from a basin and watched water dribbled from her eyelashes and down her neck.

She clawed the tight pins from her head, letting down her red tendrils. Outside, cheers shimmered across the terrace and floated down the lawn. Fluttering, sighing curtains separated them from her. Them. Good society. Perfect representations of the grace and pose humans are capable of.

Ivy wiped hot tears away.

The curtains yawned. Sharp footsteps approached in the corridor outside the powder room. Harriet strutted in and paused by the door to eye her up and down, then passed by for one of the mirrors. She fixed her eyes on herself.

Ivy glanced over. "Is the terrace too hot for you?"

"This entire day is too hot for me." She sighed dramatically. "I dread it."

"Why not ask your husband to escort you home?"

Harriet fixed her cleavage. "I would be too bored." She smirked. "I saw you exit the terrace, and I thought you might be doing something devilish in here to cure my boredom for this day."

Ivy shrugged. She knew it best not to engage Harriet Prattle during one of her flares of boredom. "I swore off my devilish habits."

Harriet looked unconvinced. "Forever?"

"For a time, at least."

"A shame. You do know how to get us all talking." Harriet removed her bonnet and dipped her palms in the basin of water by Ivy. She splashed her face. Dried it. Airy gusts played at her white dress.

"How cool it is inside, Ivy." Harriet's eyes settled on her in the mirror. "Are you cool?"

"Far from it."

"Mr. Dainty called intermission," said Harriet.

"I thought as much."

"You left in the middle of Miss Windihill's turn."

"I had to," she blurted before thinking better of it.

Harriet splashed her chest. "Were you angry with her for wagering on you?"

"No."

"You looked angry. You still look angry. I do wish you had been more cross when we..."

Ivy folded her arms. "You can hardly say it, Harriet."

"Anger suits you. You were so timid and kind with me."

"Because I cared for you." Ivy turned to her. "And you used me."

Harriet's eyes rolled. "Always so emotional. It might do you well to reign in your passions, Ivy."

"I thought you liked me angry."

She patted her chest dry. "I see the way you look at her, you know."

Ivy steeled. She retreated to the chaise in the middle of the room and avoided Harriet's eyes in the mirror. "Who?" The last thing she needed was Harriet Prattle spreading gossip about Sicili and her.

Harriet laughed. "Pretending not to care, Ivy? I know you. You hate pretend." She turned, stared Ivy down. "You used to look at me the same way." She moved closer. Forsook her mirror for Ivy. "Did you burn? Your skin is like paper to flame. I remember quite fondly how we used to sit on the cliffside together and soak up the sun and..." Harriet trailed off as she settled next to Ivy on the chaise. She ran a hand down Ivy's arm, resting her palm on Ivy's knuckles.

Ivy's skin tingled. "Your husband must be missing you."

"Phillip?" She scoffed. "Phillip never misses me. What a tedious man. Always on about business. Had I known him better, I never would have married him. Mother thought him a good match and I thought him handsome. If only a handsome face was enough to––"

"Why not divorce him?"

Harriet played with the fringe of Ivy's sleeve. "Women are not to initiate divorce."

"Any women can take her life into her own hands."

"Not a woman who wants to be liked by society." Harriet simpered. "Although, I suppose you have no inclination of such, Ivy."

Ivy let Harriet cup her cheek. "Do you love him?"

Harriet's smile chilled. "I do. From time to time. But..." she gave Ivy's hand a squeeze. "I miss our friendship from time to time as well."

She leaned toward Harriet, and Harriet leaned into her lips.

But she passed Harriet's lips for her ear. "Only when you find yourself bored?"

Harriet paused.

Ivy reclaimed her hand. "I know you just as well as you know me, Mrs. Prattle. Only you would insult me and try to kiss me in the same moment." With purpose, she got up. "If you say anything about the way I look at Sicili Windihill to a living soul, I shall visit Mr. Prattle at his place of business and murmur all the things we used to do and say to each other before you married him. My mother will be with me to recount all the events she saw. People believe my mother."

Harriet's eyes simmered with rage. She stared at Ivy for a good while, willing Ivy to let up her position and yield to the feelings she once harbored for the witch, but Ivy had learned long ago to steel herself against Harriet Prattle's advances. Harriet uttered a soft *hmmph.* She composed the humiliation of being outwitted by Ivy and returned to her reflection. She pinched her cheeks and played with her hair.

She said with sharp revenge, "I play against Miss Windihill in the next round."

"You forfeited."

"I changed my mind. I feel quite refreshed now." She winked and strutted out of the powder room.

***

When Ivy returned to her mother's side, Sicili was already on the field with Harriet, a Miss Becker, and Mr. Ferthing. She stole Charlotte's iced tea and held it dearly to her red chest.

Charlotte's suspicious eyes were on Harriet. "What kept you, Ivy?"

"Thinking. Plenty of thinking."

"And?"

"A feral witch."

Charlotte patted her hand. "I could not agree more. Her eyes are blazing in the sun."

Sicili picked off Mr. Ferthing and Miss Becker quite easily. Then she wiped the lawn with Harriet. A lovely sight. The terrace applauded, and Ivy joined in. Sicili curtsied and searched the terrace. Her eyes settled on Ivy with an indiscreet pause. Harriet, appalled and humiliated, sought comfort from a group of admirers––none of them her husband––who assured her of her talent and prestige, especially for its being such a hot day.

Harriet kept glancing over at Ivy, then at Sicili.

Ivy battled Louis Dainty, Henry Fuller––who managed to conquer the other unfortunate players––and her father. Louis, shrewd and calculated, had saved his strength until the last. He took to the lawn with a fine grin and a skip to his step. He looked cool and refreshed. While his competitors had toiled in the hot, hot sun, he had sipped iced tea and analyzed them from every angle, which meant he knew Ivy favored her right arm and lacked control with her left.

Halfway through the round, Ivy suffered sudden fatigue. She gave her ball a tap with her left arm, not her right, and watched it sail off course. To out-wit Louis Dainty at his own game would bring her little delight. The tournament belonged to him, after all, and the game was a farce of faux benevolence. She prodded and poked at her ball and suffered harassment from the terrace while Louis succeeded at every strike.

The crowd wildly loved him. They hooted and yelled and danced for him. Her true victory came at leaving Henry Fuller in the dust. Her father finished last, jolly, and still as light-hearted as ever.

Sicili and Louis Dainty were the last match of the tournament. They seamlessly rivaled for precisely one quarter of an hour. Sicili managed to look at cool as Louis. Her ball flew with such acuity that Louis watched wide-eyed and mouth dropped. He loosened his cravat and paid more attention to Sicili's form than his own. The terrace gasped in shock when he missed a ring. Perhaps, over the years, he had grown tired of winning. Or perhaps he fell victim to the trademark Windihill intimidation. Whatever the cause, the effect came as no surprise to anyone.

"I do present the worthy victor, Miss Sicili Windihill," he announced as the match ended. He raised Sicili's hand in his own and applause scattered over the lawn and into the valley beyond. Henry Fuller clapped the loudest, his face radiant with admiration.

Louis adjusted his spectacles. "Now. Shall we retreat to the cool of the drawing room for much-needed refreshments?"

"What a timely idea," agreed Sicili, and swept her brow with the back of her hand.

The guests mobilized toward the Dainty's residence, chattering about the glorious final match. A crowd formed around Sicili and sailed with her into the breezy indoors, glasses sparkling, and voices filled with laughter and grace.

Fourteen

Heat Stroke

As the Dainty's drawing room proved too intimate to host thirty dehydrated, fatigued guests, Mrs. Dainty suggested a migration to the ballroom just off the tea parlor. Arrangements were made, fussed about, and a table set up with refreshments as everyone glittered into the modest Dainty ballroom.

George Windihill gladly gloated, "Mr. Dainty, I must point out, your ballroom is half the size of my grand and stately ballroom at Windsworth."

Mr. Dainty's eye twitched as he dabbed his sweaty temples.

Ivy scoured the ballroom for her father and scowled when he would not be found. The clever man. He must have ducked out the front entry while Sicili shone her brightest and stole the wealthiest hearts of Wiltshire with her soft smile and graceful swing. Ivy clung to the sidelines of the ballroom. Small talk began. The possibility of a dance, when the heat wore off, spread from ear to ear and brought about wild smiles. The *dreadful heat* was another favorable subject, as well as Sicili's victory. Avid debates were soon in progress, of which Ivy steered clear.

George Windihill and Mr. Peacock stood with their backs to her.

"How good and wise it is to have a woman win these sorts of sports," George vigorously said, "every year or two. It should be a rule."

"A rule regarding who should win? Truly, Mr. Windihill?"

"Truly."

"Has your daughter encouraged this outlandish idea?"

"Not at all. I imagined it of my own will." George turned to Ivy, his eyes full and his beard scattered with pastry crumbs. "What do you think, Ivy Ferthing?"

She blinked at him.

"Surely you have an opinion, girl."

She nursed a glass of iced tea, amazed that he had addressed her after the incident at Windsworth last month. "Opinion fails me at the moment, Mr. Windihill."

His laugh filled the ballroom and echoed off the high ceiling. "I had it on good authority that opinion is your forte, Miss Ferthing." He turned back to Mr. Peacock. "You think my ideas outlandish, Mr. Peacock?"

Sicili stood across the room on Henry Fuller's steady arm, being insincerely congratulated by a sour faced Harriet Prattle.

A wild uncertainty seized Sicili's eyes. She disentangled from Henry and floated across the ballroom, leaving Harriet mid-sentence. Henry Fuller smiled mirthlessly and tried to pick up the conversation with Harriet and Mrs. Windihill while Sicili floated toward Ivy.

Ivy veered for the refreshments, only to be met by Sicili at the table. They locked eyes.

"Is my father being cruel to you?" Sicili asked.

She selected a melted macaroon. "As expected," she said with a full mouth, hoping the lack of etiquette might detour Sicili.

Sicili only smiled and arranged delicate treats on her plate. "A shame to see my wager go to waste."

Ivy shrugged. "Your ten pounds will go to the poor, regardless."

Across the room, Harriet watched them engage. She raised an eyebrow at Ivy––a silent threat.

"I care nothing for the wager," Sicili said. She reached for a macaroon at the same time Ivy did, and their hands brushed. Ivy wiped the hand on her dress, and Sicili went on, "It's the principle I find myself troubled by. I watched you all afternoon. You have quite the aim, and plenty of spirit. Do you want to know what I think?"

"Not particularly."

"I think you let Mr. Dainty best you."

Ivy stopped chewing. So, Sicili Windihill had been quietly observing her from cool shadows of the tournament, without saying, "hello" or "how are you?", and all while keeping Mr. Fuller at an arm's length, waiting for her answer to his proposal. It sickened Ivy. It made her pale and hot. "Are you mocking me?"

Sicili's soft expression hardened. "Why would I want to mock you, Ivy? I only wish to celebrate your abilities."

"Because you thought them beyond me?"

She scanned the ballroom, innately aware that her mother's eyes would be on her no matter where she resided. Sure enough, she spotted Charlotte watching them like a hawk from the comfort of a pale chaise, her fan swishing wildly, her lips pursed. Francine Windihill observed them as well, although more discreetly from behind Mr. Fuller's arm, her gaze darting back and forth from Mr. Fuller's company to the spot where Ivy and Sicili stood.

Sicili stepped closer. "I think you misunderstand me, Ivy. I––"

Ivy retracted a step, keeping the distance between them measurable. "Everyone watches us. We stand on a stage with the eyes of Wiltshire upon us."

Sicili laughed with nonchalant entitlement. "Let them gawk."

She played with her food, rearranging them to avoid Sicili's bold gaze. "My musings in Dainty's powder were correct, then," she said softly.

"You mused about me in the Dainty's powder room?"

Ivy took a stern inhale. "You have never considered the disdainful eyes of society and what they can do to you, have you Miss Windihill? You have never suffered the consequences."

The plate dropped to her side as Sicili stuttered for words. Her dejected treats scattered on the floor.

Ivy said firmly, "If you continue engaging me, you will."

"Sicili," Mrs. Windihill called from across the room, clearly impatient with how long they had been alone at the table. "Mr. Fuller needs your opinion on an undetermined matter."

Sweat slipped down Sicili's temple. Her mouth opened. It closed with determination. The curiosity in her eyes faded, and she turned with a cool air, retreating to the far side of the ballroom and Mr. Fuller. Frowning, Mr. Windihill dabbed her neck and chest. She leaned in and whispered something secret to Sicili.

Sicili nodded once and turned to Mr. Fuller with a polite smile.

"Ivy," Harriet said above the hum of conversation, "that drab of a dress truly looks uncomfortable."

Conversation lulled as heads turned. Harriet fanned herself and waited for complete silence, and when the ballroom hung on her every word, she raised her voice like the flickering star of a stage performer who knew her final act had come to an end. All eyes on her, she strutted across the ballroom.

"You are sweating in all the wrong places, Ivy. I advise you to change into something more comfortable. And familiar." Dark intention flooded her eyes. "Have you a pair of trousers tucked away some place? In a pocket or a glove?"

A trickle of laughter rippled through the room.

Ivy's voice wavered. "Harriet, please, do desist."

"Go on." Harriet's smile provoked. "I am more than certain you wear a pair under your sweaty, uncomfortable frock. Give us a show. We are in dire need of entertainment now that the tournament is won."

The room burst into unconstrained laughter. Comments flew. "What a grand show it would be," and, "Ivy Ferthing at her best!" and, "The rumors come to life!" and, "What I would give to see the infamous trousers at long last."

Across the ballroom, her mother sat on the chaise, completely absorbed in devouring a pear, her frown distinct and her eyes downcast. Someone dared to give her a light-hearted nudge, and her green eyes lifted. Sadness welled in them, and a quick headshake begged Ivy to resist.

She swallowed all the things she had to say to Harriet Prattle, like she had swallowed all the things she wanted to say to Sicili, like she had kept her tongue tied around Mr. Windihill and his "wild" idea to *let* a woman win at a sport every few years for the "good of society". She could do it for her mother.

She hated them all. She hated the ruse and the *need* to be entertained after being entertained.

She set down her plate. "Excuse me, Mrs. Prattle, while I powder my nose."

As she brushed past, Harriet grasped her wrist and whispered tight in her ear, "Miss Windihill is nothing more than a dream. An illusion. Look at her, Ivy, stiff and frightened and confused. You confuse her. She cannot understand what we used to have."

Harriet let her free, smirked and retired to her husband, who whispered something laughable. The momentum of conversation and good spirits at Ivy's expense prevailed, and she slipped into the aftermath of a hot summer day. Quickly forgotten, she wilted out of the ballroom and strode with much despair through the breezy drapedness of the Dainty's mansion. On the terrace, she shaded her eyes and advanced upon the strewn mallets and forgotten croquet balls. With a huff, she began the journey to Vineyard Estate.

***

It was an uncomfortable walk home. Ivy braved the heat with various grunts of discomfort and exhaustion. She decided this mess of a hot day was due penance for her initial churning, aching, squeezing emotions. She had to stop dangerously dwelling on the unavailable Miss Windihill. She had to resist wondering what another conversation in a moon lit study might produce between the two of them. She had to suppress dwelling on Sicili altogether. The facts were what they were. Knowing society, she knew that her churning, aching, squeezing emotions would do nothing for her——they would only make her miserable.

As much as she hated to agree with a *feral witch*, Harriet Prattle happened to be correct. Sicili Windihill was an illusion.

She trudged up the rolling hills to Vineyard Estate. Her arms were burnt, as well as her ankles, nose, and cheeks——but she had survived the journey, and she found herself at the bottom of her father's stately vineyard. She opened her arms and twirled about.

"There you are, Ivy," William Ferthing called out. He tended to his grapes. "I wondered when you would quit that dastardly tournament––that farce." He bent and cradled a wilted vine of grapes. "All the while I was away, I worried on and ever on."

"About what, Father?"

"What this heat was doing to my vineyard, so I took a long walk home. You know me, Ivy. I cannot stand those social affairs for too long. It is your mother who likes them. I go for her, but my heart belongs to this vineyard––rain or shine."

"I commend you, Father, for the luxury of finding your true self."

He laughed and gave her a quick wink. "Do not mistake me, Ivy. When I was your age, I had not the smallest inkling I would end up a celebrated wine merchant."

"Are you saying I shall have to grow up?"

"We all must grow up, my dear. Be a sport and bring me that canvas, will you?"

Ivy hiked up her dress and set to work. By the end of the day, she had burned to a crisp, been defeated at croquet, pushed about by Harriet Prattle, provoked by Sicili Windihill, stained by gossip, and attacked by vines. And now, as she wiped a hand across her brow, she reflected with some surprise that she stood tall, with a confidence she had not felt in some time.

And she was much in need of a glass of her father's excellent wine.

Fifteen

A Much-Needed Stride

The old man, named Mr. Ponder, strode up the side of a patchy hill, thrashing wheat husks with his makeshift cane. Old troubles and a sore back slowed him. He wore canvas trousers and an elbow patched tailcoat and shoes too big for his blistered feet, but he climbed regardless——because he had to.

He had to.

At the top of his destination, a crest of rock formed the side of a cliff, and when he shuffled to the crest, a wind came up and blew off his top hat. Red hair tumbled loose and tangled with the gust. The cliff overlooked the poorer half of Wiltshire——rolling green and gold farmlands where little cottages puffed smoke from chimneys, where farmers plowed the land, planted seed, and tended the flock. A lovely view. A simple life. Off in the distance, somewhere out there, London spread over miles and miles——busy streets and social happenings and Madam Desiree'ss where girls with bright eyes and strange hearts were welcomed. Not frowned upon. Not gossiped about. Not told they were scandalous and wicked.

Old troubles pinched at his heart. Old, familiar sorrows.

Breathless from his stride up the hillside, he sat on the crest and picked a blade of grass, pinched it between his thumbs and blew. A sweet, sweet melody. His troubles slipped away, away with the wind, over the side of the cliff and down into the valley of farmlands. Let them have all his worries. Let them feast on his sorrows. Sunshine warmed his face and tickled his soul––all he needed was the sun and the open hills and the distant sound of roaring London.

An unpleasant voice carried over the wind. "Ivy, *oooooooh*, Ivy. Breakfast gets cold."

Ivy lurched out of character. The melody pitched and broke off. Leave it to her mother to spoil peace and quiet and Mr. Ponder. She glanced over her shoulder, down the patchy hillside, and sighed heavily at the opposite dip of hill. Sunlight reflected off Vineyard Estate, blinded, and brought on a wild urge. What if she never ascended the hillside? What if she devoted herself to the guise of Mr. Ponder and forgot she had a prying Mother and a needy Father? What if she caught the fastest coach into London and found a small flat to live in, cheap and plain, and worked hard to survive? Her heart skipped. She could wear trousers, every color and make, without being shunned because no one, not a soul, would know her. She could cut her hair short and live, truly live, and breathe and never again wear a sufferable corset. She could be herself in the morning, the afternoon, and well into the evening. Wear what she wanted. Say what she wanted. *Kiss* who she wanted.

She split the blade of grass down the middle and pretended the halves were women who danced in the wind.

"*Ivvvvvvvvy!* I can see you perched on that blasted hilltop. Come inside at once or I'll have you banished!"

The vineyard waved in the wind and beckoned, and desired to strangle her in vines and bittersweet juices. She frowned. Slouched. Sighed. Vineyard Estate, her prison. Her penance for being Naughty Ivy, the outcast and scandal of Wiltshire. "More like Westshite..." she mumbled. Another glance over her shoulder caused a squeeze of guilt. They would never survive without her——those two lumps. Her father was getting on in his age. Years of endless work in the vineyard were catching up to him, slowly but surely. His hair grew thin and the lines on his brow thickened. If she abandoned him like her brothers had, she would never forgive herself. He needed her more than ever, and he trusted her. He saw promise and competence when he looked at her.

He believed in her.

Unlike her despicable mother. Her irate, un-nurturing nemesis. Despite predictable denial, Charlotte relied on her. Wholly. If she ran away, who else would the old bag yell at and threaten and call horrid names? Who would listen to her fretting and her vexations and her selfish concerns? Who would keep her company at boring, hapless balls? Who would she hassle and dress up and pamper with pinches?

Wistfully, Ivy blew the valley a kiss and turned her back on the green and gold farmlands, the little chimneys and the cows and pigs and ducks, the blue sky and the torrent wind. She left a piece of herself sitting on the crest, staring out over the valley and wishing for a better existence. She found her top hat and strode down the hillside toward the vineyard, thrashing wheat as she trudged.

***

Ivy joined her mother in the breakfast parlor, who proceeded to judge her with a vexed expression. "What are you wearing, Ivy?"

She removed her top hat and bowed. "Mr. Ponder is pleased to make your acquaintance. How do I look? Old?"

"Dreadfully young. Take off that drab tailcoat. How long have you been making up characters in that wild head of yours?"

She sat across from her mother and dove into her cold plate of eggs. "Always have."

"Naming them?"

"Always will."

"You strange girl."

They savored a silent breakfast. Sunlight tickled the table-top and leafed onto the walls. Mother and daughter, sharing tense glances, smiling when the other smiled, only to frown when the other looked out the window. Together, but distant. Her father had taken to the vineyard at dawn, after encouraging Ivy to spend a day with her mother.

Charlotte cleared her throat. "What were you doing on that hilltop? And so early?"

"Just thinking, Mother."

"About?"

"The day I shan't have you breathing down my back."

"Mothers are meant to guide their offspring. We have been doing so since the beginning of time. Do you want to know what day I look forward to?"

"I'll pass."

"I look forward to the day you shall be struck with it."

"Struck with what?"

"The realization of how wonderful I am to you."

She snorted a laugh. "You might be waiting a good while."

Charlotte stirred her tea with a wounded huff. "You might be pleased to know Sicili Windihill refused Henry Fuller." She stopped stirring, pinning Ivy with a vigilant stare. A test.

Ivy scooped eggs into her mouth and chewed loudly. "I suppose that means she'll be onto the next one." She leaned back in the chair and placed an ankle over her knee.

With dismay, Charlotte glowered at the way she sat, but said nothing. She had been nagging Ivy less since the Dainty's tournament. Ivy suspected Charlotte felt poorly for staying quiet when Harriet Prattle had made a mockery of her.

Charlotte continued stirring her tea. "Which is not to say you should resume secret trysts with Miss Windihill––

"Wasn't planning on it, Mother."

"––because the Prattle's ball is Saturday next. They expect you to attend."

"I do despise the Prattle's."

"You despise everyone."

"They despise me in return. It's better I avoid another mingle with Harriet. I cannot be expected to hold my tongue every time she lashes out at me."

"Better if you do. Harriet Prattle can be silenced. Good society cannot. Be on your best, Ivy."

She wet her fingers and slicked back her eyebrows, slumping further into Mr. Ponder's character with a grand old grin. "This is my best."

Charlotte raised an eyebrow. "You will stay away from Sicili Windihill?"

Truth be told, Sicili had failed to visit her thoughts of late. She had been too busy helping William with their latest harvest, dressing up despite her mother's frowns, and visiting Westbury's fine but tiny library. "Anything for you, Mother."

"Anything?" Her mother gasped. "Will you marry a man?"

"Except that."

"I thought not."

"I cannot be entirely selfless."

"You can refrain from chaos at the Prattle's. Do be good to me."

"I shall try my hardest. For you, Mother."

And she meant it. She truly meant it.

Sixteen

Mr. Perrycot

Despite promising her mother she would stay away from the girl, Sicili's thoughts had been plagued by Ivy Ferthing since the Dainty's tournament. Three things had been insufferable: the heat, Henry Fuller's attentions, and Harriet Prattle.

Ivy's reaction to Harriet's jesting about trousers had been nothing short of unexpected, and Sicili had despised every moment of it. The Ivan Miller she had met at Madam Desiree's would have railed against Harriet. She would have shown a leg or spit in the punch bowl, but the way she had endured the laughter of the ballroom and then slipped away un-announced and so unlike herself had vexed Sicili. It had left her wanting. And the last thing she needed was to be wanting Ivy Ferthing.

"You need to eat, Sicili," Francine insisted.

She sat with her mother in the breakfast parlor. Her eggs and porridge were untouched, her tea cold.

"I have no appetite, Mother."

She had been dreaming about the Ivy, too, and how the girl had rebuffed her kindness that day. *"You have never considered the disdainful eyes of society and what they can do to you, have you Miss Windihill?"* That question had bewitched Sicili for too many nights in a row, keeping her awake and restless. It haunted her. It made her think of the painting at the end of the West wing.

Francine purposefully clattered her teacup with its saucer. "Perhaps Francis Perrycot will raise your spirits."

Sicili emerged from her musing. "Francis?"

"You expect him this afternoon. Have you forgotten?"

She pinched her nose. "I was about to."

"Refrain from purposefully forgetting, darling."

"Fret not, Mother. I shall not shirk my duties as the old man's only heir."

Instead of breakfasting, she wandered Windsworth like she used to as a little girl. The mansion was her ominous playground. Around every corner she turned, an empty room met her. Along every corridor she walked, the silence echoed.

And before long she found herself in the West wing staring up at *Grace*, feeling the burden of the last two months––longing for the simplicity of her once stood still life.

"What is it, Grace?" she whispered. "What do you *want* from me?"

The painting stood over her, silent and confident. A hand flew to Sicili's mouth as the revolution struck her. Grace, the subject of the painting, the focal point, the essence, reminded her of Ivy. Every part of the painting pointed to that ridiculous trouser-wearing girl who had found a secret entrance into Sicili's dreams. The attitude, the indecency, the defiance, the vibrant brush strokes. Sicili moved closer, leaned in. She traced Grace's lips with her finger.

"Darling, there you are," Francine said.

Sicili pulled back. Her mother stood at the end of the West wing; eyebrows raised.

"Mr. Perrycot has arrived," Francine announced. "He awaits you in the drawing room."

"Already?"

"The clock is half-past twelve. Have you been staring at that painting all morning?"

"It feels longer than one morning," Sicili said. "Almost all my life sounds more accurate."

"Are you unwell, Sicili? I can ask Mr. Perrycot to return another day. Perhaps when your mood is less preoccupied by wandering."

"No, Mother. I feel fine. I shall never be better than fine."

***

Francis Perrycot was a vain man, to say the least. He looked at himself in the mirror above the mantel every moment he could. Primped his hair, fussed with his collar. Despite his vanity, he was the son of the Earl of Norbury, and his features were daringly handsome, if not a little too direct and pretty. A sharpness slanted his eyelids upward. Redness puckered his lips. His hair formed delicate, face-framing curls.

By invitation from George, Francis had come from Norbury to meet Sicili in person.

"Your good father refuses to stop pestering me with letters about your beauty," he said after he had primped himself once or twice in the mirror above the fire. He hadn't sat down, and it made Sicili nervous. He had a fluttery way about him. He couldn't seem to keep his legs and arms from moving.

"Rather bold of him," Sicili said after pouring herself a second cup of tea. She could hardly keep her eyes open. What a dreadful night's sleep it had been.

Francis took a gallant sip of tea. "I find myself in the neighborhood to visit my widowed grandmother, you see, and I thought it high time I visit the important Miss Windihill."

Sicili yawned. "I think he meant to write how important *he* is. He does fancy himself a madman."

"Besides, I love Wiltshire's little shops. The trinkets are so varied, nothing like Norbury's fussy shops."

They made plans to go shopping in Westbury. He would buy her whatever she liked on one condition: she must accompany him to tea with his grandmother the next day. "She nags me about why I never bring a lady around," he said with a silly laugh.

"Surely I cannot be of any help in that explanation."

"You shall do perfectly. She likes girls with round faces and sparkling eyes."

Sicili wasn't sure if she should be flattered or offended. Was he trying to compliment her? He certainly failed to possess the charm her other suitors had. She let out a sigh of relief. He carried himself a bit flamboyantly, and his statements were more decided than they were teasing. He seemed different somehow, in some way Sicili endeavored to put her finger on but fell grossly short of.

The stretch of boutiques on the main street of Westbury was depressing. They were nothing like London's boutiques. Francis kept himself occupied, darting from one shop to the next, finding joy in the cutest wonders. A miniature tea set. A bracelet made of seashells from the ocean. "Mother will love it," he explained, and purchased the bracelet on the spot.

They darted to Mr. Stellaway's Fashions. Francis tried on a set of sailor cuffs and Sicili wandered. She looked over and saw Ivy shopping at the end of the aisle. She sorted through a handful of men's bow ties.

"Miss Ferthing?"

Ivy glanced over. Her lips pursed, then she seemed to think better of it and offered Sicili a polite nod before turning her shoulder. Sicili ventured over, touching seashells and tiny picture frames as she neared, trying to keep herself busy. She didn't want to see Ivy go without a friendly conversation, not after three weeks of thinking and dreaming about her. They hadn't seen each other since the Dainty's croquet tournament.

Ivy glanced over her shoulder. Her cheeks grew warm with color and her eyes widened with dread, and she pursed her lips again. *Keep your distance*, her eyes seemed to say. Sicili did. She stopped by the lace gloves. They shared a long stare, equally as disconcerting as comfortable, like seeing each other had brought them home after a long, treacherous journey. She wanted to make the moment last, but it was gone in an instant, gone as quickly as it began.

Ivy blinked, returning to her task of meddling through the bow ties. "You look a fright, Miss Windihill."

She laughed. This was the Ivy she knew, not the Ivy from the tournament. "My sleep has been perturbed of late."

"Dare I ask why?"

She found it impossible to give Ivy Ferthing the satisfaction of knowing she dreamed about a trouser wearing lad. "Nothing worth mentioning." She fiddled with the gloves, tried one on and wiggled it off. "What are you shopping for?"

Ivy reluctantly turned. "Father's birthday is next week."

"How lovely. Will he be celebrating?"

"He likes quiet affairs." Ivy held up two bow ties. "I managed to narrow it down. This one or this one?"

"Both are dashing."

"Which one?"

But Sicili wasn't focused on the bows. Ivy wore her hair down, like she had that night at Madam Desiree's. She looked quite lovely with the red curls framing her freckled, rosy cheeks.

"Neither?" Ivy said.

"That one," and Sicili pointed.

Ivy looked past her at Francis, who still fussed with the sailor cuffs. "I thought you were determined to form a union with Henry Fuller."

Sicili left the gloves and ventured to the silk ribbons. She placed herself in front of Ivy. "That idea came and went. Francis Perrycot is my most recent captor."

Ivy's mouth curved. "Is there to be an end to them?"

She shrugged, then pinned Ivy with a curt look. "Is that jealousy I hear tainting your voice?"

Ivy struggled with a grin. At the mention of his name, Francis perked up. He pranced over and settled at Sicili's side.

"Have you found something you like?" he asked.

"I think so," she said wistfully. She held up a ribbon, but her eyes were on Ivy, and Francis seemed to notice. He followed her gaze, and one eyebrow lifted.

Ivy cleared her throat.

"Look at your hair, you lovely beast," Francis said to Ivy. "You could do wonders with it, yet you wear it so drab. Were you thinking the same, Miss Windihill?"

"I like it down," she replied.

Francis began to grin.

She pulled herself together. "Francis, this is Ivy Ferthing."

"*The* Ivy Ferthing?" he exclaimed. He shook her hand vigorously, then grasped his cravat. "A pleasure to meet you in person. I dare say you are much prettier than the rumors make you out."

Ivy scowled. "I suppose every soul in England has heard those blasted rumors."

"You are right on that account." Francis leaned an elbow on Sicili's shoulder. "You know, I happen to be a great fan of what you do."

"What I do?" Ivy asked.

"You know," he lowered his voice, "standing up for *who* you are."

Ivy's eyes went wide, then they settled on Francis and she smiled like she knew a dark secret of his. They shared a good laugh.

Sicili interrupted. "What are we laughing about?"

"Secrets." Francis turned his wily eyes on her. "Do you have any secrets, Miss Windihill?"

Sicili picked out a different ribbon, avoiding Ivy's curious stare. "I try not to."

Francis pried. "What do you think, Ivy?"

Ivy crossed her arms. "I say she has one or two."

"*Everyone* has one or two," Sicili said.

"Not like yours," Ivy retorted.

"*Mine?* And what about *yours?*"

"I'm not afraid of mine."

Francis was staring at both with profound enjoyment. "I take it you two know each other?"

"Hardly," Sicili and Ivy said at the same time.

His eyebrows went up.

"That is––" Sicili said.

"We run into each other every here and there," Ivy interrupted.

Francis placed a hand under chin and turned on Sicili, narrowing his eyes on her. She returned the glower. He seemed to look at her in a new light. "I see I interrupted a rather lovely parley. Pick whatever you like, Sicili. Catch me over here trying on a jacket or two." Within seconds, he was preoccupied with his image in a tall mirror.

"Rather pretty," Ivy whispered.

"He happens to be the next Earl to Norbury."

"You do realize..." Ivy looked over her shoulder at him.

"Realize what?"

Ivy got closer. She took the ribbon Sicili fiddled with and returned it to the shelf. "How do I put it? Well, he doesn't fancy you."

Francis was slicking his hair in the mirror with a comb he had produced from his pocket. He turned and winked at Sicili like she was his little sister.

Sicili gasped. "How right you are. Is he––?"

Ivy nodded.

"How can you be sure?"

Ivy shrugged. "There's so few of us in the countryside, and it's rather obvious when we find each other. There's a knowing. Like we're out of place. And we've found someone else who is as well, and one just knows." Ivy shrugged.

Sicili rolled her eyes. "You make it sound like a secret society."

"It is."

"That one needs an invitation to attend."

Ivy's eyebrows jumped. "Anyone who is one of us can join. Are you interested, Miss Windihill?"

She playfully shoved Ivy away from the bow ties. Her sights settled on a rogue fabric, and she wrapped it around her wrists. "If I were curious...?" She felt Ivy's eyes on her, but refused to meet them.

Ivy leaned against the shelf. She tapped the point of Sicili's shoe. "Is that a question for me or for you?"

Exasperated with herself, Sicili cleared her throat and picked out a top hat and placed it on her head, then on Ivy's, and the sight of Ivy in a hat reminded her too much of that night at Madam Desiree's. Warmth flooded her cheeks. Ivy smiled like she, too, was thinking of that night.

"I wanted to say..." Sicili played with the hat's feather. "That night at Windsworth..."

They shared that long stare again, the disconcerting one, like they were coming home to one another after a long day. Sicili tried to finish. She had wanted to apologize at the Dainty's for the things she had said that night, but Henry Fuller had hung to her and Francine had been adamant she stay away from Ivy.

Ivy's smile dropped. The bell above the entrance rang and Charlotte Ferthing stepped in with a frenzy of shopping bags. Ivy removed the hat and handed it to Sicili before noticeably assuming a reserved air.

"Ivy," Charlotte said, looking strict in the light from the street, "have you picked something?"

Ivy held up the bow tie Sicili had selected.

"That will do," Charlotte said. "Hurry up and pay for it." She assessed Sicili in a begrudging manner. "Good day, Miss Windihill."

"How do you do, Mrs. Ferthing?"

"Well, thank you." Charlotte stayed by the door while Ivy paid. "The Prattle's ball is next month. Will you be attending?"

"I believe so."

Charlotte held the door open. Ivy glanced at Sicili on the way out. Charlotte seemed to notice and pressed a protective hand of bags at Ivy's back, guiding her through the door as if Sicili were a beast and might pounce. "Perhaps you will have steady courting by then," Charlotte clipped as the door closed.

"Doubtful," Sicili said, more to herself than in reply. Mr. Stellaway observed her from the register. He offered her a polite but confused smile. She had stepped toward the door involuntarily. She gave up the hopeful advancement and wandered down the aisle until she found Francis fussing with a vest. The world seemed less interesting without Ivy in it, she realized with a dreadful start.

Francis decided against the sailor cuffs. They were two "obvious." He settled for a plaid scarf.

Sicili laughed at him. "You do realize the summer heat is upon us," she said. "You might perish of unfathomable layers."

Francis offered her a wink. "In my short life, I have learned this is never a time one cannot purchase a flattering scarf. By the bye, I am willing to be your beau for the Prattles' ball. I took the liberty of overhearing that you happen to need one."

"You mean you eavesdropped, Mr. Perrycot."

He tied the scarf in pretty loops around his clean-shaven chin, then tucked it into his formal layers so that it puffed at his chest, making him look elegant and ever important. He *would* make for delectable eye-candy on her arm at the Prattle's, and it would get most of the countryside gossiping, but after what Ivy had revealed, the idea felt wayward. "As the next Earl of Norbury, I must assume you have more important parties to attend," she said, looping her arm in his as they exited the shop.

"I can rearrange my plans with a snap of my fingers." And he demonstrated. "Anything for the important Miss Windihill."

"Mr. Perrycot," she halted in the open street, "Let us be frank. The two of us are..."

He raised his eyebrows for her to continue. When she could not, he ventured a guess. "The two of us are single and under immense pressure to please our families?"

She bristled. "The two of us do not suit each other."

He tapped her nose and bid them continue down the street. "There, I believe you mistaken, Miss Windihill. We understand each other, and that is a start to any suitable union. I *did* come to Wiltshire to meet you for a reason, and I *am* looking for a blushing bride." He announced it as if he were proud of the fact, but she caught him wincing, and he coughed into the scarf, which suddenly looked too large for him. He seemed to disappear inside of it.

She stopped them again. "But a bride is the last inconvenience you desire. If we understand each other, be honest with me, Mr. Perrycot."

Francis clucked. "Did Ivy whisper one of my secrets away?"

"Unfortunately."

His eyes sparkled, and he found something to laugh about. "Our way of life is never a misfortune, Miss Windihill. When you embrace it, you shall know."

"*Our* way?" She squirmed at his inclusion of her. "Pardon me?"

Francis tugged them along. "Did I say something?"

They spent the rest of the afternoon searching for something to catch Sicili's eye. Francis insisted. "Our little arrangement cannot be fair otherwise. My grandmother may be harmless, but she is equally exhausting," he assured her. Finally, Sicili found a gold locket with engraved floral details on the outside and room for two drawings inside. She imagined a sketch of Ivy with her hair down. She would look beautiful in the locket.

"I saw the way you looked at Ivy Ferthing," Francis said on the carriage ride home.

"I never look at Ivy Ferthing," she lied.

His laugh filled the carriage. "I thought we had an understanding, you and I. To be honest? You know how you look at her, too. Such respect and admiration."

"For Ivy?"

"I daresay." Francis pulled off the plaid scarf and folded it particularly on his lap.

"Ultimately, you will have to ask yourself the question: Is she worth it?" He let the silence take its toll. "I thought Winston was worth it," he said in a dreamy voice. "We courted for two years in secret. Finally, I could no longer stand the lie. I was desperate to be free to love him in the eyes of my family, for them to meet him and to receive their approval. I wrote a lengthy letter to my father confessing my undying love for Winston Bellview, the man I wanted to spend every moment with." He sighed at the memory. "For all I know, my father burned the letter. He turned his back on me for a year. He ignored my visits to Norbury, refused to return my letters, and as far as I am aware, stopped asking my mother about my well-being. It devastated me. Winston stayed with me through the whole ordeal." He ran a hand through his hair. "He is a better person than I will ever be. But my thirst for my family's affection drove him away. The last time was spoke to him..." he trailed off. He picked up the scarf again, flicked it open, then refolded it. "So, is Miss Ferthing worth it?"

Sicili saw the heartache fill his eyes, the despair, and she felt her own ache for him. She could not possibly answer, and when she did not, Francis took her silence as affirmation and stared out the window. They rode home in thoughtful silence. With every jostle, the locket in Sicili's lap bounced. Finally, she clapped her hand around it and felt as it warmed in her palm. *Was Ivy Ferthing worth losing her family for?*

At Windsworth, he opened the carriage door and helped her down the stairs. "Remember our little tea date with my grandmother, Sicili." He said her given name with a warmth, a familiarity. As he hopped back into the carriage, he announced in a light tone, "I shell pick you up at ten o'clock."

She waved farewell, her heart heavy with confusion. Then, turned to Windsworth and steeled. Her prison.

Francine lounged in the drawing room and gave Sicili a second's pause before calling out, "How was it, darling?"

Sicili sagged against the entry doors. A tiredness overcame her. "I like him, immensely, but he is not the one."

Francine cooed. "I thought he was a bit... off."

"Not off, Mother, different." And she liked the way the word left her lips. *Different, like Ivy*, she thought. *Like... me?*

Francine glanced up from her needlework. "Did you get anything?"

"A gold locket." Sicili pulled it from her bag.

"How pretty, darling. Was it expensive?"

"Two pounds."

Francine scoffed. "I knew you would refuse him, but I thought you might swindle him for a new wardrobe or something grand." Her wry smile irritated Sicili. "He certainly seemed willing."

"I would rather swindle you and Father. After I marry, you two will be forever in my debt." She made for the stairs. "Do tell Father to stop writing letters to earls and dukes and princes. I have endured enough of his list. I plan to find a suitor for myself, and he is going to impress."

Francine squealed with delight at the idea. She clapped her hands to her mouth. "I hoped you would come to that, darling."

"Goodnight, Mother."

"Goodnight?" Francine peered out the drawing room window, then at the clock above the mantle. "Sicili, you realize it is only four in the afternoon?"

She paused at the foot of the winding staircase to the upper rooms. It felt like the deep of night, like twenty-two years of a longing and confusion she did not understand, like a standstill she had grown weary of, like an ache in a body she had yet to come home to. "I need to rest. And... think."

Francine gave her a long, considering look. Her brow scrunched, and Sicili feared she would ask how she was feeling. But the look passed, replaced by a motherly voice, "Wilber will leave you be, then."

In the privacy of her room, Sicili placed the locket in her palm and stared at it until the sun went down. She put the locket away in a neat box inside her vanity and dragged herself to bed. Her skin felt heavy, as if it belonged to the body of an ancient woman who had never known herself, never dared to ask herself questions, never dared to wonder. Francis had said *our way of life*. She had included her. A wave of confusion took over and suddenly she found herself weeping like a little girl. She wept for hours, then curled up on her bed without changing and fell asleep on top of the covers, sobs still raking her body. She slept through dinner and woke up the next morning to puffy eyes and a swollen lip. There seemed little to do about it, so she wore a hat to conceal the evidence of her miserable night.

Francis picked her up at precisely ten o'clock. "You look lovely, Sicili," he said as he helped her into the carriage, "if not a bit sad. Is my company that dismal?"

That started the weeping all over again. "I think–I think–I think––" horrible sobs "––I think I may be *different*, Francis."

"There, there." He rubbed her hands in the kindest manner. "The newness will wear off. Tomorrow this will be remembered as a bad day, nothing more."

"I think—I think I'm having a bad life."

"Is it all bad? Nothing to be salvaged." His sympathy in his eyes shattered her.

She hiccupped. "I find it deathly confusing."

He rubbed. "Grandmama will be a welcome distraction, then I shall have you straight home to your loving parents."

She sobbed. "Loving parents, my *bottom*."

Francis laughed. "I do like you, Sicili." He produced a pouch of powder and a brush from his jacket.

"Do you have a whole vanity on your person?" Sicili said, catching his contagious laugh.

"I might." He dusted the brush upon her swollen cheeks. "There. That will do. Your bad day never happened."

She wished it were that simple.

***

Francis's grandmother, Lady Anne, carried the air of a relaxed feline, ever observant and astute, but petite and charming. Not unlike her grandson. However, where Francis charmed, Lady Anne admired. She put Sicili at ease with a long, warm hug, then held her at arm's length for inspection.

"Oh, Grandmama," Francis complained, "spare her the rudeness of an examination."

"I do this to all the girls," she explained to Sicili.

Francis whooped. "What girls?"

Lady Anne squeezed Sicili's wrists, still holding her out. "Twenty-eight years and you are the first lady he deigned to bring for a visit." She laughed at her own joke. "You have beautiful skin, my dear."

Flattered by Lady Anne's kindness wrapped in wit, Sicili touched her cheek. "Do I?"

"Better not to notice than primp and torture it. The girls in my day were all about blemishes." She gave Francis a tight squeeze. "You look distressed, Francis."

"Perhaps I am, Grandmama."

"To see me? What have I ever done to cause you distress? That father of yours is the true culprit." She kissed his cheek. "Am I wrong?"

"Well, you did bring him into this world."

She chuckled, low and soft. "I carried him, yes, but it was your grandfather's dirty work that created him. Come in, you two. Come and sit. I have the tea out. Do you like chamomile tea, Miss Windihill? I only drink chamomile. Black tea is too hard on my nerves."

Sicili trailed behind as Lady Anne led them through a grand estate, larger by threefold compared to Windsworth, and she wondered how Lady Anne managed it all at her age, with so few servants present. "Chamomile is lovely," she replied.

Lady Anne leaned into Francis and whispered just loud enough. "*She* is lovely, Francis." She gave Sicili a quick wink. "So compliant."

After a jaw-dropping tour of cathedral like corridors with ceilings painted by the late Leonardo da Vinci, they settled in an open drawing room with natural light and a grand piano surrounded by glorious sofas.

"Play us something on the pianoforte, Francis," Lady Anne said.

Francis beamed with delight. He sat at the piano and ran his delicate fingers over the keys. Lady Anne led Sicili to a pink sofa.

"How well he plays," Sicili said.

"I taught him when he was a boy," Lady Anne replied. "He used to love visiting me. He would serenade me all afternoon. Now that he is grown and important, he stays away." Lady Anne raised her voice so Francis would hear. "I think he may be afraid of me, for some *unspoken* reason."

Francis smiled. He stuck his tongue out at his grand-mama and she laughed.

"Oh, I was wrong. He has not grown up at all." She kept on laughing.

He began playing softly, and the music filled the room.

Lady Anne passed her a cup of steaming chamomile. "So, you are a Windihill." She said it with decided familiarity.

Sicili sipped and bristled at the statement, as though being a Windihill was something to strive against. "I am," Sicili said with an edge of pride.

"How is George?"

"Particularly evil of late."

"Still?" Lady Anne stirred her tea, keeping her eyes on Francis as he played. "He always had a talent for schemes. I thought he might give them up once he married your mother. What a soft creature she is."

"I fear they grow worse. Her soft nature enables him." Sicili sipped. "This is my first learning of your acquaintance with my father. Do you know each other well?"

"Oh, it feels like another lifetime ago, I suppose. I knew your grandfather. Of course, George and I lost touch once he passed."

Francis lost himself to the music, and Lady Anne watched him with undivided love. Sicili listened and tried to feel at ease, but the tea was hot and burned her lap, and she felt the moment between grandmama and grandson too intimate for the likes of a stranger like herself. She felt like an intruder. She hardly knew the first thing about Francis, except that he enjoyed the company of men. In fact, she felt like a snake, a serpent, a willful collaborator in his ploy to fool his doting grandmother. An ache of guilt burned through her chest.

Lady Anne leaned in, as though she had read Sicili's mind, and whispered, "My dear, do not trouble yourself. I see that frown on your young face. I am happy to admit I have known all along." She patted Sicili's hand. "There was no need for you to come on his behalf. How very long I have waited for him to confess his true nature. I do love to pester him and watch him squirm, but the boy is proud." The immense love in her eyes shone. "And, scared, I wager. I would be scared, too. Society does not have a place for men like him."

Having said her piece, Lady Anne relaxed into the sofa and watched Francis until she dozed off into a peaceful nap.

Francis showed Sicili around the mansion while his grandmama slept. "The old gal is a notorious art collector," Francis said as he led Sicili from room to room, dedicated to highly affluent artists. One painting stood out among the rest. Sicili stopped in front of it, feeling shy and giddy at the same moment. *Grace*. The exact replica of the painting hanging at Windsworth, save the wood frame.

"Where did Lady Anne get this painting?" Sicili asked Francis.

"This old thing." He dusted the name plaque with a wet finger. "Have you not heard?"

"No."

"My grandmama and your dear grandfather George, the first, were sweethearts once upon a time. They fell in love with *Grace* on a trip to London and had a second painting commissioned. They gifted them to each other."

Sicili smiled up at *Grace's* twin. "A story that failed to circulate the Windihill lineage." She touched the garment falling from *Grace's* shoulder, revealing skin.

"I gather it was the way back then."

"How do you mean?"

"Well, people married more for power and convenience than for love." Francis gave a pretty cough.

Sicili scoffed, thinking of her father and how much he cared about his name and fortune living on. "*Back then* has hardly changed."

"I suppose you have a point, and we are the evidence."

"How lovely that they both kept the paintings. Its match is hung in Windsworth."

"Is it?" Francis said with a laugh.

They stayed until Lady Anne woke from her nap, for Francis couldn't bring himself to depart without saying goodbye. She gave him a grateful kiss on the cheek and pressed him to come again, "soon."

"When I can, Grandmama."

"You never know when I may pass, Francis. Your next visit might be your last."

Francis pecked her cheek in return. "You clever thing."

Lady Anne patted Sicili's hand. "My grandson is lucky to have you," she said, then winked.

The carriage ride to Windsworth was long and riddled with bumpy terrain, and the cracking of wheels against rocks made her heart uncomfortable. Her eyes still felt puffy from last night's crying. The powder had worn off, and she was certain she looked a fright. Fresh tears loomed. She felt France's eyes on her and tried to avoid them as she struggled to forget what Lady Anne had whispered to her while he poured out his heart to the piano.

His grandmama knew.

She wiped a tear away. Did her mother know? Did Wilber?

At first, Francis sat across from her. He fiddled with his hat. He rubbed his palms on his trousers. He coughed far too many times. Then, abruptly, he moved to sit beside her, as though he no longer had control of his own actions.

"Mr. Perrycot. Please." She moved closer to the carriage window, and he breached that gap as well.

"Do listen, Sicili. This sort of talk takes courage. In his letters to me, your father took the liberty of explaining your desperate desire for a male companion."

She sighed. She was through with the evil man.

"He seems greatly misinformed," Francis continued. "I have to admit, I was confused after meeting you yesterday, given your attachment to Ivy."

"There is no attach––"

"Do hear me out, Sicili. I considered the whole dilemma over breakfast this morning, and I can only assume you have some sort of arrangement with your father, though I dare not go as far as to assume what it is."

"How good of you."

She opened the carriage window. She needed air.

"What I mean to say, Sicili, is that I think we would make an understanding pair. You could have your Ivy, and I would have my men. Both our families would suffer the blow of our undermining skills, without even knowing it."

She sighed. Wind whistled through her hair. It blew off her hat and exposed her swollen face. "A tempting offer, Mr. Perrycot."

He clasped her hand, desperate. "Will you give it some thought?"

"In the end, Francis––" she cupped his cheek, knowing they shared a deep bond, knowing she cared more for him than any of the other suitors––"you want to keep your secrets."

Tears sprung to his eyes, and her heart broke for him. "Dearly," he said. "My secrets are what keep my heart from failing. I believe you and I are the same in that regard."

"I think we are."

Sicili squeezed his hand. They sat hand in hand in silence. She leaned against the window and watched the countryside roll by. She thought of that day she went riding and had seen Ivy in the distance, waving a brazen hand at her––red hair flying free, boots and dress covered in dirt. She thought of the way Ivy had kissed her when they first had met in her father's study: bold and soft, and full of promise. She thought of having Ivy to herself, like Francis suggested, but not having her at all because no one would ever know. Endless, agonizing secrecy

like Francis' was the last thing she wanted. If she did indeed
want Ivy, she would want the world to know.

Seventeen

All the Suitable Suitors

In the morning, Sicili refused breakfast and tea. She marched straight to her father's study and walked in unannounced. George sat at his desk. Sicili had a quick memory of Ivy slipping out of the study window, her red hair flamboyant in the wind. She blushed and sat.

"Did Wilber tell me to expect you?" George said, sparing her a glance from his stack of paperwork. His mustache poked in odd directions, which meant she had caught him at a bad time.

"He had no warning of I my coming."

"I see." Instead of brushing aside the mound of papers on his desk, he scribbled harder and faster. He seemed rather caught up, but she refused care. He smiled at her and said rather distractedly, "You look well, Sicili. I take it you recovered from last night's extravagance with Mr. Perrycot."

"I am not well, Father. How can you not see it?"

"Whatever do you mean?"

"I find myself lost, and... frightened. I am anything but well."

He glanced up. "Shall I call the doctor?"

"No. I will have you call off this game of yours."

His quill broke. He gave her an unsettled look. "What game?"

"Be serious, Father. You cannot mean to go through with disinheriting me. This has all been a ruse to keep me in Wiltshire longer than intended. Have you had your fun?

Now pull off your villainous cape."

"I *am* being serious," George said. He set down his quill with a deliberate motion. "I fear you are the one who has failed to take me seriously, my angel."

"How am I to take you seriously? This is all so ridiculous. A list of suitors and letters to earls and a croquet game you *forced* me to play."

"All in order for them witness how worthy you are."

She threw up her hands. "Mother thinks you are ridiculous, too. Have you asked her how foolish you make her feel?"

"Quite the contrary." The glint in his eye had turned cold. He tapped his fingers on the stack of papers, pausing in thought. His mustache wiggled. His eyebrows loomed. "I see I have been too easy on you, and I now recognize my fault in the matter."

She gripped the arms of the chair. "Father."

He leaped up from his desk and turned to stare out the study window. He stood there for a dreadful five minutes. Sicili held her breath. She could hear the wheels in his evil mind churning.

"Father?"

With a dramatic inhale, he said, "Let's have a ball for your birthday."

"Let's not."

He turned to face her, laughing. The glint in his eye had grown warm once more and looked abhorrently refreshed. "It will be a grand affair," he said. "All the single gentlemen in Wiltshire will be there. Not to mention, all the men you will have courted and strung along."

Her knuckles turned white as the armchair suffered. "How unnecessary."

"And, at the twelfth hour of that very night, you will announce which one of them has won your undivided affection and your hand in marriage." He quipped, "Till death do you part," and held his belly as he laughed.

She gasped. "In front of them all?"

"Yes."

"Are you so cruel?"

"Quite the contrary. I am benevolent. My devotion to your eternal happiness is my driving force."

The blood in her face drained. "How can you know me so little?"

He laughed off a beseeching expression and added, "You will thank me in the end, Sicili, when you have children to content you and a husband doting on your every need."

She stood. The chair scraped the wood floor, left a mark. She could no longer sit there and let the evil old man get away with trying to put his words in her mouth. "The end has nothing to do with me, does it? It has everything to do with *your* contentment and *your* money."

George sat down, resolved in his decision. He took up a new quill and focused on the business he had briefly forsaken. "As your father, it falls to me to see that you are settled and happy with a fine, eager gentleman who has a nice home and a bountiful inheritance and who I will take pride in calling my son-in-law." He spoke as he worked, keeping his eyes low. "As my daughter, it is your duty to comply, whether you like it or not."

Tears stung her eyes. How could he sit there so cool, so unbothered, so slick and carefree, with an attitude for only to himself? When was the last time he had thought of her well-being and happiness? When had he stopped to think of what she might feel? She wanted him to know what heartache felt like. She wanted to wound his pride, so she dug deep. "Why am I your only child?" she said coolly. "What kept you from having sons?"

His quill paused. He had always wanted a son. A child he could relate to and pass the Windihill name and estate to. A son who would be proud to be married and have children of his own. A son who wanted to live at Windsworth and care for his parents in old age. He would never admit to it, but Francine had. He pressed a hand against his desk to steady himself.

His eyes met hers with a steel she had rarely experienced from him. "I tried, Sicili. I wonder, some days, if I should have tried with other women. But I am a man of morals. I believe in being faithful. And it cost me. That is why I do not fear your anger."

"What about my hate?" She faced him with all the confidence she could muster. "I am dangerously close to hating you, old man."

"I find myself prepared to weather that storm."

"Have you looked at yourself in the mirror recently? First you ripped me from my home as a girl, then you tore me from my friends and my life in the city, and now you force me to marry a stranger. You. Are. A. Monster."

He dipped his quill and motioned to the door. "Is that all, my angel?"

As she stormed from the study, her dress swirling, and her fury palpable, it came to her. She would marry a stranger. Someone who tolerated her, not someone who *thought* he loved her. A man in it purely for the convenience, the money, and status. The last thing he would want was to kiss her every moment or make love to her every night. Yes, they would tolerate each other. They would make their children happy and go about living as if they were single. He could have a mistress, if he liked. She would have her friends and card games. It would be the perfect arrangement, and it would put George Windihill at ease. There had to be such a man out there. She would find him to spite her father, and when they were married, George would never see them. He would never know his grandchildren. They would never visit Windsworth, and every letter from Windsworth imploring them to be hosts would be burned in the fires of her wrath. He would be too frail by then to threaten her with disinheritance, and too proud of her to meddle or scheme.

She would give George Windihill exactly what he wanted. A pliable daughter who would grow to hate him.

***

For the next week, Sicili turned the drawing room into her office. She interviewed some twenty gentlemen. She got right to the point. No smoothing over the truth with witty banter and small talk. Wiltshire and George Windihill had turned her bitter, and the illusion society liked to through over its victims had fallen from her eyes like scales. She had no desire to be entrap an unwitting man.

"I'm on the hunt for a husband," she frankly told every interviewee. "Not a doting man. One who will do what nature requires of him and provide me with offspring. One or two. Nothing extravagant."

Most of the men who met with her were delighted she had deigned to think of them. They endured her presence in nervous fits and answered her questions as though their lives depended on pleasing her. They were the first to be she crossed off her list. She had grown bored with flattery, and frankly it irritated her, and she had no desire to entertain someone who needed her to feel better about himself. She would be impressed by a man who exhibited his self-worth, intelligence, and indifference.

Three candidates naturally rose to the top:

First, a philosopher who had studied in London because he had the time and money to do so. He talked her ear off about unusual ideas that had nothing to do with reality but rather with perception. He would certainly keep himself occupied in their marriage, but Sicili feared he would look to her for advice on his self-inflicted problems.

~~Frankline Herbert Jones.~~

Second, a jeweler who spent most of the year traveling abroad to purchase one-of-a-kind gemstones. He owned a franchise of businesses in England and Europe that were "uniquely" successful. Though she would never tire of jewels with him, Sicili thought he had a shifty look to him. She had the impression that he had committed too many crimes to name and was perfectly all right with it.

~~Benedict Fervent Delaigo.~~

Third and finally, a Lord Richard Caraway, who lived off his late grandfather's empire of foreign investments and treated his hobbies as if they were an occupation. His parents had died during his childhood, and his grandfather had raised him.

Lord Caraway sat with a slight lean to the left and a finger tapping his cheekbone while he watched Sicili with decided interest. He looked the part of a prosperous hobbyist. His features were sharp, not welcoming, and his attitude had a pretension to it, which she admired, but above all, he held himself with a subtle confidence that did not ask for permission. It was simply available to him. She liked a man who could sit tall and stare her in the eyes, as though she were his equal, not his lesser or his superior. He happened to be twice her age, which meant knew what he wanted, or rather that he wanted for nothing and looked at ease about it.

She took the liberty of asking direct questions. "Why have you not you married, Lord Caraway?"

He smiled lazily, despite her formal attitude. "Easily answered." His finger tapped. "I have never been in love with women."

She scribbled a note. "No?"

"Not at my core. At my core, I am in love with money. I was born with a fever to keep myself engaged in more engrossing affairs than the trap of tedious women who want only my title and social influence. I find the games society plays exhausting."

Her eyebrows shot up. "Well said."

"Naturally, I need a woman to carry on my title."

"Naturally."

"Which brings me to this crossroads." He offered a languid gesture, motioning to her sitting across from him, a quill and paper in hand.

She checked off "indifferent" on her notes. "You would not be at this interview if an offspring was not required of you," she stated.

Lord Caraway's smile looked polite, but she detected a meanness under the surface of it. "You have a decided opinion of me, Miss Windihill."

"It is my business to have an opinion. After all, you would be my husband."

He assessed her with his grey eyes. "How old are you?"

"I am the inquisitor, Lord Caraway, not you."

"You look old enough to be married."

She slid her eyes to his, narrowing them on his simmering smile. "I could say the same to you."

"You already have."

"I used no such words."

"You implied them."

She marked off "intelligent" and "exhibits self-worth", then added, *too much of it*.

"Lord Caraway," she said. "Twenty suitable men would die to be sitting across from me at this very moment. But you? I understand you are a reluctant bachelor."

"Did you speak to all your interviewees this way, with such smoldering inquisition, or did you dismiss them as soon as they groveled and begged? I am not a groveler, Miss Windihill, if that is what you mean to insinuate. And I believe my reluctance is why you like me." His finger tapped. "Am I wrong?"

Sicili looked at her notes. Indeed. She had written only positive scribbles. He had a good nose and grey eyes that could sever a heart, and his intellectual banter would keep her adequately engaged on the days she found herself bored. He had a way of leaning in to show interest but keeping back just a touch to create the perfect distance. Because he could.

"Your opinion of me is severe, Miss Windihill," Lord Caraway said. "I may exude arrogance, but I assure you it is observation in disguise. I know how to read people. You are an intelligent woman, and I find myself drawn to your confidence. Most women your age have no idea what they want. Their desires are second-hand whims passed down by their parents."

She huffed. "Since we are being blunt, I can tell you I am no exception. I, too, experience times of confusion about what I want." She thought of Ivy. "What I truly want." Her voice had wavered, and she endeavored to compose it.

Lord Caraway made a soft *hmmm*. "Not accepting what you want does not make you want it any less. I offer this truth as someone twice your age, Miss Windihill."

She remembered the way Ivy's hair had looked in Mr. Stellaway's shop. The dream of Ivy in trousers came crashing back to her. She reached for her tea and cleared her throat. The task at hand was finding herself a husband, not thinking about the incorrigible Ivy Ferthing. "Do you court, Lord Caraway?"

"I used to. I found it too consuming. I was forced to neglect the things I most love in life."

"Which is playing with things."

"Things, not people. Ask any of the women I courted. I was honest about my intentions."

She sipped. "I take it none of them were willing to fit into your decidedly demanding lifestyle."

"No."

"And you have yet to meet someone who does?"

"Indeed." Lord Caraway leaned forward and rested a finger on the cleft of his chin. "In fact, you should think of this as being *your* interview, not mine."

Just as he said it, Francine strolled into the drawing room. "Are you still at it, Sicili? Have you not grown weary?"

"Not quite," Sicili said, keeping her eyes on Lord Caraway.

He returned her gaze with deliberate confidence.

"I need the drawing room for company tonight," Francine said as she came around the sofa. She addressed Lord Caraway, "I would introduce myself, Sir, but my daughter has had me introduced so many times I hardly know my name anymore."

"Quite all right," he said, and got up. "I was just leaving."

"Are you letting my mother scare you off, Lord Caraway?" Sicili asked. "She's the nice one. My father is the evil one."

"Fret not, Miss Windihill, I frighten less and less with age." He winked and swept up Sicili's hand in a kiss. "Thank you for the enlightening interview."

As he took his coat and hat from Wilber, Sicili had an idea. "Lord Caraway," she called after him. "Will you escort me to the Prattle's ball next month?"

He paused by the door. "Let me think on it. I may be occupied with a chess tournament that day."

She scoffed, offended that a chess tournament might take president over escorting her to a ball. However, it did suit his character, and if she were indeed being interviewed, he was likely testing her fortitude for his hobbies. She got brittle. "You are the first and only interview I asked. If that makes the matter easier for you to decide."

His lips turned upward, and he tipped his hat to her, then bid Wilber a good day as the butler held the front door open for him.

Francine watched him through the drawing room window, holding the curtain back with a smile. "Is he as old as I am, Sicili?"

"Possibly, and I think it agrees with him. He has already inherited his grandfather's fortune. And he does not faint over my attention. And he cares more for his money than flattery. And he has a way of seeing through me that I find appealing."

Francine let the curtain drop. "Quite a lot of *ands*, darling. Remember to breathe."

"There is something to being old, Mother."

"Sicili, you go about this all wrong."

"Do I? Tell me how to go about it when I have less than two months before my damnation."

"I thought you knew yourself better than to waste your time on interviews," Francine said with gentle concern.

"Lord Caraway shall not be looked down upon because I discovered from an interview. Father has been preening and grooming and interviewing this whole time, and his suitors have been rubbish. I deem Lord Caraway the best fit thus far. He is ancient, yes, but I dare say he stimulates my mind."

"Keep it from your father, darling." Francine poured herself a glass of wine. It was two in the afternoon. "He wants you making babies, not debating physics with an ancient."

Sicili ignored her mother. The truth was, Lord Caraway had left a lasting impression. Not romantically, but intellectually. They both understood that money meant freedom. Her only qualm was that he seemed like a calmer version of her father. She would rather be married to Francis Perrycot, unhappily, than a man who reminded her of her evil father.

Eighteen

A Tete-To-Tete in the Summer Heat

"Have you heard?"

"Heard what, Harriet Prattle?"

"Ivy Ferthing is a..." Harriet leaned into Simon Becker's ear. "A tom."

Simon Becker gasped. "What in all of Wiltshire is a tom?"

"It means she likes girls, not boys, and she would rather be married to a girl than dance with a boy at a ball. You see the way she shirks poor Patrick Derby every time he approaches."

"I would never want to be lousy Mr. Derby."

"You certainly would not. Now go off and tell your mother, Simon. I look forward to hearing her squeal."

"This will make Mother squeal?"

"Be assured," Harriet said with a wicked wink.

Simon took off with a skip and a laugh, and Harriet wended the path to the Becker's mansion, knowing that she wanted to be in earshot of Mrs. Becker's scream. It had been far too long since worthy scandal had spread in Wiltshire, and Harriet felt less and less like herself without someone to gossip about. Or someone to ruin. She had wanted to ruin Ivy ever since they were girls, once she realized she had to give her up because society's smiles and nods were more important than young love. Ever since Sicili Windihill had returned from London, Ivy had been smitten, and watching Ivy fall in love vexed Harriet to her rotten soul. She remembered how Ivy used to look at her, with such abandon and wonder, and if Harriet could no longer be the object of such devotion, no one could.

Ruin came naturally to a woman stuck in a loveless marriage. If she had to suffer, Ivy would suffer with her. And if Ivy responded in like, they would go down together, and at least they would suffer together instead of a part.

Nineteen

Ivy Speaks Her Mind

Ivy was nineteen when society turned its back on her for the second time.

News had spread like a windstorm over the hillsides, as it always did in Wiltshire, that Ivy fancied women instead of men. The chatter had not stopped in three weeks. It flared up at parties and tea visits and on lavish croquet fields. Five years after her first debauchery, Ivy was the talk of the countryside once again.

"Can you imagine? A woman with a woman?"

"What a sorted lot those Ferthings are, and they let her get away with it?"

"Is it a wonder she dresses in trousers now? Surely, her fancying a lady is the reason!"

All social calls had been refused. All invitations had been withdrawn. The lights in Vineyard Estate were dimmed, and the servants were given a long, indefinite vacation. Charlotte refused to see anyone, even William. She kept to her bedchamber, sobbing into the pillows and cursing Ivy's name. She barred the door and only took tea and crumpets. William kept his head down and busied himself with the vineyard, and when Ivy offered to help, he would give her a severe, "You have done enough already, Ivy," which was so unlike William it made her pale with dismay.

Not only society rejected her for a second time, but she had also been cast into bitter neglect by her own family. They dared not look upon or to speak with her, and it made her feel invisible. All she could do was accept her lot in life. She had been given five merciful years of practice.

On the night of the Prattle's ball, Ivy found herself at Madam Desiree's, nursing a tumble of scotch. Everywhere she went, the chatter followed her, so she dressed up whenever she left Vineyard Estate, assuming the part of one of her characters. Tonight, she was Charles. Just Charles. Charles owned the grand age of eighty-three. He had a severe limp, a slouched back, and walked with a marble-handled cane. Despite his immeasurable wealth, Charles wore mismatched socks, shoes that gave him blisters, and an old plaid vest that collided with his plaid tailcoat. He didn't like people to know how good life had been to him because. In fact, since his wife had passed three years ago, he felt a tremendous loneliness.

Embracing Charles' slouched back, Ivy sipped the scotch. She was happy to be Charles tonight. The alternative would have been her stuffed into another one of her mother's contraptions, and Charles' wardrobe was quite breezy and free in comparison. With relief, she savored the burn of loneliness, but the liquor settled in her stomach and kept burning. Once upon a time she had dreaded the Prattle's ball; only the daring thought of seeing Sicili Windihill had made it seem bearable. Now, she reckoned, good society would never permit the dejected, pervasive tomboy of Wiltshire to be in the presence of the desired Miss Windihill. So, with a darkness across her face, she drank, and drank, and drank, and muttered guesses at who had spoiled her deepest secret.

She sat alone. Anyone who approached her end of the bar saw her gloomy state and mumbled apologies. Some of them gave her odd looks, stared too long at her bright red mustache, but most of them avoided her dark eyes and hobbled away from her, leaving her to the mercy of Eveline's keen gaze.

She hadn't been back to Madam Desiree's since the night Sicili had exposed her, and she exchanged a long, beseeching look with Eveline. She had nowhere else to go. Madam Desiree's had been a home to her for so many years, a refuge from her mother's nagging and anxieties. She needed to be left alone to drink and sulk.

Eveline returned her look with a soft smile. She made her way to Ivy's end of the bar and draped a hand over Ivy's shoulders. Leaning in, she whispered, "Between you and me, if you had told me about your preferences, we could have come to an arrangement much sooner."

With a sigh of relief, Ivy relaxed. She grinned from ear to ear. "I liked being chased down the street by men in uniform." She tipped her suede top hat and pretended at Charles' voice. "A lick of adrenaline keeps this old heart young."

Eveline tucked a loose curl under the hat. "Who should I call you tonight, then?"

Ivy glanced behind at the table of fellows playing cards. They were in the thick of losing their money to the man with an abhorrent mustache, too engrossed to notice sorry, old Charles by himself.

"Call me Charles."

Eveline winked. "Just Charles?"

"Indeed. Harmless, lonely Charles who lives alone with five Great Danes in a mansion overlooking the ocean. He needs no one, and no one needs him."

"It sounds like a miserable life."

"It could be worse. Old Charles here could be dead and rotting in the ground."

"Well, then, Charles––another round of scotch?"

Ivy held up her glass. Eveline reached across the bar and swept up the scotch decanter. She kept close and lowered her voice to a purr, "You're the talk of Wiltshire, you know."

Ivy said nothing. A grunt was all she could manage. She chugged the scotch, and Eveline aptly refilled it. "How does it feel?"

Another grunt. "Rather foreboding."

"Foreboding?"

"Like life has just begun."

Eveline gave her pointy nose a gentle pinch. "Have you not been waiting for life to start all this time?"

Ivy's throat bobbed. "I think I have, and I'm confounded. I haven't the slightest clue how to go about it."

Eveline leaned in with a smile. "Would you like to know what I think, Charles?" Her eyes twinkled.

"I've always liked hearing you talk, Evie."

"I think they can all roll in their graves. Let them talk in their high houses with their lofty views. Who are they to say who you can and cannot be?" She took Ivy's hands and squeezed. "You were made for more than snotty Wiltshire. Now you are free. Now you can *truly* live."

The bell above the entry doors jingled, and Eveline gave Ivy a quick kiss on the cheek. "Find me later if you're still lonely." She winked and attended to the arrival of a flock of rowdy gentleman who had done their share of drinking elsewhere and were already handling the ladies.

Eveline's view of her made Ivy sit taller. It made the over-sized tailcoat and musty vest feel tight and heavy. It made her eyes shine and her hair itch with the desire to be free of the suede top hat. She cracked her cane against the bar top and whelped with joy. The fellows playing the game behind her paused and sent her perturbed looks. She glared them all down, and they must have seen Charles with his formal years and his demand for respect, because they all broke her gaze with flinches and concern and returned to their game and conversation.

Which Ivy listened to because of the following name:

"You say George Windihill graced this very alehouse last night?" The tall, slinky one said.

"Indeed," the abhorrent mustache said. "He quits Windsworth every month or so to patronize our mediocre company with the exuberant affairs of his self-indulgent schemes."

"That man could spend all day scheming," the one who was losing grumbled.

"Yes, well, he guzzled two decanters of whisky and danced with a dozen ladies, at least, before belting out his latest scheme." The mustache wiggled as its wearer held his belly and laughed. "It was quite a show." He paused for effect. "Would you know his latest design?"

"We would," said the tall, slinky one. "Tell us so we can feel better about walking out of here poorer because of you."

The abhorrent mustache went on, "He has locked up his one and only daughter at Windsworth with a looming ultimatum: she must marry by her twenty-third birthday or be disinherited."

"Disinherited?"

"You heard right. And he boasted about the affair as if he were a conductor of a great symphony, as if it would make the world good and right again, and not crush the poor girl."

"Rather a lousy father," the losing one said.

"Let's not pretend George Windhill knows the first thing about raising a child. He did send the girl away for six years to be rid of her."

Ivy reeled around. Her heart erupted with all the thundering emotions she had kept at bay, and she finished the last of her scotch with a whopping smile. She howled a laugh and smacked the glass down, which brought the stares of the alehouse upon her. But all they could see was a downcast old man, so she walloped again, and this time smacked her knee. All this time she imagined Sicili *wanted* to be married, that she courted Princeton Evergreen and Henry Fuller and whoever else because she fancied a union with a man, that she had flirted and strung Ivy along out of a need for attention like Harriet, but the illusion came crashing down, and Ivy could see right through it. George Windihill *forced* Sicili to find a match, which meant Ivy had a sliver of chance. Perhaps a very small one, but she had to do something about it. Eveline was right. She could live, she could love, she could tear off the confines of society and truly embrace herself.

She stumbled off the stool, lost her balance and smashed against the bar. Eveline came to her rescue, hoisting an arm around her waist and helping her to stand upright. Ivy gave a laugh and slipped.

"The scotch has settled over me, dear lady," she said in her deepest voice.

"Are you trying to get home in this state, Charles?" Eveline clucked. "Best to sleep it off in the back."

"On the contrary," Charles announced, "I'll be needing your finest horse."

She would be attending the Prattle's ball after all.

***

Ivy rode against the wind. Storm clouds formed over Westbury and followed to her across the rolling countryside. She sobered some, with the wind thrashing at her clothes and hat, enough to hold onto the horse for dear life but not enough to think better of her plan to face Sicili in the getup of an old man. She lost the suede hat halfway to the Prattles, not caring to retrieve it, her eyes set on the grey horizon and the wistful thought of seeing Sicili after a month without her company, after repressing the yearning to be close to her and tell her all she felt.

When she arrived at the Prattle's attractive estate, Charles' mustache had fallen off in the wind, and anyone who was anyone could see that the old man was in fact Ivy Ferthing. Her hair stuck out in all directions, weathered by the ride, and riddled with unruly knots. Her shirt had untucked from her trousers and the plaid vest had somehow undone and re-buttoned in the wrong places. The tailcoat swallowed her whole. She tossed off the blistering shoes and dismounted Eveline's horse without a care for who saw her. She ignored the shrieks of the girls in the garden as she passed by them barefoot and half herself, half Charles.

Arms akimbo, she stopped in the garden entrance to the Prattle's stately ballroom. Huffing, she took in the scene. To her disadvantage, it was an intimate affair. The Prattles had far less space than the Windihill's. Guests rubbed up against other guests and were forced into small talk, which meant Ivy's arrival brought on the gazes of all.

Silence followed her dramatic entrance. Complete silence. The torchlight from the garden illuminated her backside as she stood wide-legged in the entryway. Guests near her backed up and bumped into one another, their wine spilling and frills clashing. They exchanged wild expressions.

The mustache, which had actually got stuck to the arm of Charles' tailcoat, slapped to the floor. An astonished, unified gasp filled the silence. The entire ballroom of guests, holding their chests and fanning their faces, stared wide-eyed at her.

Harriet Prattle stood at the far end of the ballroom, an arm hooked around her Mr. Prattle and a palm to her mouth.

People began to stir.

"Is it...?" They held up their eyeglasses.

"Naughty Ivy in the flesh?"

"What in all of Wiltshire is *she* doing here? And in such an audacious performance?"

The scotch still coursed through Ivy's veins, so she surrendered to it and let it do the talking. "I emerged from my exile to see Sicili Windihill," she announced with a sway.

A hush, then the crowd of guests parted to the left where Sicili sat fanning herself on a sofa next to a stately man Ivy had never seen. He looked as slick and as oily as a fox. Silver hair and a shiny forehead. A finger pressed his temple, and he tapped it, as though the evening's delights had no effect on him. He looked fascinatingly bored. Sicili stopped fanning and wiggled to the edge of the sofa. Her gaze landed on Ivy with afflicted awe. She looked both aggravated and riveted.

Ivy cleared her throat. Guests recoiled. She regarded Sicili's visible awe as an invitation to proceed. She took the path and weathered the whispers.

"Is it must I smell wafting from her clothes?"

"Is she *trying* to be an old man?"

"Where is her mother? Did Charlotte Ferthing allow this outrage?"

When she arrived at Sicili, Francine Windhill had settled at her daughter's elbow, and the man to Sicili's left had leaned forward with an interested gesture and a mocking smile. Ivy had reason to believe this was the most entertained he had been all night.

She stopped before Sicili. "I need to speak with you."

"Ivy––"

She held out her hand. "It cannot wait."

Whispers fluttered. Sicili's name slipped from lip to lip. Vehement gasps filled the room. Her stricken gaze wavered from Ivy's hand to the apprehensive stares of everyone gathered. She met Ivy's eyes, then her mother's, then Ivy's. Francine muttered something tight and thin.

"I recognize that, Mother," Sicili said curtly. The man sitting next to Sicili stood up and loomed over Ivy.

"Surely, whatever you have to say to Miss Windihill can wait, Miss..." His brow farrowed.

Ivy crossed her arms. "It's Charles tonight."

"Miss Charles?"

"Just Charles."

He bowed his head as his earlier smile waned. A glint stirred in his eyes. "You have interrupted a fine evening with your show of bravado. Let me escort you out before your reputation regrets it."

"My reputation is fully in tatters, Mister, and I quite like it that way." She removed his hand from her elbow and turned to Sicili, letting some of that unworldly bravado show in her eyes. Sicili rose.

"Miss Windihill," the man said in warning.

"Lord Caraway, I know this vagabond," Sicili replied. She slipped her hand into Ivy's and gave it a comforting squeeze. "Whatever she has to say will not harm me."

"I beg to differ, darling," Francine chirped. "Look around you."

The room hung in dreadful astonishment at Sicili embracing the disastrous Naughty Ivy. The pressure of Sicili's pressing into hers set Ivy's heart roaring. Their intertwinement held the attention of every guest present. Her palm grew warm against Sicili's, and it felt right. It felt like being home. The sliver of hope had become a wedge, spurring her on, and the curiosity in Sicili's eyes had grown brighter in the presence of all who watched.

She tugged, and the crowd parted for her. She maneuvered toward the nearest exit. Harriet shadowed it. Ivy muttered a curse and veered toward it regardless, keeping her eyes set on the exit. As they passed, Harriet whispered something malicious in Mr. Prattle's ear before staring Ivy down with such loathing it caused a shiver. She quickened her pace, hoping to pass the couple without engaging them, but Harriet took a step forward and blocked the narrow path to the ballroom's exit.

Harriet raised her voice. "I revoked your invitation, Naughty Ivy, or did your mother forget to tell you?"

Ivy paused. The most elite of Wiltshire watched. They held their breath, waiting for an audacious reply, something worthy of the accused. Whatever was witnessed tonight would be spread around the countryside until the next extravaganza deserving of unhinged gossip. Though, not surprisingly, Ivy guessed Westbury would be talking about tonight for half a decade to come. Her eyes narrowed on Harriet. Whoever she took down with her would stay down, would suffer as she suffered. Harriet froze, her eyes hardened, and the slight smile on her lips dared Ivy to do it.

Sicili nudged. "Ivy..."

Ivy stepped close to Harriet and lowered her voice. "I know it was you, Harriet. Go ahead. Have your Mr. Prattle, and your stuffy parties, and the nod of good society. At the end of the day, I feel pity for you. Not contempt. Not revenge."

Harriet's eyes smoldered. She wanted Ivy to strike back, and Ivy had the means. She could tell them all what Harriet Prattle and her used to do in the vineyard when no one was watching. She could tell everyone what Harriet used to tell her. What she wanted Ivy to do to her in the dark after they had kissed themselves into fits of passion. Eveline's words resurfaced. *Now you are free. Now you can truly live.* Harriet had done her worst, and her worst had freed Ivy, but Ivy could never do the same to Harriet. She could never intentionally exile someone she once loved.

Ivy sighed. "My mother has been sobbing in bed for a week, Mrs. Prattle. Rest assured; this has broken her more than it has me."

Harriet's fists clenched. She moved aside, then laughed Ivy off. "What are you all standing around for? Dancing is to be had. What is there to see here but theatrics? Shall we return to our fine evening and let the disgraced remain disgraced?"

With a scoff, Sicili made to say something, but Ivy tugged. She veered them through the stirring crowd and headed for the door, removing them from the heat of observation as the cool of the corridor beyond the ballroom embraced them.

***

Ivy rushed them into a small sitting room. A fire blazed. Windows lined the wall, ready to be jumped out of if need be. Grey clouds had followed her from Westbury and now blustered the Prattle's modest mansion. Rain splattered against the windowpanes.

She threw open a window for fresh air.

"Not this again," Sicili said with a soft smile. "Did you bring me here to force me to escape with you?"

Footsteps echoed in the hall outside. She locked the door in a hurry.

Sicili laughed. "Am I your captor?"

"No." She slumped against the door, trying to find the words for her feelings.

"Are you intoxicated, Ivy?"

She turned to face Sicili. "Why did you keep it from me?" Her words came out more accusatorily than intended as tears sprung to her eyes and wobbled her voice.

Sicili's playful disposition turned serious, and her cheeks burned disturbingly brightly. "Truly, Ivy, even for you, this is quite untoward." She took in Ivy's clothing and tussled hair with a captivated but troubled expression. "Keep what from you?"

"Your father's scheme." Ivy crossed her arms. Her jaw tightened. "His ultimatum."

Sicili's eyes widened, then narrowed. She played off the matter, fussed with her fan. "That nonsense," she said with a flustered laugh, "happens to be a family matter. You need not concern yourself wi––"

"I would have tried harder had I known."

Sicili blushed. "Whatever do you mean?"

"I thought you impartial."

Sicili's lips thinned. "I have to be."

She took her chance. She closed the distance between them and stepped close enough to rustle against Sicili's skirt. Their lips nearly met. Her thumb traced Sicili's jaw. "If you truly desired a union, then yes, but now that I've learned your father forces your––

Sicili's breath hitched. "Ivy, be careful."

"I care for you." It spilled out in tumbles, unable to be stopped. Her chest grew warm with emotion, with the truth. "I have since that night at Madam Desiree's."

Sicili laughed. Her gaze fell, and brightness betook her cheeks again. "That was a regrettable night."

She lifted Sicili's chin. "Do you mean that, or are you playing cool to appease society?"

They stayed frozen for a handful of seconds. She ran a thumb down Sicili's throat and rested her fingers at the nape of her neck. Sicili touched her elbow tentatively, her eyes glued to Ivy's. And Ivy cursed herself. Why had she not tried harder regardless of all the courting? Why had she let her mother stop her from showing she cared? Sicili blinked, and the moment between them hiccupped as fear settled into Sicili's eyes. Pressing her away, Sicili reached for the armchair by the fire and sank into it.

"You care for me?" she asked softly, as if she needed to hear it again to believe it. A whoosh came out as she uttered the question, and part of her seemed to deflate with terror.

Ivy settled in the armchair across from her and took her hands. She kissed her palms. The skin of Sicili's hands felt clammy and cold, and Ivy wondered if the daughter of the almighty George Windihill always felt cold in his overbearing shadow. She rubbed her palms over Sicili's knuckles, warming them despite the fire.

Sicili's eyes softened, and the wonder that captured her face said she shared Ivy's affection, though she made no attempt to say it out loud.

"Is it so hard to believe?" Ivy asked.

"Yes, it is." Her hands turned to fists. "Mr. Stellaway's Fashions and the Dainty's tournament. You kept your distance. I imagined––"

"Forgive me. I wish I hadn't. I stayed away for Mother." Ivy kissed her clenched knuckles, and Sicili responded with a soft sigh.

"How is your mother?"

"On the brink of heartbreak. She cares a great deal too much about how society views me."

Sicili cooed. "Naturally."

"Naturally?" The passion she had felt at the Windsworth library got a hold of her again. She had kept it in check for far too long, and this was the consequence of turning from her wayward self.

Silence hung between them.

Sicili sighed, this time heavier, perhaps with the knowledge that she spent time alone, behind a locked door, with Naughty Ivy. She leaned in and brushed a tangle behind Ivy's ear.

And said this, "Naturally mothers care about what happens to their daughters."

"And are we daughters not allowed to decide our own fates?"

"You know how it is, Ivy, how it has always been. Let's not argue."

Passion turned haughty, righteous. Indeed, she had had held back too much for too long, and it all came tumbling out. "I refuse to be impartial to *how it is*. Need always be forever? Need we stay in the shadows and pretend our feelings have no merit?"

Sicili began to recoil. The daughter of George Windihill was not afraid of theatrics, but she was afraid of the truth, of the passions coursing through Ivy.

She withdrew her hands and sunk further into the armchair. It looked like she wanted to melt into it, to disappear.

"Not all of us are you," she said, her voice edge with a bitterness. "Not all of us want freedom so badly we will give up our harmonious privilege."

Ivy stood. She moved to the fire. She stared into it. "So, you will go through with it? You will bow to the almighty George Windihill and let him force you into unhappiness?"

Sicili bit a trembling lip. She watched Ivy with haunting admiration, but fear had got hold of the wonder, and it made her look like a lost child enveloped by a gigantic chair. Shadows flecked the side of her face, casting the rest of her into a relentless darkness. "What would you have me do?"

Ivy had already lost her, but she refused to stop fighting. "*Everything* you can. Stand up to him. Tell him no. Tell him you will disown him as a father if he persists."

Sicili's eyes broke with sorrow. "I think you are forgetting one very important fact: I'm not you, Ivy. No one is you. No one shows up to balls dressed as an old man and confesses her affection. There is only one you. And you marvel and astound and break laws. You may well be the last you, but *dear God*, for the sake of a feeble woman like myself, I hope there are more of you. I hope you never stop."

Tears blurred Ivy's vision. It would be the closest to a confession Sicili would give.

Something brushed against the other side of the door. The doorknob jiggled before what sounded like the whoosh of a dress as its wearer pressed an ear to the door. They had an audience.

Someone knocked. "Sicili?"

Sicili's jaw set. The sorrow vanished from her face as she sat up with such feigned composer it made Ivy shudder. She cleared her throat and wiped away unwanted tears. Ivy stared in stunned shock. This was Sicili's pretend, her illusion. She cast the image that her heart was impenetrable, and she did it so that others could not hurt her.

The door jiggled.

"I see," Ivy said.

"You have wasted your feelings on me, Miss Ferthing."

Another knock. More adamant. "Sicili, darling? Are you alone in there with...? You had better come out. The ballroom is simmering with whispers, and you cannot be caught up in this scandal if you wish to further impress Lord Caraway. He considers an imminent departure."

Without another moment's hesitation, Sicili moved for the door. "I needed some air, Mother."

Ivy dashed a wayward tear away as Sicili turned and swept through the door without a backward glance. The door clicked shut, and Ivy stood in the sitting room alone. The fire crackled at her, mocking her.

She dried her eyes on Charles's sleeve and allowed one sniffle, then inhaled and leaped out the open window. She had done it a dozen times, fled from balls her mother had forced her to attend, but this time her foot caught on the window ledge, and she slipped. She landed on her knees in the pouring rain. The impact shot up her thighs. She stayed in the mud for half a minute, feeling the pulse of the rain as it soaked her clothes and chilled her skin, then she rose, stumbled, and brushed the dirt from Charles's trousers. She needed the pain. Pain would remind her tomorrow of how foolish she had been to fall in love with the only daughter of George Windihill.

***

When she arrived back at Vineyard Estate, her knees throbbed. She tore off Charles' tailcoat and vest and threw them on the foyer floor. Her hair dripped all the way to the drawing room where she stacked a pile of logs in the hearth and lit a match. A puddle of rainwater formed at her feet. She extended her hands while the flames grew, and the walls took on flickering shadows. She shivered until the fire warmed her and her tears were spent.

She had completely dried when Charlotte cleared her throat. She jumped. Her mother sat in the corner rocking chair, cradling a cup of tea in the shadows.

She wiped her eyes with a sleeve. "I thought you might never come out of your lair, Mother."

Charlotte rocked the chair forward. "Where were you, girl?"

She scoffed. "Following my wayward heart." She stared into the flames.

"And?"

White knuckled, Charlotte clutched the saucer. She brought the tea to her lips. Though her eyes were puffed from crying, she looked refreshed. Younger, perhaps, or less worried. Her cheeks glowed a wholesome ruddy. Her expression was open, not narrowed, and distraught, like Ivy had grown used to.

"You truly want to know?" Ivy asked with a sniffle.

Charlotte nodded.

She turned to her mother, squared her shoulders. "I played the part, Mother. I did your bidding. I surrendered to society, and I'm still me. Now, please––" her voice wavered, "––let me live. Just let me live."

Eyes glistening, Charlotte pressed her lips. She took in Ivy's state, not the clothes or the character or the frazzled hair, but her. Just her. She stared at Ivy for a good minute, and Ivy stared back, full of hope. The clock chimed nine o'clock. Creaks from further in the house pervaded upon the drawing room.

Charlotte rocked back. "All right, my Ivy."

She paused, looked at her mother, blinked. "All right?"

"You heard me. Be yourself. Be who you are meant to be. I grow weary. It seems good society is bent on making a villain out of you." Charlotte sipped, eyes still glistening. "Damn us if we refuse to allow it."

And then Charlotte rose and did something she had failed to do in a very long time. She scooped Ivy into her arms and squeezed tightly.

Twenty

Ivy Wanders

At the crack of dawn, Ivy pulled the sacred chest of clothing out from under her bed and dressed up as a successful banker who had not a worry in the world. He had three daughters who were married off and a wife who liked to unzip and get into his trousers whenever she could. Some people had all the luck.

As the sun rose over the trees, Ivy opened her bedroom window and climbed down the gutter. Her father, already tending to his beloved grapes, whistled at the bottom of the vineyard. He peered up from his work as she trudged by in her disguise.

"Where are you off to, Ivy?"

She picked a grape and popped it in her mouth. "To do some thinking."

"Be careful with that. Be back before supper, will you?"

"Anything for you, Father."

He smiled widely.

She walked for hours upon hours, all morning and all afternoon. In town, people tipped their hats to her. They saw the successful banker in his expensive suit, eyeglasses, and tall top hat—not the girl, not the scandal. She tipped her hat back, encouraged by their lack of recognition. She really could go on fooling Wiltshire if she wanted to. But being a fool fooling other fools was the last thing she wanted. She wanted to be

Ivy Ferthing, the girl who fancied girls, not some happily rich banker.

She spent most of the day walking, not thinking. At mid-afternoon, she stopped to take in her surroundings. With a mutter under-breath, she dug her hands deep into her pockets. She had reached Windsworth Estate. It was the last place she wanted to be, but after walking most of the countryside while not thinking, Windsworth appeared to be the only place left. Having paused in the garden grounds behind the mansion, she had a nice view of an East Wing sitting parlor and the corridor that met it. She produced a pipe and lit it. Inside, Sicili strolled up and stood by the window. She wore riding clothes. Her golden hair fell over her left shoulder, and she held a hand to her throat.

For a moment, Sicili's gaze passed over Ivy and Ivy feared she had been caught, but then she squinted and saw the glossy sheen in Sicili's stare. She had perfected her illusion since last night. Her walls were icy. Her face blank. Her lips a thin line. Her eyes passed on, unseeing, to the rest of the garden. Someone interrupted her, and she looked over her shoulder, then disappeared toward the doorway of the parlor.

Ivy sucked in too much smoke and coughed on it.

Lord Glint-in-his-eye Caraway. He walked up the corridor and met Sicili halfway. Ivy bit down on a jealous grunt. Clearly, her and Sicili's rendezvous at the Prattles hadn't detoured his affections for her. He kissed her on the cheek, and she smiled pleasantly at him, playing the part, solidifying the illusion.

"You do it so well," grumbled Ivy. "No one can hurt you when you're the one hurting yourself."

Eyes stinging, Ivy turned away.

A sturdy butler stood behind her. His narrowed eyes treated her with suspicion. Dark slicked back hair and black as night eyebrows took up half his forehead. With hands behind his back, he cleared his throat.

She lowered her voice to fit the image of the successful banker. "So sorry."

"Can I help you?" the butler said.

"No, no. I was just leaving."

"You do realize..." the butler paused and looked closely at her "...sir," he managed, "that this is a private garden."

"I do now." She swept up his hand and shook it. "Thank you, my good man."

She snuffed her pipe and tucked it into the banker's pocket before hurrying past him and bounding away from Windsworth.

***

When she arrived home, the sun had set. The dining room danced with candlelight and Charlotte's lowered voice hissed through the house. Ivy paused in the hall to listen.

"Do not say a peep to her about it, William."

A chair creaked. "She might hear about it some way or another."

"Not if we can help it. This is the last thing she needs. If you had seen her last night, William. Never have I seen our girl so dejected."

"She goes out, you know, at night, and she socializes with her own kind of people."

Charlotte whimpered. "Her *own kind of people*?"

"You know––"

"Never mind, William. I dare not know." She gasped. "Did you hear something?" Then called out, "Ivy, is that you?"

Ivy strolled into the dining room as confidently as she could, pipe still hanging from her mouth. A beautiful piece of once-folded paper rested next to Charlotte's plate.

She folded her arms and leaned against the door frame. "What are you two whispering about?"

"There you are," Charlotte said. She took in Ivy's banker disguise. "I must say, Ivy, this is your weakest work. I find you not at all believable."

She tipped her tall hat. "Most of Wiltshire believed me, except one sturdy butler."

"A butler? What were you doing in a butler's business? Were you on private property again?"

"Just a private garden."

William chuckled.

"What is that paper, Mother? Father's right. I'll learn about it at Madam Desiree's."

Charlotte blanched. "Madam– –"

Ivy took a wild gait and plucked the paper from Charlotte's plate edge.

Charlotte stood. "Ivy, darling, do be mindful of how– –"

But it was too late.

The invitation was addressed to *The Ferthing Family*, from *Your Great Friends the Windihill's*. The only invitation they had had in weeks. Ivy cleared her throat. She took a seat before she began:

My dear friends of Wiltshire,

As some of you may know, my glorious angel and only child Sicili is turning twenty and

three on the 7th of September 1840. On that very night, we will be celebrating our Sicili

with a ball to end all balls. There will be dancing, costumes, and memories we will never

*forget. And, dear friends, there is another detail we will
be celebrating. As a few of you*

*   may know, my Sicili is betrothed. I will not utter the
name of her betrothed here, for it is*

*   Sicili who will announce him on the night of her ball.
Until then,*

*   George Windihill and Family*

Ivy's heart broke for Sicili. She had a mind to dash
out the door and return to Windsworth, to find Sicili and
convince her to run away to London, to shirk off her
ridiculous inheritance and embrace her heart. But then Ivy
remembered the steel she had witnessed last night. The
illusion. The pretend. Sicili knew what she was doing. She
had made a choice last night to embrace her duty as the
only daughter of George Windihill.

She set the invitation on the table. Stared at it. Her
parents stared at her, awaiting her response.

"Only George Windihill would think to make an invitation into a letter," she muttered.

"Try to see the bright side," Charlotte said.

"What bright side? He's an awful man." She crumpled the
invitation and tossed it on the floor.

"Whatever do you mean, Ivy?" Charlotte asked.

"I found out last night. George Windihill forces Sicili to
get married."

William showed a wholesome frown. "Forces?"

"If she refuses to form a union, he means to disinherit
her. Can you imagine such a cruel union? I thought *you
two* were cruel."

Charlotte huffed. "Now you know better." She returned
to her seat and shared a concerned look with William. "So,
is that why you came home so off? You faced her? And at
the Prattles ball no less?"

Ivy nodded. There was no point in hiding the truth. "Let's be honest, Mother: Haven't I always been off? Like a spoiled egg."

Charlotte refrained from arguing. She lifted her chin. "There it is," she said righteously. "All our worries put to rest. Cruel as the solution may be."

"All *your* worries, Mother. Mine have just begun."

A silent resolve came over Charlotte's face. Not fear, or shame, but constrained curiosity. Ivy could swear she saw love softening her mother's eyes. "Ivy, do you mean to say you fell in––"

"I mean to have a drink." In two long strides, she was at her father's liquor cabinet. She poured herself a glass of scotch and drank half of it right in front of them.

Charlotte watched her with those soft eyes and slumped shoulders, and Ivy realized she liked her mother better as an enemy. She was used to her mother nagging and prying and worrying. This side of Charlotte showing she cared, accepting her daughter for who she was, scared Ivy to the core.

"Do you need some tea, Ivy?" Charlotte asked. "I can bring it up."

She finished the glass. "This will do. I'm off to bed. Walking all day got me too much sun."

"What about supper? You might go hungry."

"I'm full on disappointment, Mother."

Charlotte moved to get up, but William reached across the table and stopped her. "Let her be, Charlotte," he said.

Ivy swept up the decanter of scotch and lumbered out of the dining room. In the hall, she paused once more.

Her mother sniffled. "Why would they send us an invitation at all? They know we are outcasts. And to say they are our *great friends*."

William sighed. "I think they mean to rub it in our face. I'm certain Francine Windihill already knew about Ivy and her preferences, and now with it all out in the open, she wants to make it clear that Sicili will not have her."

It was very well the cleverest and harshest thing her father had ever uttered, and it was abominably true.

In her room, Ivy drank until she fumbled around, bumping into bed posts and dressers and feeling as light as a feather. She caught a glimpse of herself in the mirror by the wardrobe and realized she was still dressed as the banker. He was a mess. Not a banker at all. He was a girl trying to be someone else so that the world hating her hurt less. She tore off the pinstriped suit. She threw the eyeglasses on the floor. She let her hair down and watched it sail over her shoulders. Down to a long shirt and bare legs, she stared at her drunken, crying self in the mirror.

"You have been thoroughly foolish, Ivy Ferthing," the banker said to her. "All this time you imagined Sicili Windihill, of all women, would see the light and fall in love with you. Not so, young creature, not so."

Twenty-One

A Pretty Fellow Falls in Love

Ivy spent the next month forgetting about Sicili. She pre-occupied herself by helping her father with his winemaking business, which had taken an insufferable toll due to Ivy's blackened reputation. Orders had trickled, locals had stopped raving about his wines, and those who hosted intimate parties scratched him off their list of suppliers. Charlotte took it the hardest. She continued to barricade in her room. William suffered it with a gruff laugh and bottled his harvest nonetheless, even though the only place of business who purchased from him was Madam Desiree's.

Ivy delighted in crushing clusters of grapes with her fists and imagining it was Lord Caraway's face she mashed.

One sunny day, she went along with her father to deliver a large order of last year's harvest to Madam Desiree's and dismally ran into Harriet Prattle, who stepped out of Mr. Stellaway's Fashions just as they dismounted the wagon.

"Yoo-hoo," Harriet said. She strutted up with an arm of parcels, as if she and Ivy were still friends. "Have you heard about Sicili Windihill's engagement?"

William shared a shrewd squint with Ivy as he passed her a crate of wine.

"Can't say I have," Ivy mumbled. She brushed past to set the crate down.

"How surprising," Harriet said, settling directly in Ivy's path. "Her engagement is the talk of Wiltshire."

Ivy grabbed another crate. "You made sure Wiltshire hates me, so naturally, no one talks to me anymore."

Harriet nursed a wounded expression. "I never told Wiltshire to hate you. I merely let them know who you truly are. I did you a favor, Ivy Ferthing."

Ivy exhaled. She stacked the crates and turned to Harriet, allowing all her exasperation to show in a frown, then she took her by the arms and moved her aside, then thought better of it and stepped close. She swept a wayward strand of hair behind Harriet's ear. "Is this what you wanted?" she said, loud enough for only Harriet to hear. "To replace her?"

Harriet froze.

"Careful. Mrs. Prattle," Ivy said, "I doubt you want to be seen conversing with a degenerate." Ivy motioned to the pedestrians who had paused on the sidewalk and created a large distance between Ivy and the wagon.

Contempt steeled Harriet's eyes as she stepped back and crossed the street with her wounded pride and her sea of parcels. William got back to it and handed Ivy another crate.

On the ride home, he cleared his throat. "You and Harriet used to be such fine friends."

Ivy chewed a blade of grass. "We were never friends, Father."

"Does that mean you and Sicili Windihill are *more* than friends?"

"Yes, it does."

Charlotte stood on the front pathway when they returned to Vineyard Estate. She waved a frantic handkerchief. A saddled horse nibbled the flowerbeds that lined the road to the barn. For half a second, Ivy's heart skipped a beat. Did the horse belong to Sicili Windihill?

Then she bit her lip and silenced her wild heart.

"What do you think she's up to, Father?"

William stopped the wagon in front of the house. "You had better go see."

"It looks ominous."

"Go on." He shoved her off the creaking wagon and rode off toward the refuge of the barn.

Charlotte hurried down the pathway. "Come quick, Ivy. Patrick Derby is in the drawing room."

"Patrick Derby? The lad I danced with at the Windihill's?"

She tried to get a view of the lad, but Charlotte pushed her up the stairs. "He has something to ask you."

"Patrick Derby is here for *me*?" She feigned a faint.

"Enough of that irksome behavior. You need to change, Ivy."

Charlotte rushed them straight to Ivy's room, where she proceeded to pull out Ivy's best dresses and set them out in a flutter of nerves.

"Is this *your* doing, Mother? It has you written all over it."

Charlotte huffed an insulted snort. "He came of his own will. I swore off trying to save you."

Ivy crossed her arms and legs as she watched Charlotte fret. "This is rather inconvenient," she said. "I was going to wander the vineyard and do some thinking."

"You cannot think and wander forever, girl. Neither will get you any further in life."

She winked. "That has yet to be determined."

"Pinch your cheeks." Charlotte did it for her. "And wear something glorious!" She scurried out of the room.

Ivy ignored the dresses. She brushed them off her bed and they fell into a heap on the floor. Instead, she set out the best of her male outfits. If Patrick Derby had something to ask her, he could ask while she stood in her finest outfit. She went with an elbow-patched tailcoat and paired it with ironed trousers.

She looked the part of a pretty fellow. In place of wearing a hat, she wore her hair down, letting it flow free and disastrous, riddled with twigs and dust from the road.

Charlotte would be horrified.

She walked into the drawing room with a cane and a saunter. Charlotte's hands flew to her mouth. Patrick rose and bowed. A huge smile spread across his freckled face, and his eyes twinkled with delight.

"How much did she pay you this time?" Ivy said to him.

"Not a penny, Miss Ferthing. I came because I wanted to see you."

The way he looked at her made her outfit feel paper thin.

Charlotte leaned against the sofa. "Oh, Ivy," she said. "I told you to change."

"I did."

Charlotte turned to Patrick. "I do apologize, Mr. Derby. I hope seeing her like this has not dampened your visit."

"Not at all," he said with a flourish as he swept up her hand and kissed it. "I saw her at the Prattle's ball."

Ivy chuckled. "You were there?"

"Everyone who is anyone was there, Miss Ferthing."

"As I hoped."

He smiled. "You were the talk of the night. You dismayed. You inspired."

She swished the compliments aside.

"The boy has something to say," Charlotte announced. "Shall I give you two some privacy?"

Patrick shook his head. A nervousness overcame his features and hands as he produced a wilted flower from his pocket and kneeled on one knee before Ivy.

She tried to pull him up, but his knee was firmly planted, and his face tilted up to meet hers. A kindness full of admiration beveled his eyes. "What society has done to you is cruel,

Ivy Ferthing, and I believe you deserve better. Will you allow me to help by marrying me?"

She stuttered, but words had no use, so she fell speechless for a good minute. For a good month, she had endeavored to forget Sicili Windihill, the woman who had enraptured her from the first moment she saw her at the Windihill's ball. Forgetting be damned. Pain be damned. She imagined Sicili in Patrick's place, and the image pinched her heart, made it burst with a warm pride. If Patrick was Sicili, Ivy would kneel and sweep her up in a kiss to mark the ages. But Patrick had too much hope in his eyes, and though it could be possible that he felt something for her, he was far too young and gentle to be throwing his life away for an unsavory.

Ivy kneeled and kissed his cheek. "Thank you, Patrick."

"Is that a yes?"

She patted his cheek. "That was a thorough no."

His eyes lowered to the flower. "Should I have brought a ring?"

"No. You did wonderfully."

"Then why are you thanking me?" A quiver threatened his voice.

She gave his shoulder a friendly squeeze. "Because you helped me realize how much I love her."

He laughed. That admiration danced in his eyes. "You love her?"

She nodded. "Inescapably."

His voice cracked. "Do you... do you think I will ever find what you have?"

"I know you will, Mr. Derby."

She smothered him in a hug and helped him up, even brushed off the pant leg he had dirtied for her, then she sent him on his way. He rode away with a dejected slope to his shoulders, but the lad would perk up in time.

When she returned, Charlotte sat in the parlor dabbing her eyes. "That was your second chance, Ivy."

She *tssked*. "Who said I wanted a second chance? I quite like this one."

"You ungrateful girl." Charlotte sniffled. "You might have entertained the idea."

The truth triumphed. It dashed formality. It had stayed in the shadows for far too long. "Have you learned nothing, Mother? I love her. Nothing can change that, and I will not settle for anyone but her."

Charlotte blinked. Her mouth opened in protest——closed. She went as white as a ghost, and then she appeared to accept what had stayed unsaid for far too long and stared into the flames of the fire crackling in the hearth.

"Then you shall suffer a great breaking, girl."

She knew her mother was right, and though she shuddered with the knowing of it, she cleared her throat and said, "I welcome it. I have never shied from what is necessary." Without another look at her foreboding mother, she went for William's top in the foyer and marched out of the front door.

"Where are you going?" Charlotte called out.

Ivy tipped the hat to the left. "I need a drink," she yelled in reply.

She purposefully forgot a mustache. If she was going to finally accept who she loved, then it was high time society accepted that Naughty Ivy lived in its midst.

***

Save for an old fellow petting a young tart in the corner, Madam Desiree's was empty. Eveline kept Ivy's glass full until dusk fell outside, and by then she felt weighty and grim and courageous all in the same heartbeat. She had a mind to swoop up her father's hat and walk to Windsworth Estate, but as soon as she stumbled up, the grey sky let forth barrels of rain.

A group of rowdy gents huddled in. "Pelting buckets out there," one of them howled. He slapped his drenched hat on the bar counter. "A round of girls to cheer us up, shall we?"

Eveline adjusted her cleavage and tended to them.

Ivy nursed her whiskey. One of the gents squeezed Eveline's backside, and she returned the gesture with a professional giggle. It was all a bit crass. Ivy sipped. She couldn't say she liked it anymore. Madama Desiree's––with its smoky, dark corners and lazy ambience––used to be her hideaway from the world. Now, it felt rather dingy, and rather a dark, sinister way to live out one's life. She poured herself another whiskey while the gents preoccupied Eveline and took a long swallow, then looked up as a lonesome, disheveled man barged into Madam Desiree's. With his suit buttoned in all the wrong places and grease coating his hair, he stumbled to a stool and sat next to her. She sniffed. *When was the last time he washed himself?* He flopped and faced her, showing her a heavy-lidded, lazy smile. She gagged. Given the smell coming off his breath, she knew he was already sloshed.

"Hell*oooo*," he slurred.

With a start, Ivy recognized him: the gentleman who had come to Sicili's rescue months ago at this very place, after Ivy had trapped her in the hall and forced a second kiss from her. She smiled at the memory.

"You," she said.

"Me?" He flopped a hand to his chest, patted it.

"Are you Princeton Evergreen?"

Princeton steadied himself against the bar counter. "The very one. Who are you, fella?"

"Ivan."

"Ivan. A pleasure. Shall we toast to us?"

She shrugged. "Why not?"

He lifted an empty glass. "To us, for coming to this godforsaken place to waste away. Does that make us brothers?"

"Well..."

"Comrades, then. Do you come for the girls?"

Ivy gave him a pat and thought it best to leave the poor fellow. After all, they were rivals for the same woman's heart, not comrades. He seemed to be in over his head. She got up to pay her bill and be off.

"Come on, you," he said. "We need to stick together, us brothers. We need support. Sit back down. Sit." He shoved her back into her chair and pressed a firm hand on her shoulder to see that she stayed put. He even grabbed her glass like it was his and sucked her whiskey back.

"I come for the girls," he said, "and the booze, and to forget. Been coming here every night since..." His eyes brimmed with angry tears. "I loved life before her. I loved riding horses."

Ivy clenched her jaw. She despised being manhandled, and she knew he was talking about Sicili. She played it cool, though. His heavy hand stayed on her shoulder.

"A nice hobby," she said.

"Not anymore. Drunkards are forbidden to compete. Can you believe they called me a drunkard?"

She peeled a finger from her shoulder. "Well––"

"Those bastards." He returned her glass, empty. "Have you heard the latest?"

She managed to lift his entire hand and return it to his own being. "Don't suppose I have," she said.

His lip quivered. "The-the love of my life is betrothed. Sicili Windihill. Up and betrothed to some Lord this or that."

She sighed. "I heard," she muttered.

"She's a floozy. A down right, dirty floozy."

"What did you call her?"

"I said..." He leaned in, gruff. "She's a dirty fucking floozy."

She braced herself. She was about to do something worthy of stupidity. Her heart rammed at her ribcage, spurring her on. She was tired of the brute breathing down on her with his hot, intoxicated stench. She was through with being pinned to her seat by one of Sicili's former lovers. She stopped thinking. A surge of power got hold of her. She threw the first punch, and her fist landed right on Princeton's beautiful nose. He stumbled off his chair and hit the ground with his shoulder.

"I said no trouble," Eveline shouted across the room.

"I was just leaving," Ivy said.

Princeton moaned. "Not so fast, you little bastard."

He got to his feet and steadied himself. With a gulp, she nursed her hand. He towered over her, drunk and provoked. Maybe it was the love she felt for Sicili. Maybe she knew there was no going back. Whatever it was, Ivy charged. She ran headfirst into him, circled his waist with her arms, and knocked him down, then pinned his neck between her legs and punched him as hard as she could.

"Take it back! Take back it or––"

"I can call that whore whatever I like," he roared.

He grabbed her by the back of her suit and flung her off him. She hit the side of a booth with a thud. By then a crowd had formed around them, and they were cheering Princeton on. "Get the bastard, get the bastard," they chanted.

Head pounding, she stumbled to her feet, but Princeton had the height and weight, and he trapped her. He lifted her by the shirt and raised her above the chanting crowd. He held her there with one arm.

Bloody spit dribbled down his chin. "Ready to die, fella?"

Eveline was yelling, "She's a girl, she's a girl!"

He smashed his knuckles across Ivy's cheek. Once, twice––a third, fourth, fifth. Ivy lost count. She tried to strike back, but Princeton had lost himself in the violence. He threw her on the ground and bent down to do more damage, hand lifted, when his eyes widened in shock.

Her hat had fallen off during the toss, and her red hair flowed free.

Eveline pulled and pushed at Princeton. "She's a girl, you brute," she shouted. "Get off her! Get off her!"

Princeton backed away. Shock registered on his bloodied face. "A girl?" He spluttered. "In here?"

"What in all of Wiltshire is a girl doing dressed up as a man?" yelled one of the men in the crowd.

"She must be Ivy Ferthing," another gent said. "It looks like her red, naughty hair."

The outraged voices dinned. Eveline kneeled and pressed a rag to Ivy's cheek.

"Ivy? Ivy?" Concern etched her voice. She grabbed Ivy's hand, and that was the last thing Ivy could stay conscious for.

Twenty-Two

The Penniless Lad

Sicili dreaded turning twenty and three.

Time had caught up to her, and her eternal doom await-ed her in less than twenty-four hours. George had made an embarrassing ordeal out of her birthday. He reeled about Windsworth, shouting orders at Wilber, and decorating the place in gold statues of naked regal men as if it was his birthday and not hers. He had gone mad for the last month arranging her birthday ball––the "ball to end all balls" he called it. She cringed. Every chance he could, he would jab her with, "Have you decided on the one, Sicili? Time has run out, I fear."

"You fear nothing, Father," she had assured him, "not even your own reflection."

"Be certain. Be concise. Should you pick the wrong suitor, there will be no going back."

"All of them are wrong."

"Even Lord Caraway?"

"Especially Lord Caraway. I have no choice in the matter, thanks to you."

Each time they had the exchange, he laughed mirthfully. "You make a valid point, my angel."

She used to like being called an angel by him. Now she hat-ed it. She wanted to find a hole and disappear into it. But, no, not the important Sicili Windihill. Not the diamond of Wilt-shire. She had to dazzle and beguile, temp and charm. Ladies who stood to inherit lavish mansions and endless wealth were never allowed to shirk their duties.

She sighed at her reflection. She played with the gold detail on her dress. She missed Ivy.

They had not spoken or seen each other since the Prattle's ball. A whole month without running into each other. It felt like a lifetime. She stared at herself in her vanity mirror, remembering the last words she had spoken to Ivy. *"You have wasted your feelings on me, Miss Ferthing."* She hated those words. The memory of them made her uncomfortably hot. She wished she could rewind time and take them back. She dashed her cheeks with powder to hide the hue of emotion Ivy caused.

A knock came at her door.

"Who is it?"

"Wilber, Miss Windihill."

"Come in."

Wilber opened her door but kept to the hall. "Lord Caraway has arrived. Breakfast is being served."

"Wilber, how do I look? Be honest."

Wilber cleared his throat. "You look flustered."

"I thought so."

"You should know, Miss Windihill. I caught a banker with petite shoulders and bright green eyes in the garden the day after the Prattle's ball. Hiding in the petunias. I meant to tell you."

Her chest squeezed. "A banker?"

"With a sharp nose and quick wit."

"What was this banker doing?"

"Watching Windsworth, I assume. For the sight of someone special, perhaps. If that helps your flustered state."

A smile bloomed. "It does."

"I should have told you, but you were out riding with Lord Caraway. When you came home, you went straight to your room. I thought it best to tell you at a more opportune moment."

"It was good of you to tell me now. Thank you, Wilber. Tell Mother I shall be down in a moment."

He nodded and shut the door. She looked at her reflection with a new confidence. Her eyes looked brighter, less glossy, and dull. The smile grew. She brushed the powder off her cheeks and let them burn vigorously.

Lord Caraway chatted with her mother in the breakfast parlor. He had become far too comfortable in the last month. A worn old couch. George sat in the far corner; his nose stuck in the *Wiltshire Post*.

"Good morning, darling," Francine said. "You look especially fresh. The last time I saw you glowing must have been months ago." Francine gave George a side glance. He failed to note it. He was far too engrossed in the morning news.

Lord Caraway rose and planted a kiss on Sicili's cheek.

"I have a game of croquet arranged for us out back," he said. "Your mother is going to keep score."

"How wonderful," she said, feigning delight. "Will you play, Mother?"

"Not without George helping me with the shots. Croquet was never my game. George is wonderful at it. Of course, he refuses to put his paper down, so he shall be of no use."

George let out a stupendous laugh and slapped his knee. He continued reading, neglecting to share the reason for his enthusiasm.

"You have an audience, Father," Sicili said.

He looked up. "Do I?"

"What is funny enough to ignore your family and guest over?"

He wiped his eye. "Your friend," George said, not setting the paper down. "That pleasantly ridiculous Ivy Ferthing."

Sicili's cheeks flared. "We were never friends," she said.

"They were never friends, George," Francine echoed.

Lord Caraway arched an eyebrow.

George laughed all the harder. "For the better, I think. She made her way into a scandalous article."

"Unsurprisingly," Francine mumbled.

"She has?" Sicili said, not able to disguise her concern.

Lord Caraway shot her a glance.

"Read it to us, George," Francine said.

In a thunderous voice, he read the title first. It was all Sicili needed to hear.

Miss Ivy Ferthing Impels Mayhem. The rumors about Miss Ivy Ferthing have circled Wiltshire for many a year, entertaining the good citizens of our countryside, who have historically reacted with confusion and the odd roll of the eyes. Now, however, we have evidence to believe the rumors are more than scandalous talk: they are based in fact, as has been revealed in a disastrous turn of events at the local Madam Desiree's. Princeton Evergreen was soberly enjoying a pint of beer when a skinny fellow claiming the name of Ivan came at him with fists high. Ivan beat Mr. Evergreen mercilessly, then fled the scene after revealing himself as Ivy Ferthing in disguise.

"I've never seen a woman so intoxicated," a frequent patron said of the event. "Miss Ferthing was aggressive and not in command of herself. The fight was terrible to watch."

Miss Ferthing was chased out of Madam Desiree's by a pair of peace officers and, after much struggle, taken into custody. For the curious reader's information, Miss Ferthing has been banned from Madam Desiree's. Whether she has been forbidden to dress the part of a man remains to be seen.

The room fell still. George laughed in great, windy gusts while the others shared looks and shifted uncomfortably.

"It says here that Princeton Evergreen was the source," George continued, after catching his breath. "Did he court you a while back, Sicili?"

"Hardly," Sicili said.

"He was the one who proposed," Francine chimed in.

"Ah yes––the poor fellow," George said. He slapped the paper on the table. "How was that for morning news? Ivy Ferthing is an endless wheelhouse of scandal. A wonder that William Ferthing stayed afloat for so long with such a daughter. What do you think, Lord Caraway?"

Lord Caraway shrugged. "Merely entertaining. I cannot say I appreciate the surprise of it. Scandal does not bode with me." He looked at Sicili in a curious way. "You look flustered," he said to her.

She flushed under his gaze. "How hot it is in here."

"Sicili, darling, it is only the morning," Francine said.

"Are you not hot?" she asked Lord Caraway.

His smile carried no mirth. "I find it quite cool."

She snatched the paper from her father and read over the article. She had to see it for herself. Why would Ivy attack Princeton Evergreen without a cause? Ivy was rash and non-sensical and against the rules, yes, but she was far from violent. She would have been provoked. Sicili rolled up the paper and tucked it underarm. She wouldn't know a moment's peace until she paid Ivy a visit. The girl's name had been drug about the mud of Wiltshire far too much and for far too long.

"I have to see her," she said.

"I thought you two were never friends," Lord Caraway reminded her.

She rose in a rustle of formulaic layers. Her corset pinched. "*Friends* is an oversimplification, my Lord."

Lord Caraway's jaw dropped. He stared dumbly at her before realizing his gaping mouth. "What about our croquet game?"

"Practice while I'm away. I doubt you shall miss me."

"Sicili, darling––"

"Do not call me *darling*, Lord Caraway. We both know this is a business arrangement."

Francine sipped her tea. She looked at George, who raised his white brows.

"I can play the game with you," George bellowed. "Count me in."

Lord Caraway followed her into the foyer. His relaxed confidence had shifted into a constrained attitude. She wanted to tear her corset off. Breathing had suddenly become so laborious. She needed fresh air. Gallons of it.

Lord Caraway helped her with a shawl and hat. Sicili noticed a tightness in his jaw.

"Our arrangement is important to me, Sicili," he said.

"I liked you better when you were indifferent, Lord Caraway."

He smiled unpleasantly. "This business with Ivy Ferthing tempts me to call it off."

She tilted her chin. "Go ahead. A hundred suitors will be at my birthday tomorrow, all ready to pluck me out of my father's open arms. Walk away and I will not follow you."

He caught her wrist as she turned from him and pulled her in. It was a boldness she had not expected from him.

"Sicili," he said in a whisper. "There is something you should know. You have become my latest hobby."

"You said women are too tedious to waste your time on."

"Tedious women are too tedious. A woman who is lost..." he brushed a lock of her hair behind her ear "...now that is a beautiful thing."

She jerked her wrist free. "Do not expect our life together to be good, Lord Caraway."

"I expect it to be cruel––both of us denying the one thing we want the most."

Ivy. She wanted Ivy more than air. More than layers. More than rules and formalities. She left Lord Caraway in the morning light with half of his face shaded by the sun. She couldn't bring herself to look into his eyes.

***

She knocked vigorously on the Ferthing's front door. Ominous clouds gathered over Vineyard Estate. Thunder cracked in the distance. She had galloped as fast as she could from Windsworth on her father's finest horse.

Mrs. Ferthing answered. The woman looked thinner than the last time Sicili had seen her at the Dainty's croquet tournament. Her cheeks were sunken and her eyes a defiant glassy, but her cheeks had a glow that appeared new.

Charlotte kept the door slightly ajar and failed to invite Sicili in for refuge from the rain.

"A surprise to see you at our front door, Miss Windihill," she said. Her lips thinned. "To what do I owe your stooping to our vineyard?"

Sicili endeavored to be as polite as possible. "I came to see Ivy."

Charlotte's eyes narrowed. "She was gone at first light."

"In this weather?"

"Ivy has never minded the weather."

"Do you know where she is?"

Charlotte moved to close the door. "I never know the whereabouts of that girl."

"I read the paper," Sicili said. She placed a foot against to the door to keep it ajar.

Charlotte scoffed. "Is that a threat?"

"No, of course not." The words came out heavy. "I worry about her. That's what I mean to say."

Charlotte paused. The defiance in her eyes briefly softened, and she showed Sicili a disarmed smile. "If you truly care for her, Miss Windihill, you will leave her be unless you absolutely mean to embrace her. My Ivy has suffered enough at the hands of a society run by social diamonds such as yourself. Good day."

"Will you tell her I--"

Charlotte shut the door on Sicili in mid-sentence. She deserved it, she realized, as she blinked at the cold grains of wood. She had earned the hate of Ivy's parents. She felt deeply for their daughter, and she had done nothing about it. She had left her in the moonlight of the Prattle's sitting room. If Ivy never spoke to her again, she would accept her rejection, but before that happened, she had to try. She rode around the back to see if she could get a glimpse of Ivy through one of the windows. The bristling vineyard waved to her, but there was no sign of a girl with red, unruly hair wearing baggy trousers and an oversized tailcoat.

Sicili swallowed the feeling of defeat.

The rain jabbed her like frozen needles. She steered her horse back toward Windsworth. She would try again once the rain cleared. The clouds followed her, and she surrendered to them. She opened her arms and let them soak her to the bone. It felt like justice. A break in the weather came a mile ahead. Patches of golden, warm sun touched the fields. In one of the patches, she made out a lone figure, backlit by the watery light. She shaded her eyes and saw a penniless lad, marching with stooped shoulders against the deluge.

"Ivy," Sicili whispered. She flicked the reins and galloped full force toward the figure.

"Ivy," she called out.

Ivy turned. A willful smiled formed on her bruised lips.

"Your face," Sicili gasped.

Ivy's right eye was swollen and black. Her left cheek was bruised as well, and her bottom lip thick with a cut. Sicili reared the horse to a halt in front of Ivy.

"Get on my horse," she said.

Ivy grinned. "Is that a demand?"

"Yes."

Ivy gave an indignant huff. Despite the grin, she looked thin and tired. She looked up at Sicili with one green eye. Sicili held out her hand, and Ivy took it, mounting the horse in one graceful leap.

"You can hold on," Sicili said.

"Are you sure?"

"Otherwise, you might fall off."

A long pause followed. Ivy rested her head on Sicili's shoulder before wrapping her arms around her waist. She linked her wrists against Sicili's corset and let out a long sigh. Rain clouds moved overhead and pelted them. She could have stayed there all day, embraced by Ivy Ferthing, but then she felt Ivy shivering against her back.

She kicked her horse into a trot.

"Where are you taking me?" Ivy asked.

"Somewhere dry."

The inn happened to be one of George Windihill's early investments. He bought it years ago and never put any work into it. It was an old log building at the edge of Westbury, secluded by a rash of tall trees. It looked ready to fall over. The innkeeper, a stout old fellow, stared at Ivy while Sicili arranged for the room.

"Do I know you?" he asked Ivy.

"By now, you should," Ivy said.

Sicili took her hand. "Never mind."

They roomed on the second floor. Number six. Sicili unlocked it and led Ivy in. The bed boasted numerous pillows and a cozy, handmade quilt. A small vanity stood on one side and a bureau on the other. The window had a view of the main street of Westbury.

"More cozy than comfortable," Ivy said.

Sicili laughed. Being alone with Ivy felt like sunlight despite the gloom outside. "Oh, do hold your tongue, Ivan Miller."

Ivy's grin could sear her soul. "I imagine all couples in danger of detection come here."

Sicili removed Ivy's cap. Her red hair cascaded down and took Sicili's breath away.

"Much better," she whispered. She pulled off Ivy's dripping tailcoat. All she wore underneath was a soaked, loose-fitting tunic. Somehow, it took Sicili off guard, made her cheeks rosy, because although she had seen Ivy down to her underthings, she had never seen her so vulnerable and wet. Ivy whimpered and shivered. Sicili wrapped the quilt around her and hugged her close.

"I read the paper," she confessed.

"Everyone has by now."

"Why did you let yourself you get into it with Princeton Evergreen?"

"He provoked me."

"Ivy, he happens to be a man. A real man."

"So I hear."

"He should have been jailed for what he did to you, not the other way around. You are just a girl."

"*Just*? Am I just a girl to you?"

She cupped Ivy's bruised cheek. "To me, you are an out-right, perverse, distinguished fool."

Ivy laughed. The joyful feeling of her chest laughing against Sicili's put the world right.

"If I was anything but foolish," Ivy said with a daring spark to her eyes, "would be in love with me?"

Sicili laughed in return. "Do push your luck harder."

"I fear I already have."

"You certainly have. The *Wiltshire Post* has it out for you. What will you do?"

Ivy pushed Sicili's sopping hair behind her ears, behind her shoulders. "I think I might move to London. There's bound to be more people like me there."

"There are people like you here," Sicili said, touching the patchwork on the quilt, then tenderly touching Ivy's cracked lip.

"One, maybe."

"One who is just not as brazen as you."

"That word again. *Just.*"

Sicili kissed Ivy's black eye, as softly as she could. "Try not to judge me for being a coward."

"I do."

Sicili drew her in, like she had been wanting to do all along. Her lips found Ivy's like mist finds the hillside. Gentle sensation washed over her as Ivy pulled her in and wanted more, letting the quilt fall as she hugged Sicili's waist, and the shivering of wet clothes grew warm and their heartbeats mighty.

If only they had surrendered sooner. If only she had been less proud. If only they had filled the distance with warmth and touch.

They would have had more time together.

Twenty-Three

A Great Breaking

Ivy woke up to the sound of Sicili's heart. After kissing every inch of her, she had dozed off in Sicili's arms. Sicili's heart had a lovely beat to it, with the odd skip here and there. She planted a kiss on the curve of her collarbone and Sicili gave a grumpy moan, her eyes still closed.

"A happy birthday to you, Miss Windihill," Ivy whispered. She nuzzled into Sicili's neck.

Sicili groaned. "Has this dreadful day truly come?"

"It has yet to be dreadful for me," she said, and pecked Sicili's nose with kisses.

Sicili pulled her into a kiss, and they got lost in the moment. The morning sun peeked in through the window and warmed the edge of their tangled bodies.

Sicili paused for air. "Were you lurking in my garden the other day?" she asked in a whimsical voice. "Wilber said he came across a pretty little banker hiding in the petunias."

"That was Mr. Fletcher," Ivy lied. "Besides, that was three weeks ago, not the other day."

"Oh, a Mr. Fletcher. I should have known." She pressed a soft hand on Ivy's bruised cheek. "How will I keep up with you?"

"Keep up? Impossible, malady."

Sicili sighed. She rolled over and tried to run fingers through her tangled hair. "What time is it?"

Ivy grinned. "Does it matter? I plan to spend all day with you." She kissed her hand and laced their fingers.

Sicili pulled free of Ivy's grip with a soft sigh. "I have to get ready," she whispered, pulling the quilt off. She got up and stretched.

Ivy stayed in the bed and watched, wishing they could stay in this hideaway inn all day and laugh together and fall asleep again in each other's arms.

"I want to stay," Sicili said, lazily picking up her clothes. The undergarments. The dress. The corset.

"Then stay."

"Mother will be wondering what happened to me."

"Let her wonder."

"Oh, Ivy," she said with a laugh, ignoring her plea. "Our clothes are still wet."

"It was pouring, remember?"

"I shall be shivering all the way home." Her hair was a beautiful mess. It fell in frazzled waves down her naked back and touched the dimples just below her waist. Ivy sighed. She could look at her for days and still not be satisfied.

"What are you going to tell your father?" she asked.

Sicili looked back at Ivy like she had just woken from a long, peaceful dream. She blinked, and the dream in her eyes slowly evaporated. "What do you mean, Ivy?"

"About Lord Caraway."

"What about him?"

"That... you changed your mind."

Sicili turned toward the light of the window. Her naked silhouette disappeared under layer after layer of formalities. She got lost in the layers and forgot to reply.

"You are going to tell him?" Ivy prompted.

"Of course not," she said softly.

Ivy sat. She watched Sicili struggle with the corset. Her stomach warmed with regret and her heart ached. "Are you going through with it?"

A long silence hung between them.

"I have to," Sicili finally managed.

"You plan to marry a man you have no love for?"

"It cannot be about love, Ivy. Not for us."

"What is it about, then?"

"I *have* to marry him. I face a union or disinheritance. You knew last night, so do not look at me like that."

"Like what?"

"Like I just pulled your heart out."

Ivy pulled the quilt around her arms and covered her chest. It has suddenly got quite cold, and she shivered with a revolution. "Mother was right." She laughed, and there was no warmth there, only regret and bitterness. She rubbed her eyes, willing the tears not to come. "I should have listened to her. I hardly believed I would ever say those words. But she was right. You are my *great* breaking."

"What does that mean?"

"Figure it out." Her jaw set.

Sicili's brow farrowed. She failed to deny it. She said nothing. The silence hurt. The silent truth. She turned her back. "Will you help me with this damn corset?"

"Corsets were never my strong-suit, Miss."

"Why are you calling me *Miss?* I dare say I am more than that to you."

"What should I call you? Secret lover?" Ivy threw the covers off and picked up her own wet clothes. She shrugged them on.

With a reserved silence, Sicili abandoned her attempts at the corset and drew close, but Ivy backed against the door. She fiddled with the knob.

"This is far from simple, Ivy," Sicili said.

She bundled her hair into the fisher's cap. Once again, she was a penniless lad. Once again, she felt invincible, tucked away from society. "I punched Princeton for you. He called you a floozy, and I clobbered him. The funny thing is, he was right. You *are* a floozy. You have seduced every man from here to London. Congratulations. You even seduced me."

Sicili's eyes teared up. Ivy swallowed the acid words. She didn't mean them. She wanted to take them back. She knew she shouldn't have used them. She was being vindictive and hurtful, but it was the truth. She was in love with the pretentious Sicili Windihill––a woman too in love with herself to know how to love in return.

Sicili sniffled. "Do come to the ball. I need you there."

She let the rest of the acid out. "All you need is your reputation and your affluence. We both know that." Then she left Sicili half-naked and slammed the door on her stricken face. The number six sign creaked.

The innkeeper at the front desk raised a set of tired eyebrows as Ivy passed.

"How was your stay, Mr.–"

"Miller," Ivy said. "The room was just fine."

He narrowed his eyes at her. Ivy took her leave before he had time to put the pieces together. She trudged all the way home with a heavy, pounding heart.

Twenty-Four

A Mother's Love

Charlotte, vexed, sat in the drawing room. When the front door opened, she inhaled, not realizing she had been holding her breath. The fire beside her roared, and the teacup in hand had long since cooled.

"Ivy?" she called.

The door shut with a heaviness. A long silence followed.

"Here, Mother," Ivy said from the foyer. She chose not to venture into the light of the drawing room.

"Where have you been, girl?"

"To hell and back," Ivy said.

"You had us worried sick."

Despair thickened Ivy's voice. "Forgive me, Mother."

Charlotte softened her tone. It had happened. The inevitable. She had known it was only a matter of time. "Will you come in and tell me about it?"

"I'm tired," Ivy replied, and then trudged heavily up the stairs.

Charlotte set her tea down with a sigh. She went to the kitchen and put a fresh kettle of water over the fire. As the kettle came to a boil, the wailing started. Deep, hard wails from her precious Ivy. Charlotte listened to them for a good hour. She knew a broken heart when she heard it. She set a tray with a teapot, saucer, and cup. She filled the pot with steaming water and added tea leaves. She sliced up an orange and arranged it nicely on a plate. Oranges were light and zesty, the perfect remedy for heartache.

She delivered the tray to Ivy's room. Ivy was curled into a ball on her bed.

"Mother, I'm not in the mood for a scolding," she moaned.

"I brought you a pot of tea."

Ivy sniffled back her sobs while Charlotte poured her a cup. What a mess of heartache the girl looked, with her black eye, tear-streaked face, and runny nose. What a precious mess. Ivy sipped her tea while Charlotte swept her red, sloppy hair off her swollen cheeks.

"You have to get ready for the ball," Charlotte said.

"We never received an invite."

"All the more reason to go."

Ivy started weeping all over again. "Not like this, Mother, not like this."

Charlotte cupped her cheeks, forcing Ivy to look at her. "You are going to that ball, Ivy Ferthing."

"I'm tired of fighting you, Mother. I cannot do it anymore. I'm done for. I'm through."

Charlotte shook her head. "You are going to that ball for Sicili Windihill, not for me. You are going to show her what she is giving up."

Ivy gave a hiccup of surprise. "Do you mean that, Mother?"

"I do, my Ivy, I truly do." She took Ivy's hand in hers. "I always knew you loved women. I was so worried when you were younger. I despised the idea of you being an outcast, and I let it drive me to a certain madness... the desperation to change you." She wiped Ivy's tears. "If you want to be an outcast, nothing I say or do can change your mind. You, my daughter, are a pariah. And I shall not be George Windihill."

Ivy hugged her so tight it felt surreal. Mother and daughter had never been natural at affection. It was William's area of expertise, not Charlotte's.

"Forgive me for ruining you and Father," Ivy said. "I never mean to."

"We needed some ruination. It helped us see clearer." She stood, a plan forming in her mind's eye, and pulled Ivy up with her. "Now. Shall we start with your hair? Would you like it down?"

Ivy's hiccups were persistent. "I get to decide?"

"Go on."

"Down. I want to wear it down, Mother."

"And what are you going to wear? Something irresistible, I think."

A beautiful light dazzled in her Ivy's eyes. Charlotte realized, perhaps a little too late, that it had always been there, waiting for her to fetch it and make it glow and never cease. She preferred that light over seeing Ivy heartbroken. With a deep breath, she let Ivy choose one of her brother's old suits and spent the rest of the afternoon tailoring it to fit Ivy's curves. In the end, her daughter looked quite dashing, save for the battered face that made her look like a convict.

When the clock struck eight, mother and daughter, hand in hand, exited Vineyard Estate, each feeling nervous in her own way but smiling at one another, because without each other, who were they?

William waited outside in the carriage, with his own grand smile set in place.

"There you are," he said to Ivy, smiling ear to ear with delight. "You look absolutely yourself, my dear."

Ivy was acting rather shyer than usual. Perhaps it was all the crying. "You think so, Father?"

"I have always thought so."

He gave her a wink, then a peck on the cheek, and helped her up into the carriage.

Charlotte watched her daughter settle herself in her seat, her hearth warm with the same light that played in Ivy's eyes. She smiled at her husband, and he smiled back. And she knew, then, that she had everything she needed.

"And you, my love," William said, turning to his wife, "you are as splendid and selfless as they come."

"Oh stop, William. Far from it. I have a world of wants and frets."

"And yet have given them up for the happiness of our Ivy."

She sighed. It felt powerful and real. "What else could I do?"

He helped her into the carriage, and the ride to Windsworth was undertaken with much lightness and only a small feeling of dread. What would Sicili Windihill do when she saw Ivy Ferthing done up exactly as Ivy?

Twenty-Five

A Ball to End All Balls

As she remembered last night at the inn, Sicili endeavored
to pull herself together. She tried to breathe properly in her
corset, but all she could think about was Ivy's hands on her,
Ivy's kisses on her neck, Ivy lying naked next to her. She
glared, teary-eyed, at her reflection in the vanity mirror. She
hated who she saw––the little girl who had grown up alone,
controlled by her father's power and society's expectations. It
was clear, now, after last night: this was not who she wanted
to be.

She wanted Ivy.

She opened one of the vanity drawers and found the neat
box she had put there last month. A gold locket sparkled
inside. Delicate and simple. She placed the locket around her
neck. It matched her red dress. Red for bitterness. Red for
anger. Red for passion.

Francine waited in the foyer. A perplexed expression pulled
at her brow. "You look beautiful, darling," she said as Sicili
descended the stairs.

"I feel trapped."

"I am sorry, Sicili. I half-expected George to call this sham
off."

"He is a selfish man, lest we forget."

Francine sighed. "Are you ready?"

Tears pricked her eyes. "I will never be ready for this."

They walked arm in arm to the ballroom and the nervous, awaiting crowd. Francine stroked her hand, but the feeble attempt at comfort far from soothed Sicili's pounding heart. She was about to give her freedom away, and there was nothing good about giving one's freedom away for the sole purpose of money. She touched the locket, wondering, romantically, if Ivy would attend. Her absence would save them further heartache, yet Sicili could not help wanting her there.

Was it selfish for her to want to look into Ivy's eyes when she announced the doom of her future husband?

The ballroom overflowed with chattering, glittering, expectant guests who turned, almost as one, to greet the reluctant Miss Windihill.

"How glorious you are, Miss Windihill."

"You do surpass all."

"How marvelously excited you must be."

They sounded far away, behind a veil, as if she were in a dream, trying desperately to wake up next to Ivy. She felt the urge to yank away from Francine and run. *How marvelously abhorred I am*, she wanted to shout. Francine had slipped a hand around Sicili's waist and laced her other hand in Sicili's. She propelled her daughter forward, into the jaws of a society that planned to swallow her whole by the end of the night.

She felt ready to faint from the tightness of her corset and the overwhelming attention. All eyes were on her. Most of the compliments came from the male sex, save for the clever, "You look like an angel, Miss Windihill," from Harriet Prattle.

Francine guided her from the frays of the crowd and into the utmost middle, where she found it hard to breathe. Air. She needed air. She felt like a showpiece at her father's most extravagant scheme to date.

George had gone mad with the decor. Panels of chiffon hung from the ceiling. Naked male statues lined the walls of the ballroom, each holding out a wanting hand. In the center of the dance floor, a singular female stature dressed in a thin layer of fabric stood alone. On display. She glowered. Polished chandeliers dripped gold candle wax. Not the safest idea, but that was George's way. He cared nothing for the danger, as long as the ballroom looked exactly the way he wanted it to.

Sicili searched the crowd for him and narrowed her eyes at the farthest end of the ballroom. At the moment, he chatted up a group of nervous gentlemen, gabbing on about "Sicili, oh my angel Sicili––yes, yes, she will make a smart wife. She on your guards, gentleman. She is a clever little thing."

Overhearing him, Sicili scowled and rolled her eyes. If she had her way, she would lop off every last one of their heads with her cleverness. In the corner, a pyramid of wine glasses sparkled at her.

"Mother, I need a drink."

"Be careful, Sicili."

"I have always been careful. I will always be careful. And it has destroyed me, Mother." She said it as bitterly as she felt. She wanted it to sink in. "If I do happen to drink too much because of this horrid ordeal, leave me to my ruin."

Francine gave her a pout, but quickly got caught up in conversation with a Miss Beacon.

She headed straight for the pyramid. Lord Caraway, dressed in his finest attire with slicked-back hair, intercepted her.

"Going for the wine already, darling?" he dared to ask.

"I told you yesterday. Do not call me *darling*."

"I must have forgotten, sometime between waiting for you and waiting some more."

She brushed past him. He followed. She snatched up the first wine glass and guzzled its contents in seconds. He watched her, his confidence ebbing.

"How was your rendezvous with Ivy Ferthing?" he asked once she grabbed a second glass. "I waited until after eight before giving up. Your mother made excuses for you, but I am no fool. I take it you were preoccupied."

"I was."

"By Miss Ferthing?"

Sicili cleared her throat. "Yes," she whispered.

"I resent being used."

"How funny. You seem to have no problem with using my womb for the growth of your offspring, and for such a small settlement."

Defiant sparks darkened his gaze. "We agreed fifty-thousand a year was well worth your time."

"I changed my mind. The usage of my womanhood is priceless."

His loosened cravat pinched at his throat. Ran a hand through his hair. He teetered on the edge of composure.

"The amount never mattered, did it?" He picked up a glass of his own. "You were never going to go through with it, were you?" He held her gaze. "You are *too* lost."

"*Too* lost? Is that possible?"

"I daresay, you manage it seamlessly."

"If you think me seamless, we truly have nothing in common."

"We can agree on that. I came tonight to tell you the arrangement is off. What I thought was beautiful about you is truly poisonous."

"You are the poisonous one, Lord Caraway. You are the one who is going to die obsessed with yourself––rich, indifferent, and alone. To think I was going to marry the replica of my father."

"Careful, Sicili. You are your father's daughter." He kissed her knuckles with what confidence he had left. "Best of luck to you."

If she had been asked, she would have admitted to not being surprised by Lord Caraway bowing out at the last possible moment. They shared an indifference. It was the foundation of their attachment, and indifference did not care who it wounded. Her indifference had goaded him on. It watched as he paid his farewells to George and Francine. They would have destroyed each other, and she could not live a life of destruction, not now, not after she had tasted love.

Francine politely said goodbye to Lord Caraway, then shot Sicili a vexed frown.

What happened? she mouthed.

Sicili raised her glass and shrugged.

The ballroom teemed with testosterone. There were plenty of men to take his place, plenty who smiled nervously at her, plenty who would never make anything close to the impression Ivy had. Ivy was wholly her own. These men were lost, more lost than Sicili, and they looked to her for validation. It sickened her.

She finished the wine and picked up another.

The plenty included Princeton Evergreen––the last man she had expected to see. He staggered about, clearly drunk. He found the table holding a grand birthday cake printed with the ironic words "Angel of mine, captured by the light". *Captured by the darkness*, it should have said. Princeton leaned against the table and looked ready to eat the cake with his fingers. His eyes were bleary from too much wine or not enough sleep; his trousers were scuffed at the knees and his shoes unmatched. This Princeton was not the man she had met three months ago, and she discovered that, instead of hating him for what he had done to Ivy, she pitied him.

She approached him. "Princeton?"

He smiled at her lazily.

"What are you doing here?" she asked.

"I received an invitation."

"Yes, but––"

"I still have a viable chance, do I not?"

She could not be so cruel as to tell him the truth, so she changed the subject. "What in all of Wiltshire happened to you?"

"Love."

She scoffed. "Love is old news."

"Love is wicked."

"Indeed, it can be, but not if you find the right person to love." It slipped out with genuine inflection. She scanned the room for Ivy as she said it.

"And I suppose you have, with all this madness."

She touched the locket. The cold metal against her fingers kept her sane. "I think I have," she said.

"Is it too bold to hope that person is me?"

She nodded.

He deflated.

"Forgive me for the way I treated you, Princeton. I should have been clearer about my intentions. The truth is, I was lost."

Princeton took the truth quite well. He staggered over to the pyramid and stared at it. He reached for a glass in the middle and the pyramid toppled over, onto itself and onto Princeton. Glass upon glass of disaster. George rushed over with flailing arms. Princeton stood there with wide, intoxicated eyes.

"By god, fellow," was all George could say.

"Did you not expect it, Father?" she said, hiding a smile. "I did."

***

As the night progressed, and the dancing started, Sicili turned down hand after hand for the comforts of wine and let a feeling of immense pain settled over her heart. She missed Ivy. After tonight, she knew, she would always miss Ivy.

"There you are, Sicili," Francis Perrycot said, coming up and snatching the wine from her hands. "How many of these have you had?"

"This is the sixth... I think."

"Oh dear," said Francis. "Have you been crying again?"

"Thinking, mostly."

"And where has that got you?"

"Nowhere."

He fished for a handkerchief. "Listen, Sicili, I have been thinking for years, and 'tis a terrible business thinking too long and too hard over things you cannot change."

She sniffled into the initialed cloth. "Thinking is for the dogs."

"Come. Let us dance away our sorrows." He held out his hand.

Francis was an amiable dance partner. He knew all the steps and had a quiet flair of his own. Dancing with him was like dancing with a friend. He refuted the part of a superior male intent on winning her hand. She felt his equal in his arms.

"By the bye," he said in her ear, "I came for the party, not the announcement. I found myself a new man. You and Ivy have inspired me."

She laughed for the first time all night. "How are we inspiring? I plan to marry a stranger, and Ivy is a criminal."

"So I hear." He laughed. "Is suits her. It appears she has stepped into her own." He brushed a strand behind her ear. "You, however, are dismal. Is this what you want?"

"I thought I could do it."

They circled the dance floor twice more and suddenly Francis grew sober. He leaned in again with a serious expression. "I was once engaged to a lovely Miss Boadice. She was lovely. My father had arranged our attachment and I could not bear being the one to break her fragile, lovely heart. I did, eventually, once I harnessed the courage that had been raging up inside me. And guess what––it was a great deal easier than I imagined it."

"Was she heartbroken?"

"Indefinitely. But when I told her, I noticed a look in her eye... I think she was relieved. I think she knew all along. She preferred a broken heart to a bitter, unhappy life as my wife. I never would have satisfied her."

Sicili had to smile. "What a fine storyteller you are, Francis."

"Just because you are human, my dear, does not make you less inspiring. I see a love in your eyes. You do love her, yes?"

She felt as though a soft, bright light were shining from her.

"There," Francis said. He could see the light as well. "You admitted to it. That is the hardest part."

"Where do I go from here?"

"Now that is a riddle. Perhaps the greatest riddle of our lives. I have yet to discover that answer for myself."

They danced another two sets. They laughed and chatted like old friends. She caught George watching her with stupendous delight. Determined not to let her father steal what joy she had left; she stuck her tongue out at him. His white eyebrows scrunched with disapproval.

"There she is," Francis whispered to her on their third set.

"Who?"

"Who do you think?"

Her chest erupted with tight warmth. "I convinced myself she would not come."

"She looks sublime."

"Where?"

Francis danced her toward the edge of the dance floor and motioned towards the huge double doors of the ballroom. The Ferthing's had just arrived and were being welcomed by her infamous father. Slightly apart, on the other side of one of the chiffon panels, Ivy stood tall and proud, resplendent in a black suit tailored to fit her worldly personality: she wore a bow tie at her chin, a top hat decorated with a gold band and a feather, a dashing tailcoat, and the finest pair of trousers Sicili had seen her into date. Her flaming red hair fell over her shoulders, loose and free. She had come to make an impression. Despite her bruised face, Ivy was divine.

Sicili's corset pinched. She could not bring herself to meet Ivy's searching gaze. She needed air. Fresh air.

"How has it got so hot in here, Francis?"

"Go to her," Francis urged. "Tell her."

She clung to him. "How?"

"Come on, then."

"We parted on painful terms last night."

"Shall we change that?"

Francis danced them right into the Ferthing party, who by then had made their way to the edge of the dance floor next to George. Her father observed with approval as they approached.

"Such a glorious pair you two make," George said, "looking so fresh and innocent." He all but rubbed his hands together. "I see you have stolen a fair amount of my Sicili's time tonight, Mr. Perrycot."

Francis laughed, obviously tickled by George's naivety.

Charlotte looked ruffled by the interaction. She pressed a protective hand to Ivy's.

"Shall we get some refreshments, Ivy?" Charlotte said. She tugged.

"You go along," Ivy said.

Charlotte gave Sicili a sidelong glance. "Are you sure, Ivy?"

"Certain, Mother."

William had to pry Charlotte away from Ivy and whisper something comforting in her ear. He gave Sicili an apologetic nod. She understood. A good mother does everything in her power to protect her only daughter.

A long, strangely comfortable moment lapsed between Sicili and Ivy, as they stared at each other like lost souls in a swarm of nervous, hovering men. Francis soon had the moment under control.

He took Ivy in hand and kissed her cheek. "The infamous Ivy herself. You, darling, are stunning. The suit becomes you."

Ivy cracked a grateful smile. "So good to see you, Francis," she said. A hollow look devoured her one open eye, like her heart had been torn out by cruel hands and ripped to shreds. Her gaze kept getting caught in Sicili's. There seemed no helping it.

"It thrills me to see you, and so as yourself," he returned. "I was beginning to wonder if you would come. We were both wondering. Sicili has not been herself without––"

"Quiet, Francis, please," Sicili said, reddening.

Francis gave a wry smile. "Deny it if you like, Sicili."

"Is it true?" Ivy asked.

Sicili's cheeks burned. Her heart pounded. She was certain Ivy could see it ramming against the chest line of her dress. She reached for Ivy's hand.

"It is good to see you," she managed.

Francis buttoned his tailcoat. "I take it you two need some time alone."

Ivy looked at Sicili's hand but neglected to take it.

"We had plenty of time to ourselves," Ivy said. Her jaw set.

Francis looked from Sicili to Ivy. "Can I get you another glass of wine, Sicili?"

"Please," she said.

Francis raised his brows. "Ivy?"

Ivy continued to stare into Sicili's soul, so calmly. Francis took her silence as a no and skipped off. The room moved around them, and they stayed still. Anyone watching would have known.

Sicili took the locket in her fingers. "I have something for you," she said.

"It's *your* birthday, not mine."

"I never cared much for birthdays. Father is the one who likes to make a grand affair out of them. As you can see."

She unclasped the locket. Ivy's eyebrows raised. She opened Ivy's balled fist and set the locket there, safe and beautiful in her palm. "You should have it. I bought it with you in mind. A sketch of you would look very pretty in it."

Tears welled in Ivy's eyes. "A sketch that small?"

"Yes. That small. There are artists who make them specially to fit."

Ivy clasped the locket, closed her hand into a fist. "I understand. A trinket to remember you by." She sniffed. "Where is Lord Caraway?"

"Gone."

"What do you mean, gone?"

"I mean gone."

A light of hope dazzled in Ivy's good eye.

George interrupted, pushing up to them with a following of half a dozen men.

"Sicili, my angel," he boomed, "these fine fellows have been waiting all night for a dance. Now that Francis Perrycot is done with you, surely you can oblige."

"Father, I'm tired."

"Try not to be surly, darling. Whatever grudge you have with me has nothing to do with these fine men."

"It has *everything* to do with them."

"Your friend will understand," George insisted, and then turned to Ivy with a reptilian smile. "Miss Ferthing, how are you? Such a dismay, all those rumors kept you out of society these last few months."

Ivy crossed her arms. "Rumors are based in hearsay. I can confirm, in fact, that I do fancy women."

George gasped. His mouth fell, then closed, then gasped again at Ivy's show of confidence. Finally, he managed, "*Ooooh*, that face. That bad, was it?"

"Rather bad," Ivy said. The hope in her eyes flickered and died. "Go on," she said to Sicili. "They came for you."

Sicili was bullied into five more sets. By ten o'clock, her feet stung, and her ribs chaffed, yet her father refused to run out of men for her to dance with. From the looks of it, he had invited half of London's male population. They crushed up against one another in the ballroom and began to flow out into the West wing corridor and into the rooms beyond. George laughed and hosted like a hound from hell. All he cared for was that Sicili had the attention of every eligible male from Wiltshire to Dover.

Ivy got lost somewhere in the throng of potential husbands. Every now and then, here and there, she would see a flash of red hair, and Sicili's heart would seize. But before she knew it, the clock struck twelve, and she felt like the cinder girl from the fairy tale her mother used to tell her before bed: out of time.

George, the Persistent, the Cruel, stood on a raised dais, motioning for the instruments to halt. He *clanked* a gold fork against his wine glass. The ringing of her doom settled over the eager crowd. The music died. The ballroom stood still.

"My fine guests," George's exuberant voice rang out.

Sicili's heart stopped.

"Thank you kindly for joining us for my daughter's twenty-third birthday. What a splendid time it has been. Shall we have a toast to Sicili?"

"Hear, hear," a chorus of voices concurred.

The ballroom held up their glasses and *clinked, clanked*. Nervous shuffles and dewy, expectant eyes engulfed Sicili. Bodies pressed in on her. The corset constricted the blood flow to her heart.

Where was Ivy? She searched for Ivy. Had she left?

She couldn't breathe. She couldn't find Ivy.

George raised his infamous white brows to her as he held out his glass. "Now, for the moment you have all been waiting for. My angelic Sicili has an announcement to make. Do try to hold in your excitement."

Laughter rippled through the ballroom. A pathway cleared for her, a parting of flittering souls and anxious gawkers. She held her throat, willing herself to breathe. A frog of anxiety and fear croaked, stuck between her chest and tonsils.

One breath at a time, she stood tall. She lifted her chin. She ignored the pinched of the corset, digging into her flesh. This was not going to be how she stopped living––a martyr to her father's will.

One step at a time, she rose above the crowd.

***

Whatever hope Ivy had left, which was outrageously still existent, was extinguished the moment Sicili took to the stage. Sicili had a lost look to her. She stared over the audience with glazed eyes. Her expression softened and cleared when she found Ivy in the crowd. They stared at each other. Ivy felt like the only one in the room.

She felt sick with helplessness. Why had she let her mother convince her to stand by and watch Sicili sign her happiness away? What a horrible mistake this had been. Thinking she would arrive as herself and win Sicili over. Francis had an arm around Ivy's shoulders. Even the spirited future Earl of Norbury was glum.

"I truly did think... I truly did, Ivy." He attempted to comfort her, and possibly himself. "I truly did. You must know."

It didn't matter anymore. Whatever he thought would never change the fact that Sicili stood on the dais before them all, about to announce her decision to the world.

"I need some fresh air," she mumbled to Francis.

"Now?"

"Yes, now."

"Ivy, wait. Do wait. Ivy– –"

Ivy peeled her eyes from Sicili and pushed through the tightly packed guests, all waiting breathlessly for Sicili's words. She pushed for the door, through it, into the corridor, and along into the West wing. Sicili's voice faded, a distant dream. Ivy pressed her hands over her ears. She slipped through a paneled door and into a room she vaguely remembered. A moon lit study. She had planted her first kiss on the pretentious lips of Sicili Windihill in this room. She huffed out an outrageous laugh.

It had only been a few months ago, and yet their first meeting felt like years ago.

***

Sicili watched Ivy's head of unruly hair bob against the crowd. With a sinking heart, she saw her burst into the corridor and head toward the West wing without so much as a look back. Sicili stood frozen on the stage. She was the highlight of the night. All eyes were on her. The air itself seemed compressed, stilled, awaiting her words.

She opened her mouth.

"I am... rather lost for words." She fiddled with her dress. The sea of men blinked at her––waiting, hoping.

"Go on, my angel," George urged.

Sicili pressed a hand to her chest, feeling for her locket, needing its strength. It...was gone. Where was it? *Oh god.* She had given it away.

"I..." Francis met her gaze. A redness pricked at his eyes. His eyebrows pinched. She stuttered. George motioned for her to continue. She squeezed her eyes shut and cleared her throat. "I thought I could do this. Once. What feels like years ago, before I met an outrageous, iron-willed, dashing, beautiful person. Who unfortunately has just stepped out." She stared toward the ballroom doors, hoping Ivy had heard her and would reappear. She waited. There was no Ivy. "But..." Sicili looked at George. The glint in his eye was stronger than ever, urging her on.

In that awful moment, she realized she would never be free of that glint––not when she married, not when she had children, not when, finally, inevitably, her life was bitter and pointless. Not *ever*.

"I cannot do this," she said. A great weight lifted from her chest, forcing a laugh from her. "Did you hear me, George

Windihill? I will not do this. I *will not* marry. None of you will have my hand." Her chest filled with a lightness, a final sensation of freedom. "I am happy to be penniless. Did you hear that, you evil man? *Penniless--*especially if it means being with the woman I love."

"Woman?" George stuttered. The crowd fell utterly silent, every eye now fixed on father and daughter. "Do be considerate, darling." He cleared his throat.

"I have been nothing but considerate. I have stood by like a good little girl and let you control me with your hollow threats. *You* are the inconsiderate one, Father. *You* are the one who strung these fine gentlemen along by dangling your daughter in their faces."

The guests glanced at one another as though waking from a dream. Almost as one, they looked to Sicili with bewildered admiration.

"I am ashamed to be your daughter, George Windihill," she said, her voice as clear as a bell. George's face had gone all kinds of red. He looked a mix of embarrassed or enraged. Possibly more enraged. She laughed, because her heart felt like a dove, fluttering and free. "Gentlemen, let me apologize on my father's behalf, as he will likely never admit to his folly. Thank you all for coming. Have yourselves one last drink and be on your way. The show is over. Personally, I need some fresh air."

A stunned silence followed, and then the room erupted in startling cheers from the gentlemen and eager whispers from the ladies. Naughty Ivy would no longer be the only scandal of the countryside. The instruments attempted to start up again, perhaps at George's bidding, but quickly fell short because the lead cellist had fainted right there in front of everyone, which made a few of the on-looking ladies faint. Quite the scene, quite the outrage, and Sicili stood tall, watching it all unfold, and feeling proud of herself for the first time in possibly her entire life.

"Well done, Sicili," Francis shouted, clapping. "Well said. Good show, good show."

As she stepped off the dais, a fuming George immediately met her.

"Sicili, Sicili," he stammered. "I daresay, Sicili, if you do not get back up there and mend the damage..." he blustered. "If you do not this very moment... I will cross your name this very night, this very *hour*, off my will."

"Go ahead, Father."

"Go ahead?"

"Your money is not worth my happiness."

Changing tacks, George clasped her hands in his. "My angel," he implored her. "Think about what you will do to our name? A woman? *A woman?*"

"The Ferthings seem to have weathered the damage quite well."

"But-but *Ivy Ferthing* of all women? Has she put a trance on you? Has she bewitched you?"

Sicili cupped his cheek. All the hate she had felt for him had disappeared, replaced with an immense pity for his mental health. "She has, and I must find her."

George stammered and stammered some more as he realized that his beautiful daughter was not going to back down. His face turned from red to white and then back again. Francine appeared with a fresh glass of wine for him. He guzzled it, sweating.

"Sicili, are you sure?" Francine said.

"I cannot be more certain, Mother."

"But... a woman? Did I hear you say you are in love with a *woman?*"

"You did."

"Why am I only hearing about this now?"

"I was afraid before."

"And are you not afraid now?"

"I am, but I know it will pass."

Francine kissed Sicili's cheek. "I'm afraid too, darling."

She trapped her mother in a hug. Francine gave a little gasp, then melted into it.

"When Father recovers, tell him I love him more than I hate him."

Francine smiled. "I will."

Across the room, one of the chiffon panels burst into flame. Fire swelled up the panel and cause a commotion of screams and movement. A general scramble ensued as a group of gentlemen stamped the fire out; the crowd thinned as guests pushed their way outside into the garden, fanning themselves and coughing from the smoke. Sicili smiled, feeling strangely disconnected from it all. She made her way toward the West wing. In the corridor, she was met by an enthusiastic Francis, who took her arm and kissed her full on the mouth.

"Well done, Sicili," he said again, smiling. "I knew that defiance was hiding somewhere in you. Quite the show."

"Where is she?" she said.

"She left. She mentioned something about fresh air."

"I have to find her."

"Of course you do. Go, go."

The West wing was next to empty. Ivy was nowhere to be seen. Sicili retraced her steps into the corridor and checked every door: the library, the back parlor, the kitchen just off the parlor, even the pantry––Ivy was Ivy, after all. The powder rooms. The tea parlor where her mother liked to read in the middle of the afternoon. The storage room where Wilber kept a wash bucket and mop.

George's study was the last door she tried. Of course. She should have known. On the floor, Ivy had discarded her bow tie and tailcoat. She had shed them on her way out. Night air gusted in through the propped open window. Sicili leaned over the window ledge and peeked out.

A burst of freedom had her laughing.

"Ivy?"

But of course, Ivy was long gone. Sicili imagined her running across the countryside in her crisp white shirt and tailored black trousers, her hair flying wild. She wiped the tears streaming down her face, accompanied by the uncontrollable laughter.

"Wait for me, Ivy," she shouted, not caring who heard.

She would never make it out the window in her dress. The buttons. The puffed sleeves. The formal layers. The petticoat. The pinching heels. She tore them all off, but she still felt trapped and restless. Her hands fumbled at the damn corset. Her mother had fastened the back, and it was nearly impossible to reach the ribbons without someone else to help. Something shined on the desk in front of the window. A letter opener. She grabbed at it and cut at the front panels, shredding them without a care. She yanked the panels open and shrugged out of the last layer, tossing both on the floor. A breeze found her bare arms and chest and cooled her hot skin.

She breathed. Better. Much better. Now, she could breathe.

Down to her undergarments, she climbed out the window. Instead of feeling silly, she felt airy, feather-like, no longer contained. She felt free.

"Wait for me, Ivy."

Epilogue

Sicili and Ivy ran away together and lived for a year in London with Sicili's friend Catherine, who had always suspected Sicili didn't like men. George Windihill was true to his word and disinherited his one and only daughter. A year after his daughter and Ivy ran away, George had a stroke. On his deathbed, he apologized to Sicili for forcing his hand but did not condone her loving and living with a woman.

"Of all women, the ridiculous Ivy Ferthing."

He died at peace with his daughter.

Sicili inherited her father's wealth and the Windsworth estate at the age of twenty and five, according to George's will.

Francine also came to terms with the whole matter, although it took her some years. She had always assumed Sicili was different from the other girls, but never to such an extent. She tolerated Ivy at first. Toward the end, they were honest friends.

Sicili and Ivy moved to Windsworth and lived with Francine for many years, not venturing to include themselves in society. They were content to enjoy the peace of Windsworth and each other. Sicili taught Ivy everything there was to know about riding a horse. The countryside was their canvas.

When William Ferthing fell ill due to years and years of working long and rainy days in his vineyard, Sicili helped Charlotte to nurse him while Ivy tended loyally to the vineyard. Ivy's brothers visited every now and then, less and less as the years passed. Eventually Sicili and Charlotte let their guard down and, in the end, they got along wonderfully.

Ivy and Sicili loved one another until they died. They were never able to legally wed, of course, but they arranged a small family ceremony where they exchanged rings. In their hearts, they were married. Sicili kept a copy of the article entitled "Miss Ivy Ferthing Impels Mayhem." For Ivy's eightieth birthday, Sicili had it framed and hung it next to the painting of Grace. It stayed there until 1915, when a couple with money from overseas took a tour of Windsworth and decided to purchase it. They chuckled at the article and replaced it with a painting of their twin girls.

The rumors about Ivy Ferthing live on to this day. She is still referred to as Naughty Ivy.

Acknowledgements

I could not be happier this book made it out into the wild. An enormous thank you to Carl and Andrew of Spectrum Books for making *Sicili and the Penniless Lad* happen.

To Andrew, thank you for tinkering so much with the cover design and making my vision for it happen. For your kindness in communication and for always being available to answer my questions.

A heartfelt thank you to my copy editor Jennifer who told me she laugh-choked on coffee many times while reading my manuscript. To know I brought laughter and joy to someone I had only met online gave me the push ten years later to revise *Sicili and the Penniless Lad* and submit to it publishers. Thank you for all your kind suggestions and the wonderful edits you did for these characters to make them come more alive.

Thank you always to my sister Laurie for believing in my talent as a writer, and for encouraging me to write even on the hard days. Your belief in me helped me to come back from a year long hiatus from writing. Thank you forever for your support, big sis.

I'm compelled to thank my upbringing in a conservative family for the shape of this book—the sadness I faced after coming out to my parents and the lessons I learned while choosing love. There was a lot of messy, but I'm grateful I went through it and let it shape my voice.

To my sweet Mama who reminds me so dearly of Charlotte. I know you have always tried to protect me from the scary things. I see your fear. Equally, I see your love. Thank you for bringing me into this world with your best and your strongest love. One day, you will joke about life. We're already getting there.

And finally, thank you to all the women I have learned from in love. When it hurt, it hurt good, and it taught me to express myself and be bold in my dreams.

About the Author

Rachel C. Neale writes queer fantasy and sapphic romance. She released her debut novella, *Beyond the Grove*, in 2022. She is passionate about capturing storylines driven by female leads who go against the grain and question conventionality. Rachel studied at Simon Fraser University to start her own editing business that helps authors thrive during the plotting stage. When not writing or editing, Rachel can be found scouring thrift stores, flailing to music, supporting the arts, and learning book design.

Excellent LGBTQ+ fiction by unique, wonderful authors.
Thrillers
Mystery
Romance
Young Adult
& More

Join our mailing list here for news, offers and free books!

Visit our website for more Spectrum Books
www.spectrum-books.com

Or find us on Instagram
@spectrumbookpublisher